Fatherless

By Josh Conley Jr

This is a work of fiction. All characters, organizations, and situations portrayed in this novel are a product of the author's imagination or are used fictitiously.

FATHERLESS

Graphic Design by Kim Li

Editor(s) Ester Kiburi and Susan Strecker

Contents

"Confess your faults one to another, and pray one for another, that ye may be healed. The effectual fervent prayer of a righteous man availeth much." – James 5:16

FATHERLESS

Chapter 1: Seven

A shrill high-pitched sound pierced through the air, interrupting the peaceful silence that had settled around Seven. He looked at his down-turned phone on the couch armrest beside him wondering who it could be. He shrugged, returning his focus to the newspaper in his hands. *Whoever it is will leave a message,* he thought. But after multiple rings, he couldn't ignore the persistent jingling any longer. He folded the newspaper in two and grabbed for his phone. Jumi's face illuminated the screen.

"Jumi? What's up? Why you calling so early?" His voice had a tinge of annoyance to it. After a hard week at work, he needed a quiet morning to himself.

"Seven, Dad was rushed to the emergency room!" Jumi responded in one breath.

"What? What happened?!" Seven sprung to his feet.

The neatly folded newspaper fell to the floor in a pile of mess, a forgotten relic of what was meant to be a tranquil morning.

"I don't know all the details, but he's being prepped for emergency surgery, so you need to get over here quick! All I can tell you is that it's not looking too good. Just get here. Drive sa…"

Seven hung up the phone before Jumi could finish. He had no time to waste, he needed to be there yesterday. His body moved on autopilot, as Seven searched for his keys. He looked in his jacket pocket, then to his desk, then his closet. He could feel the fog engulfing his short-term memory.

Where are they? Calm down, deep breath, he thought to himself, taking in a soothing lungful of air to satiate his nerves.

After he had taken a few deep breaths, he cleared his mind and then remembered that his keys were in his laptop bag. He placed them in his pocket, grabbed his coat, and ran down the stairwell to the garage. He was so flustered that he stumbled and grabbed the banister to keep from falling.

"Crap!"

He was in a slight panic, his heart pounded, and mind raced as he reached the car. He pulled the keys out of his pocket to open the car door but immediately dropped them. He quickly bent over to pick them up, and at that moment, he realized that his hands were shaking. He wondered what was going on.

He was in deep thought as he picked up his keys. He then hit the clicker and unlocked the door. He quickly entered the car and placed the key into the ignition, which started the engine.

He opened the garage, and pulled out. Seven sped through intersection after intersection, headed for the bridge that led him to the highway. Completely lost in his thoughts, Seven merged onto the bridge into traffic.

Why now? I've recently got him back into my life, am I going to lose him already? As long as I can remember, all I ever wanted was my dad in my life, and as long as I can remember, he has never been there for me. I can't lose him! Not yet, he thought to himself. The words 'not yet' reverberated in his mind, egging him to drive faster.

As he continued to think, a single tear rolls down his cheek. "I don't want to lose my dad", he whimpered under his breath. He attempted to wipe away the tear and noticed a truck drifting into his lane. He immediately pressed down hard on his horn, but it didn't help. The truck barreled towards him and rammed into the car.

"Watch out!" Seven screamed, putting his arms up to his face on reflex.

His car swerved, and hit a van in the other lane. Seven found himself trapped between two vehicles. He tried to turn the wheel and accelerate, but the three vehicles plied together. A symphony of horns and metal crunching filled the air, intensifying as the seconds ticked by. People watched in horror as all three vehicles, stuck together, continued to rumble down the side of the bridge. The force of the impact had them headed straight for the divider on the edge of the bridge.

They hit the divider hard. The van went over immediately. It pulled Seven's car partially over the edge of the bridge as it plunged into the river. The momentum of the hit dangled Seven's car over the edge. The only thing that kept it from also falling into the river was the fact that it was stuck to the front of the truck.

Seven's passenger door flung open, unbalancing his car even more. Seven was afraid and as he looked up, he saw the face of the truck driver. The driver's eyes were wide with panic, his expression contorted with fear and regret. His hands gripped the steering wheel in an attempt to reverse, but gravity had other plans. The truck slowly slid forward and caused the crowd to gasp in fright.

"Help me! Somebody help me!" Seven had no recourse but to scream. The crippling fear within him had reached its peak, yearning for a release.

He reached for his seatbelt and the car made a creaking sound. His slight movement caused the car to move, putting more pressure on the hinges of his opened door. Paralyzed with fear, he leaned back in his seat, closed his eyes, and took a deep breath.

"Mercedes, call Faith."

"Calling Faith Now."

Seconds later, the call connected.

"Seve..." Her sweet voice provided a much-needed reprieve to the crunching and swelling of metallic sounds.

"Babe," he said and prayed. "Lord, please don't let me die here. I'm scared and don't know what to do. Please send help!"

As he continued to pray there was a louder *"Crack"*. The

door hinge at the bottom of the door had broken off. The car then dangled violently.

"Seven… what's going on? Seve… what was that?" asked Faith, her voice dripping with concern.

Seven opened his eyes briefly but the movement of the car, in addition to looking up at the sky, caused him to become dizzy, so he closed his eyes again. In the darkness, he heard a snap and then he free fell into the river below.

The Hospital

"Hey Jumi. Did you speak to your brother?" asked Rehi.

"Yes, I just got off the phone with him. He said he's on his way." Replied Jumi.

"How did he sound?"

"How do you think he sounded, Mom? Seven went into a panic as per usual. I told him to drive safe, but get over here quickly."

Jumi shook her head, clearly worried about the state of mind that her brother was most likely in. Since they were young, Seven had always been the worrier, always anxious, and thinking about the worst-case scenario. The siblings were fond of each other, but Jumi wondered if Seven would ever get over his excessive anxiety. Rehi reached out and took Jumi's hand in a comforting gesture. They had no recourse but to wait.

The doctors had finished operating and stitched the entry area. Jerri was now prepped to go into recovery when he flung his eyes open. Unfortunately for the medical staff that were present, it wasn't a confusion-laden rousing, but one that stunned and forced them to take a step back.

"Seven! Seven! Seven!" Jerri screamed.

Tears cascaded down his face and his heart pounded. The doctor, medical assistant and surgical techs stared at him.

"Please," Jerri said. "Can someone call my son?"

"Your son?" asked a nurse.

"Yes nurse, my son. His name is Seven. Seven Bradford." He folded over onto his side, weeping. He whispered, "God please… no no no I'm sorry. I'm so… so… sorry baby boy. God please… no no no."

The doctor placed his hand on Jerri's shoulder and tried to console him.

"Mr. Bradford, I will send the nurse out to speak with your family about your surgery, and also your son, while we take you over to recovery. In the meantime, please hold still because I don't want you to tear your stitches. But how do you feel?"

Jerri sniffled as he's body shook.

"I'm okay, Doctor. I need to see my son. Please have someone call him right now," he responded in a shaky voice.

"Absolutely, I'll send the nurse immediately," he turned on his heels and gave the present nurse brief instructions.

The nurse met the family in the waiting room. Only Jumi was around.

"Nurse Hope. I'm so happy to see you. How did things go with my dad?" asked Jumi.

"Really well," she said. "The doctor will be out shortly to give you specific answers about the surgery. Jerri is being taken over to the recovery room but you should be able to see him really soon since he seems fully aware. But I do have a question. Your dad awoke from the anesthesia asking for his son. He seemed *concerned.* Is he here?"

"Really? Um… not yet. But he should be here soon," Jumi checked her watch. "I'll call him again."

After Hope left, Jumi called her brother but got his voicemail. "Seven, where are you? We've been here waiting for you for the last two hours. Where are you, bro? Call me or *something* okay? Anyway, Dad is out of surgery and stable, but he is asking for you. So, call me or hurry up and get here."

As Jumi pressed the end call button, the doctor approached her and spoke. "Surgery went well. Your dad is fully awake from the anesthesia so we didn't see the need to keep him in recovery. So you can go see him as he's headed to his room now."

Jumi clapped her hands in excitement as relief flooded through her.

"That's great! So, what are the next steps?" she asked.

"Well, I suggest that he takes it easy for the next six weeks. We have prescribed him some pain meds that should help with the discomfort and a stool softener to help with going to the bathroom. Other than that, he should be okay as the cancer did not spread past his left kidney."

"Wow, that's great! I can't wait to tell Seven. He'll be relieved since it seems to be not as bad as we initially thought. My dad was in so much pain, so I didn't know what was happening. Thank you again doctor."

"Make no mistake it was very serious, but the cancer was contained only to his left kidney. So, I'm confident that he will make a complete recovery. We'll keep him through the night and if all goes as expected he should be okay to go home tomorrow. I'll send the nurse in to check on him soon."

As the doctor walked away, Jumi went to find her mom and share the good news.

"Thank you, Lord. You are excellent! I'm so happy he's going to be okay," Rehi uttered out loud. A smile spread across Jumi's lips, glad to see her mom happy. It was good news after all. Just then, her ringtone caught her attention, she reached for her phone and without looking at the screen, answered it. She expected it to be Seven.

"Seven-"

"Jumi! Oh my God", the voice whimpered.

"Faith? What's wrong girl?" asked Jumi.

The Bridge

As his car disappeared into the black water, Seven struggled to undo his seatbelt. The more the water poured into his car, the more he struggled to free himself. As the water rushed in, Seven had no choice but to take in lungful's of air. He clicked the release button repeatedly, but nothing happened. He couldn't hold his breath for much longer. So, he frantically searched for something that he could use to pry the seatbelt loose. He opened the console and saw his pocketknife. He sawed on the belt and was almost through it.

One last piece. His lungs burned and he involuntarily inhaled, taking in water instead of air. A jolt of shock reverberated through his body as his lungs filled with water. Seven could feel his body resist, deprived of the much-needed oxygen. A fog settled around him, nestling his thoughts like a warm blanket. His eyes struggled to stay open, as his body shut down. As he blacked out, he heard his mother's voice.

*****Fall of 1979*****

"Seven? Seven? I know you hear me. Seven!" yelled Sissy.

Seven gritted his teeth. He could sense from his mom's tone that he had waited too long to respond.

"Yes Momma?" He answered, slightly apprehensive.

"Boy next time I call you, you come!" His mom stared down at him, clearly agitated by his sluggish response.

"Yes ma'am," he responded, almost instantaneously. He was not going to make the same mistake twice.

"Okay it's time for me to go to work so your aunt is coming over to watch you until I get off," his mom responded after a few minutes of eyeing him up and down. He breathed out a sigh of relief, glad to have missed out on a tongue-lashing.

"Yes! Auntie Iris is fun. We go to the store and she gives me ice cream. I love it when Auntie Iris comes over. I love her so much," Seven brimmed with joy, his most recent blunder a fleeting thought of the past.

"Yes, I know you love your Auntie Iris. But umm… tonight, your Auntie Iris isn't watching you."

"Why not Momma? Who will be watching me then?"

"Your Auntie Ivy is coming to watch you tonight."

"Auntie Ivy? No Momma, I don't want Auntie Ivy to watch me. She's never watched me before. She doesn't know what I like to eat, what I like to drink, she doesn't even know to rub my tummy so I can go to sleep. I don't want Auntie Ivy to watch me," his face dropped as his heart sunk, and the image of an ice cream cone in his hand vanished.

"It will be okay baby, I'll be home before you know it. Now, promise me that you are going to be a good boy while Momma is at work," his mother reached out for an embrace, but Seven folded his arms and shrugged as he walked to the living room. "I'm always a good boy. Especially when Auntie *Iris* watches me."

"Boy, I swear you are too stubborn for a five-year-old. Now go change into your night clothes because your aunt will be here soon."

In the midst of chuckling at her son's behavior, Sissy heard a knock on the door. Before she could answer it, the person knocked again.

"Hurry up Sissy, I need to use the bathroom!" Sissy rushed to the door and undid the locks. Before she could unclasp the chain lock, the door pushed open, but stopped.

"Dang Sissy. You always acting like you hiding from the mob or something. Why you always use so many locks on the door? You got a million dollars under your mattress or something?" asked Ivy.

"Shut up Ivy. Move so I can take the chain lock off too. And please, you act like you don't know how crazy it is out here with all the robberies and stick up kids looking to jack people. Girl you can doubt the desperation of others all you want, but not me." Sissy responded.

Ivy took a reluctant step back, her shadow hovering at the entrance. Sissy unclasped the chain lock, shaking her head.

"Thank you. Now get out the way," Ivy darted past Sissy to the bathroom. She danced as she struggled to undo her pants.

Minutes later, Seven walked in. "Eww… Momma she sounds like a boy peeing in there."

"She does, doesn't she baby?"

"Make sure you wash your hands *Uncle Ivy*." Seven yelled.

Sissy and Seven laughed loudly, the sound echoing through the bathroom door.

"Shut up both of you. Y'all ain't funny at all." Ivy retorted, walking into the living room while wiping her recently washed hands on her jeans.

"Sounds funny to me. Anyway, I'm heading out and will see you guys in the morning." Said Sissy.

"Okay Sissy. See you later and have a good day." Replied Ivy.

"Bye Ivy. And you little man, remember what I told you."

"Yes, Momma. Be a good boy for Auntie Ivy, I know."

Sissy kissed Seven on the forehead and headed out to the bus stop where her coworker, Sheryl, was waiting.

The bus stop wasn't far away, and with Sissy's briskness, she was there in under 5 minutes. As she greeted her friend, she realized that she had forgotten something.

"Crap," she said. "I left my badge in the house. Sheryl, you think you can stall them a few minutes in case I'm not back by the time they get here?"

"Sure, Sissy. But you know how these drivers are. If you ain't here I doubt they gonna' wait. So, hurry up!" Cheryl urged.

As Sissy raced back to her house, Ivy and Seven were already bickering.

"I told you it's time for bed," Ivy told him.

"No, you told me to get ready for bed. And I am. See?" He motioned to his clothes. "I'm already in my pajamas, *Uncle Ivy*."

"Um, no. You need to go to bed now, please and thank you!" Ivy spat, clearly agitated by Seven's attitude.

"But I'm not sleepy yet," Seven crossed his arms to challenge her.

"I don't care twerp. Get your butt in your bed now!" Ivy raised her voice, shaking her finger at him.

"Stop calling me a twerp! *Uncle Ivy*," said Seven in a snarky tone.

"Don't disrespect me again. I'm your aunt and not a man.

You probably don't even know the difference between boys and girls, anyway. Now get your butt in the bed!" Ivy inched closer, her hands akimbo.

"I do know the difference. Girls are pretty like my mom. And since you are ugly, you must be a boy!"

"Oh yeah? Get your butt over here!" She grabbed his arm.

Finally, Sissy reached her house and started up the steps. As she pulled out her keys, she heard Seven's voice.

"Stop it! I'm telling!

Sissy fumbled to undo all the locks and pushed open the door. "What the hell is going on in here?!"

Chapter 2: Faith

It was 6:40 a.m. Seven's alarm clock sounded, disturbing the tranquility of the early morning atmosphere. He stretched his hand and turned it off, willing his sleepy eyes to open. He went to the bathroom and looked at himself in the mirror. His eyes fully open now, a warm feeling spread through his chest.

"Today is going to be a great day!" he said aloud, teetering on the much-anticipated day.

He walked back to bed where his beautiful wife Faith lay. He still couldn't believe that she had said yes to him all those years ago. He thought he'd find her asleep, but she was wide awake, a pearly smile on her lips. In her outstretched hand, she held out a card.

"Happy birthday baby."

He opened the envelope and read the card. Immediately, tears welled up in his eyes. He looked away and wiped them before they fell down his cheek, and then turned back to his love and hugged her. She squeezed him back, holding him tight in a warm embrace.

"Seven, I love you so much. Do you know that?" asked Faith.

"Yes, I do. And, I love you so much in return." Seven replied.

"How do you know? Do you feel my love?"

"I do baby."

They looked into each other's eyes and shared a long and deep kiss. Afterwards, he continued to look deeply into her eyes, drowning in the depths of her soul. Almost immediately, he could sense a discomfort within her that sent warning bells ringing in his head.

"What's wrong?" he asked, cupping her cheek in his right hand.

"Nothing… Well, I had a bad dream. Nevertheless, it seemed so real. The weirdest part of the dream was that every moment I looked at the time, it was always the same, 2:33 p.m. It was like, it was 2:33 for my entire dream," Faith uttered, after a few moments of silence.

"So, what happened?" Seven queried, his curiosity piquing.

"Everything seemed so real. As if I was hovering over my body, watching myself. I felt so paranoid. We were driving all over for some reason and I was so afraid. At one point, you took me to a park, so that I could get out the car and get some air. However, once I was outside the car… I don't know…I felt like something bad was about to happen. So, I ran back in the car," her eyes were downcast, as she fiddled with her thumbs to maintain some sense of composure.

"Really? Well, what was I doing while you were going

through this?" Seven asked, soothingly. He seemed concerned, but avoided displaying it through his voice.

"Trying to comfort me. You seemed worried and confused. I guess because I couldn't explain what I was afraid of. And every time I looked at the time, the sight of 2:33 intensified my feelings. It's felt déjà vu-*esque*. As if I knew what was about to happen but couldn't really remember it to explain, but it felt like I experienced it before. Anyway, it was only a crazy dream," Faith shrugged, her body language taking a 360° turn. She reached out and planted a kiss on his lips once more and got out of the bed.

"I enjoy our morning conversations babe. I can talk to you for hours lying in this bed, but not today. Momma needs to get up and go because I have a big meeting this morning."

Seven stared at his wife. Her hips swayed from left to right as she walked to the bathroom.

Mhmm. I love that woman. God thank you for blessing me with such a gift, he thought to himself.

She turned on the shower so he raised his voice to be heard. "Wow that does sound like a crazy dream. But, what's your plan for the day babe?" asked Seven.

"Going to work early for this meeting, but I may be free a little after lunch," she responded, her voice slightly muffled.

"Well I figured that much."

"So, what about you, birthday boy? Taking off today?"

"No, at least I don't think so. I didn't really plan anything."

"Of course, you didn't. Well, I say, you should take the day off and relax. Once I'm done with work, I'll come pick you up and we can do something nice."

"Something nice? How nice are we talking? Like nice? Or *nice, nice*?" Seven itched with anticipation. Past memories of birthday celebrations assured him that this year would be no different. Faith always knew how to make this day special, and one to remember.

"You will just have to wait and see then, won't you?" Her voice broke through the reverie, and Seven could almost detect an undertone of teasing.

"I don't mind waiting. As long as it's worth it!" His body jostled with excitement.

Minutes later, Faith got out of the shower. She grabbed a towel and walked over to the bed. She then kissed him ever so slightly on the lips.

"Am I not worth the wait?" she asked, her mouth in a pout.

"Oh, you are worth it, but I can't wait. So, I think you should take off too and we can stay in bed all day. And, you know that I'm worth it," Seven teased, inching his fingers up her thighs.

"Boy bye!"

Faith kissed Seven on his forehead and walked away chuckling. She went to her walk-in closet and picked out a pin-stripe skirt suit that extenuated her figure in all the right places. She picked out 5-inch heels and understated jewelry to complete the ensemble. She quickly dressed and applied a subtle layer of make-up. She had no time for her usual morning pampering as she needed to meet her assistant at the office to prep. As she walked out of her closet Seven startled her.

"Really? That's your response? But it's my birthday." he pouted.

"Fool, you scared me! Anyway, it will still be your birthday later."

"Wow, you're wrong for that. Well can you at least make me some breakfast?" he yelled as she walked out of the bedroom.

"I'll order you something."

"Order? Never mind, I'll make myself breakfast, so order me lunch, okay?"

"Okay, I got you covered baby," she called out before shutting the main front door.

Faith made it to her office in record time, and pulled into her assigned parking space and had a thought. *That was a really weird dream. God are you trying to tell me something?* As her mind wandered in contemplation about the meaning of her dream, a knock on her window startled her.

"Faith, Faith. You okay girl?"

Faith jumped and then looked up to see that it was only her assistant, Wendy. She looked at her, smirked, and then hopped out of the car.

"You okay boss lady? You seem a little nervous." Wendy stated.

"Yeah I'm okay." Faith replied.

"I mean I know this is a big morning for you, so are you sure?"

"Nope, I'm not sure. But it will be fine."

Faith and Wendy walked to the elevator and headed to the penthouse floor. Since she worked for the most prestigious consulting firm in the nation, it awarded Faith with plenty of respect and admiration by all of those who worked with and for her. She was made the youngest VP in the history of her company three years prior. She was the epitome of black excellence, and most of the partners in the firm, fully supported her. Of course, there was one exception. All in all, her team adored her for she truly believed in rewarding those who worked hard and maintained the level of excellence that she expected. Faith and her assistant finally reached the top floor and quickly turned into the first conference room off the elevator.

"It's 7:55 so let's get to it. I only have thirty minutes to prepare so show me what you got Wendy."

"Okay, so this is what I put together based on the notes you provided. Here are all the numbers on this slide, the percentages of long-term deals closed without you, and the comparison to those closed by you. All showing the longevity of the clients on average."

Wendy scrolled through the presentation, pointing and enhancing the slides. Faith couldn't help but pat herself on the back. Seeing her achievements summarized in this way, symbolized to her just how far she had come. Most times, she felt like she had stagnated, stuck in a vicious cycle of trying to prove her worth. But this right here, was what she had worked so hard to show. Today was going to be monumental.

"Great. This looks really good." Faith said with her voice full of pride.

"Thanks boss lady." Replied Wendy.

"No really. You did a great job and I appreciate how you have stepped up these last few months."

"Faith, I'm the one who is appreciative of you. I mean, I wouldn't even be here without your belief and guidance. Not to mention that fat… excuse me… *sizeable* increase. You are absolutely the best leader that I have ever worked for."

"Awe thanks Wendy."

"No, thank you."

Wendy beamed, her hand on her chest. A moment of respect

and mutual gratification lingered for a few seconds before they refocused their attention to the matter at hand.

As they wrapped up previewing the presentation, they heard the ping of the elevator. “Sounds like your 8:30 has arrived.” Said Wendy.

“Actually, I’m his 8:30, but I know what you mean.” Replied Faith.

In walked Lucian. He was the principle partner of the firm and the lone person who continued to give Faith pushback. She frowned as he entered the office. He was one of few people that actually got under her skin. He was the highest-ranking individual at her company, the top of the “food” chain, and she needed his buy-in to move forward. He noticed them, but did not speak as he walked past the conference room.

“He looks especially prickly this morning,” Wendy tried to repress a chuckle.

“Wendy, he looks especially prickly every morning,” Faith chuckled slightly, encouraging Wendy to join in for a brief moment. It was a much-needed respite from the half-hour prepping they had completed.

“Yeah I suppose you right about that. Hey, would you please order lunch for Seven today. It’s his birthday so he’s taking the day off.” Faith explained.

“The Italian place he likes? One o’clock?” asked Wendy.

"Perfect."

"Will do. Oh, and Faith…"

"Yes Wendy?"

"Good luck girl!" Wendy gave an ear-splitting smile as a form of encouragement. Faith reciprocated, feeling a sense of calm settle in her bones. She had the best team supporting her, and she wouldn't have made it this far if it wasn't for them.

Faith packed up her laptop and walked to her office to drop off her jacket and grab her notes. She made it to her office, quickly got her things in order, and then headed down for her 8:30 pitch with Lucian. She arrived at his office and waited outside his glass doors. Lucian continued to speak with someone on the phone when he waved her into his office.

"Listen Charles, I don't care what the rest of the board says about this, you have to trust me," he placed his hand on his forehead and glanced up at Faith. "Yeah well, we can continue this later, shall we? My 8:30 has walked in so…" He gestured to Faith to sit. "Okay great, talk to you later Charles."

He hung up and directed his attention to Faith. "So, what do you have for me *Ms. Free-man*?"

The way that he said her name reminded her of the first time he addressed her directly. It was at the company holiday party after Faith had been promoted to VP. It was announced with most employees, and invited guests, in attendance. Charles made a beautiful speech, and everyone listened attentively to see who would be promoted to the VP position. After a few minutes, Charles made the announcement.

"I would like you all to help me congratulate our new Vice President, Mrs. Faith Freeman-Bradford!"

As those in attendance clapped and cheered, a "tipsy" Lucian went to the microphone. "Congrats Faith. You've been here for some time and have done great work. I look forward to the great work that you will do going forward. But there is one thing that I have always wondered, are you truly *Free-man* or do you have a price tag?"

He then staggered off the stage, clearly pleased with himself, but many of the attendees were in shock at what took place. Murmurs filled the room, an air of disapproval co-mingled with astonishment. Faith remained embarrassed and slighted throughout the rest of the evening, and even three years later, she couldn't shake off those feelings. If it hadn't been for Charles, she might not have stayed with the company for this long.

"Ms. *Free-man*, again, what do you have for me?" His gnarly voice broke through her recollection.

"Again, it's *Mrs. Freeman-Bradford*. And I wanted to meet with you to discuss the potential for another partner to join the board. With you being the principle partner, I thought that it would be advantageous to have a conversation with you about how I may be a good fit and to also get some direct feedback from you. As you know, my teams are performing at a record-breaking pace in terms of added revenue, and have been doing so since I have been leading them. Furthermore, my mentorship of a few of the other leaders have assisted them in improving the performance of their teams as well. I believe my impact has been not just for my teams alone, but rather portfolio-wide."

Faith then displayed her additional material on the projection screen. She walked to the screen to add emphasis on the specific slides that displayed her success as a leader and those of her teams. As she spoke, she occasionally turned to look at the information that she was presenting and when she turned back, she couldn't help but notice that Lucian didn't seem interested at all. She turned away once more to point out the difference between her team's revenue accomplishments versus other teams within the portfolio and accidentally dropped her electronic pointer.

"Crap!"

She picked up her pen and once she stood, she turned to find that Lucian seemed very attentive—sitting straight in his chair, making eye contact, and even had a slight smirk on his face. That made her wonder, confused as to his sudden spike in attention.

His phone rang and when he saw the caller ID he said, "Faith, I really need to take this."

"Sure Lucian, thanks for meeting with me and I hope that

you would consider me when the time comes."

"That's what I like about you *Free-man*. You are always direct and full of confidence," he took a deep breath and sighed, all while maintaining a slight smile on his face.

"Okay, I would like to hear more about why you believe you deserve to be a partner. I'm only free at lunch time today. So, would you like to go for lunch with me?"

Faith paused for a second as she thought about the offer. "Umm, sure."

"Well don't sound so enthusiastic. My car will pick us up in the front of the building at 12 sharp. Don't be late!" he demanded.

"I'm *never* late." She retorted in a snarky tone.

"Great. See you then. Oh, and please shut the door on your way out," he swiveled in his chair, cradling the phone receiver under his ear.

"Jerk." She mumbled under her breath as she left his office.

Lunch Time

Faith went about her morning as usual, filled with back-to-back team meetings. Her head was buried in a pile of paperwork when she looked up at her wall-clock. It was time for her to meet with Lucian. She grabbed her jacket and walked to the elevator.

Why am I even bothering to go to lunch with this jerk? Take it easy girl… Just a means to an end… Now play your cards right and get this partnership, she thought to herself.

Her mind was conflicted, but she knew she couldn't miss out on this opportunity. Usually, she liked to give herself a pep talk when she was alone in the elevator. Today, it was critical that she talked to herself. Faith got in the back seat of a waiting town car beside Lucian.

"Quick pit stop before we go to lunch. We need to stop at my loft so I can grab my briefcase. It'll only take a minute."

Faith thought that was a rookie mistake, but she didn't say anything.

"Anyway, let's get to it. You are very intelligent and you really know how to push a team to achieve great success. The problem is that I feel like you lack that killer instinct. That one quality that separates you from the rest of us. I worry you won't get the job done at any cost."

"My record speaks for itself. Men lie, women lie, but numbers don't." Faith glanced out the window, upset by his implication.

"You have a line that you won't cross. Me on the other hand? There is no line that I won't cross to get the job done and take my firm into the stratosphere."

The driver stopped in front of Lucian's apartment. "Come,"

he said. "Let's walk and talk."

Faith exited the car and followed him into the elevator. Following a few steps behind, she began to wonder what Lucian was after. An unsettling feeling descended into the pit of her stomach. She tried to shake off those feelings, but her sixth sense spiked causing her to slow her footsteps. Soon, they were walking through the lobby and her attention was diverted.

The white colored walls, and tiles to match, exhilarated an air of opulence and luxury that matched her boss' ego. She expected nothing less from a man in his position. He pushed the button for the penthouse floor.

"Faith, have you ever lived in one of these before?" he asked.

"No, I haven't. I prefer to live in a home. Not really a loft or corporate building type of person." She replied.

"Just wait until you see this view."

They entered the penthouse and Lucian started to give her a tour. Much like the lobby, Lucian's place was a sight for sore eyes. With floor-to-ceiling windows inviting the mid-day sunlight, the penthouse lived up to the lavishness that the lobby exemplified—spotless, vibrant and with wall-to-wall art work that Faith thought must have cost a fortune. They walked from his living area, through the kitchen, and her eyes widened with each step as she admired the breathtaking view. The penthouse overlooked the city, towering above most surrounding residential areas. Faith couldn't help but think how the view looked like at night. She could imagine the flurry of scattered yellows, reds and blues dancing in the horizon, epitomizing a city that never sleeps. Somehow, in the daze of the extravagant tour, they ended up at the bedroom.

"Now, isn't this view amazing?" asked Lucian.

"It is actually. I have to say that I've never seen anything like it." Replied Faith slightly amazed.

"Somethings in life are worth the sacrifice. Now, what are you willing to sacrifice to become a partner at my firm?"

"Anything," Faith blurted, but wished she could take it back. That feeling earlier crept up her spine. *Damn!*

"Oh really?" Lucius grabbed Faith by the hand and sat on the bed.

"Excuse me, but what the hell do you think you are doing?" Faith asked as she snatched her hand away.

"Nothing, we're just talking right?"

I can't do this. This is wrong. No matter how much I want this partnership. No matter how much he "thinks" I want this partnership. Lord get me out of this situation, she thought.

"So, do we have a deal?" he whispered ever so seductively while taking a slight nibble on her earlobe.

She jerked back and stood. "I don't know what you were

thinking, but I am *not* that kind of person."

"No one starts out a particular way but everyone evolves. Besides, together we can be unstoppable." Lucian removed his jacket and moved towards Faith. He placed his left hand on her shoulder, and attempted to pull her closer to him. They locked eyes and he continued to pull her closer to him despite her resistance.

"Stop it!" she insisted.

"Come on, I know you like me." Lucian said confidently.

"I said stop!"

"Don't be that way."

"For the last time, let go of me!" Faith demanded.

They looked at each other at an impasse. Lucian's expression remained amused, like a predator after prey. Faith wanted to smack that expression off his face, but for fear of retribution she held herself together. She smoothened out the creases on her skirt suit, and stood tall, preparing to give Lucian a piece of her mind. But her ringtone echoed through the lavish bedroom. *Saved by the bell,* she thought.

Faith looked down at her phone as it rang—Seven's smiling face illuminated the screen.

"I need to answer this. It's my *husband*. I'm married, *remember*!"

"Of course it is," Lucian sneered and huffed before walking

out of the bedroom into the kitchen and poured two glasses of wine.

"Hey, honey. Um, I'm in a meeting right now can I call you back in a few?" asked Faith.

"Lord, please don't let me die here. I'm scared and don't know what to do. Please send help!" he prayed.

"Seven? What's going on?" He didn't answer. She looked down to make sure the call was still connected. "Seven? Seven?" She heard a loud noise like something breaking followed by a loud scream. "Seven!?" she yelled concerned about what just happened.

The phone disconnected. She tried to call him back multiple times, but the phone continued to go straight to his voicemail. She sat back on the bed and stared at her phone while she tried to make sense of it all.

Lucian walked back in with the glasses of wine.

"I need to go. So, let's leave." Faith insisted.

"I figured we'd have some wine and continue with the discussion."

"What part of *no* don't you understand?"

"I never take no for an answer. If I did, I wouldn't be as successful as I am today." Lucian boasted, taking a step towards Faith.

"You spoiled little pompous prick! Not now nor will I ever, become involved with the likes of you. Just because you have money you think you can sexually harass me?" Faith's rage boiled, co-mingling with worry.

"Whoa, harassment? You came here under your own volition. I didn't force you here," he chuckled as if she had said something amusing.

"I want to leave. Now!" A note of finality in her tone. She didn't have time to deal with this. She had to find out what had happened to Seven.

"Okay fine. I'll drop you off wherever you need to go."

Chapter 3: Hope

The nurses lounge buzzed with conversation, lockers opening and closing and coffee brewing nearby. The smell of freshly made coffee wafted around the co-workers, as their conversations ebbed-and-flowed. It was the typical atmosphere during shift breaks.

"Girl, did you see that?" Hope asked, leaning against her locker.

"Hell yeah. That's why I'm in here with you," replied the other nurse.

"I've never seen anyone coming off anesthesia while screaming before."

"Me either. That must've been a crazy dream he was having. Or, maybe he was hallucinating?"

"Nah, he was still under. It's like he was forced out from under the anesthesia by whatever was going on in his mind. Besides, you have to be awake to hallucinate *silly*. And he clearly was not."

"Oh. Well yeah. Hope I knew that," she chuckled.

Hope looked at her quizzically, but opted not to point out anything. It had been a long day for both of them.

"Sure… you did. Well anyway, I'm about to take a walk to the bus stop and relax my mind," Hope responded, turning to open her locker.

“Okay Hope. I’m going home so I’ll see you tomorrow.”

“See ya girl!”

Hope gathered her things from her locker and walked out of the room, headed toward the elevators. She thought the patient must have really loved his son to be shaken up like that. She held the elevator as others were entering, still lost in her thoughts.

Once she got to the lobby, she realized she still had a few minutes before her lunch started. She used her new vape pen and inhaled deeply. A few minutes later, the much-needed warmness flooded her chest and shot straight to her head. She could feel her nerves settle from the reprieve. *Man, I needed that*, she thought.

Suddenly, she saw someone out of her peripheral, so she put the pen back in her pocket.

“Nurse Hope?”

“Yes, hey. Umm… Jumi, right?”

“Yep.” Jumi confirmed as she walked closer to Hope.

“How are you?” asked Hope.

“I’m okay under the current circumstances,” Jumi responded.

“Yeah, I hear ya. Stay positive. Things with your dad are looking pretty good.”

“I am. I did get to speak with him, so I think he’s doing okay for the most part.”

“Great. Oh, have you heard from your brother yet?”

"No, actually. I'm going to his house now to check on him."

"Well, I hope everything is okay. By the way, I'm on shift tomorrow, so I'll be your dad's nurse again. Hope to see you then."

"Okay great, so I'll see you tomorrow."

Hope and Jumi nodded at each other and waved good-bye. Hope turned away, but turned back in Jumi's direction as her phone rang. Jumi quickly picked up and continued to walk up the street headed to her car.

Hope walked back up the path that led to the hospital entrance and made her way to the cafeteria. After the day she had, she was on the hunt for some food. Her belly grumbled in protest. She said hello to the cashier as she checked out the menu. "I can't decide, Terrence. What do you recommend?" she asked him.

"Sorry, I'm not on the menu," he teased.

"Boy don't nobody want you. Now, I'll have the cheesesteak please," she replied, sucking her teeth in the process.

"Cheesesteak coming right up. Now, would you like fries with that?"

"Cheddar fries please."

"Oh, somebody is hungry today huh?"

"Yeah, I didn't eat breakfast this morning, so I'm starved."

"Either that or you got the munchies," he whispered in a joking tone.

“Whatever, make my food please”.

Hope smiled at him as she waited for her food to be prepared. Her attention was captured by a breaking news story broadcasted on the cafeteria TV.

“We are live on the city bridge where an hour ago, a man was pulled out of the river. As you can see, this crane behind us pulled out his car. According to witnesses, the person’s car had collided with a truck on the left of the bridge and then dangled over the edge for a few moments before eventually plummeting into the river some forty feet below. Paramedics have reportedly rushed the person to a nearby hospital. However, we do not currently have any updates on his status. There was also another person that was rescued from the water. The van that they occupied was the first to hit the water however they were able to free themselves and swim out. This started as a three-vehicle collision and quickly turned into a rescue operation-”

“Hope. Your cheesesteak and fries are ready.”

Hope was yanked out of the trance that the news had kept her in. She fluttered slightly in response, “oh… okay. Thanks Terrence.”

“Did you see that accident on the news? They have been talking about it for the past hour or so.” He stated.

“Yeah they said it was a little over an hour ago when it happened. I wouldn’t be surprised if the people involved were here.”

She replied.

Hope carried her food to a table to eat as the intercom called for a code blue. She took a bite of her cheesesteak, and then ran toward the ER. She saw a man being carried in on a gurney. She gloved up and asked a nurse what was happening.

"Near drowning," the nurse told Hope. "Car fell off the bridge with the victim pinned inside. We revived him on the scene, but we lost him twice in-route. At the moment, his pulse is weak."

A doctor approached and ferried out instructions, "Okay let's get him hooked up immediately. Hope, we need an epinephrine shot and an EEG. What's his name?"

"Seven," the other nurse said. "Seven Bradford according to his license."

"Okay. Seven? Mr. Bradford? Can you hear me?" The doctor leaned over Seven, opened his eyes and examined his pupils. Then the heart monitor let out one long beep.

"He's coding!" the doctor shouted. "Nurse, get the defibrillator."

Hope turned to the medical draw, grabbed the paddles, and quickly handed them to the doctor. He shocked Seven once, but nothing happened.

"Charge to two-hundred," the doctor shouted to Hope. She did as asked, and the doctor shocked him again. Seven's body contracted with a little more force. One of the receptors on his chest came off during the action. Until finally a response. "Okay he's back!" He worked on the patient for a few more minutes until he stabilized.

"Great work people. He's not completely out of the woods yet, but his vitals seem to be stable currently."

Hope felt relieved and realized there was a certain familiarity to his face—the thickness of his eyebrows, the curving of the corner of his lips, even the shape of his nose. She wondered where she had seen him before.

She reached down to grab the receptor that fell off of him, all the while secretly scanning his face. Everyone else in the room was focused on their assigned tasks and hadn't noticed her curiosity in him. She positioned the receptor to reapply it to his chest. Near his right shoulder, she noticed a crescent-shaped mark—not really a scar, but more of a birth mark. She reapplied the receptor as it hit her.

She wondered if it were possible. She dismissed it. She told herself to not jump to conclusions. She cleaned the room, but caught herself as she stared at him again.

There's something tranquil and peaceful about this man. I feel like his spirit is warm and loving, she thought to herself and continued to stare. For some reason, she felt the need to pray for him. So she did just that and prayed in her thoughts.

Chapter 4: Jumi

Jumi looked down at her phone as she walked to her car and saw that it was Faith calling. She side-eyed her phone and contemplated answering. She let the phone ring some more, then reluctantly answered as she got into her car and pulled out of the parking lot.

"Hey girl."

"Jumi! Have you heard from Seven?" asked Faith in a slight panic.

"No actually. Haven't you? Jumi replied.

"Kind of, but not really."

"And what does that mean?" Jumi stifled an eye-roll.

"He called me, but I couldn't make out what he was saying. Any idea where he might be?"

"He's your husband not mine. I would think *you* should know."

"Jumi, I don't have time for your attitude. I'm worried because I don't know where he is."

"Yeah, yeah. I just left the hospital. My dad is doing okay by the way. Thanks for *asking*. Anyway, I'll call Seven and see if I can get him."

Jumi abruptly hung up and continued to head over to Seven's house.

She got the nerve to call me about Seven and not even ask how my dad was doing. That's why I never liked her. She only thinks about herself. Questioning me about his whereabouts like it was my turn to watch him. Shoot, he's a grown man! I hope he off finding a new you, she thought to herself.

Jumi arrived at the house and pulled into the driveway. She walked to the side door and looked into the garage to see if she could get in, but it was locked. She peeked through the small garage window and noticed that Seven's car was gone. She rang the doorbell several times, but no one answered. Her sixth sense tingled slightly as she thought how odd it was that he wasn't at home. She shook her head in disbelief wondering what had happened to him.

She was about to leave when Faith pulled up with Lucian. Jumi noticed Faith's hair and clothes were a little disheveled. Jumi thought, *Mhmm, they were in the middle of having sex! I'm telling my brother whenever I find his crazy self.*

"I tried calling and he didn't answer, so I came over," Jumi said to Faith. "I have no idea where he could be." Her hands slumped in defeat. As her eyes fleeted around, she noticed something on the front steps and went to it.

"Ohh… what's this?" Jumi asked Faith, as she picked up the brown paper bag.

"It's his birthday lunch. It was delivered a little while ago. That means it's been quite a while since he's been here," Faith answered, nervously pacing back and forth.

Jumi thought the bigger question was where Faith had been and why she was showing up with her boss. But she was worried about her brother, so she didn't say anything.

"That's so strange. Have you talked to him today?" asked Jumi.

"Not since this morning. I've been working all morning."

"Really? Oh, I assumed that you would have spoken to him. At least by now. Okay well, I called Seven this morning because our dad is in the hospital. I told him what had happened and he said he was going to come to the hospital. But he never showed."

"Jumi we gotta' find him. I feel like something is wrong!" Faith sobbed and leaned into Jumi. Jumi reluctantly wrapped her arms around her for comfort.

"Okay, so let's talk this through. I spoke to him a little after eleven to tell him to come to the hospital. He had to have left the house a few minutes after that because his food is here. What time did he call you?" Jumi rubbed her sister-in-law's back, not without some discomfort.

"It was around 12:30 or so. I was in the middle of a . . . um . . . meeting and I left to speak with him. But when I picked up, it sounded like he was in the middle of a prayer and then the phone disconnected," Faith wiped at her cheeks with her suit sleeve, stepping back from Jumi's taciturn embrace.

"Have you checked your social media? Did he post anything today being that it's his birthday? Maybe he's out with one of his friends?" asked Jumi.

"Yeah, I checked, but I didn't see anything from him at all. Some of his friends wished him a happy 49th birthday but he never responded. Everyone else is posting about this stupid car crash."

"Okay, well I'm sure he'll turn up. He might be at the strip club or something. Probably smacking some booty for his birthday. You know how men are. Anyway, I need to get back to the hospital. I haven't spent much time with my dad since he came out of recovery because I came here looking for Seven," Jumi raised her shoulders in a blasé sort of way.

"Really, you're going to leave?" Faith asked, stunned by her sister-in-law's attitude.

"Girl, what else am I supposed to do? Sit here with you and do nothing? Listen, I don't know where my brother is, and I'm sure he'll turn up somewhere. But I need to get back to my dad."

"I thought you said Jerri was okay."

"Yeah, I did say he was okay, but that doesn't mean that I don't need to be by his side. You never even once asked if he was okay or anything. This is why I don't deal with you. You're only ever worried about yourself and things that affect you. You're so selfish. So, again, yes, I'm worried about my brother, but I'm going to be with *our* dad. Maybe he'll turn up at the hospital anyway because he said that he was coming. And unlike you he is a person of his word," Jumi's voice belied the calm expression she was exhibiting.

"I'm not selfish. I'm worried about my husband!" Faith took a step back, her eyes emptied of the tears. It's as if Jumi's nonchalant attitude had air-dried her tear ducts.

"You couldn't have been too worried about him. Out doing God knows what, with your boss. And on his birthday? You're just dirty. Perhaps my brother doesn't want to be found. Maybe he knows what you were up to. Did you ever think about that?" Jumi spat. She couldn't believe the nerve of the woman in front of her. *How dare she flounce around with other men and pretend to care for my brother?* She thought.

"You know what. You're right. I'll deal with *my* missing husband and you go ahead and leave to take care of *your* dad. Lord knows he's been anything but a father to Seven. So, go ahead. Roll out. We'll be fine over here," Faith took everything in stride. This wasn't her first rodeo with her *dear* sister-in-law.

"Yeah let me leave, before you make me lose my salvation." Replied Jumi.

Jumi walked to the side of the house, entered her car, and headed back to the hospital.

The nerve of that girl. I can't believe her. Talking crap about my father like she knows us or something. She just got here. I don't know what my brother sees in her. Jumi was lost in her thoughts rehashing the interaction with Faith as she headed back to the hospital. She was both pissed and infuriated, her mood refusing to settle on one emotion.

For the second time today, Jumi pulled up to the hospital and parked her car. She took a deep breath and tried to clear her thoughts while she walked back to the hospital entrance.

'It's after one now, Seven, where are you?' Jumi muttered under her breath, as if expecting an answer to fleet to her.

Her dad was alone when she got to his room. She walked to the side of his bed and looked at him, lost in thought.

He always looks so peaceful when he's sleeping. Like my big head brother. He may look exactly like you dad, and may even have some of your tendencies, but my brother is so very different from you.

Jumi sighed, and started to shake her head as the thoughts continued to run rapid through her mind. She pulled out her journal and began to compile her thoughts on its pages.

I love you so much and I'm so happy that you are okay. You've done so much for me and have been so committed to me. Even in that, there is a side to you that I can't understand. The side that is venomous, vindictive, and so very petty. Yeah, you and Seven are so different from each other. I wonder if you even realize some of the things that you have done. As much as you say you love God, do you ever reflect to understand your fault and shortcomings to progress as a person?

I love you so much Dad, truthfully, even though you are a piece of work. At times, I feel so sorry for you. Because it never seems like you have grown out of your malevolent habits. At other times, I feel you will one day reap what you have sown. The one thing that I absolutely don't understand is the rift between you and your son. You say your heart is filled with much love, but when it comes to him, I don't always see it.

She sat at the foot of his bed, and sighed as she admired the curves of his face. Saddened by her continual thoughts, she continued to write.

I wonder what you were thinking about if you truly awoke the way the doctor said you did–screaming his name and asking for him. What did you see? What did you witness? What was it that scared you? Who am I kidding? Even if asked you all of these questions, I doubt you would really answer them with any sense of ownership or acknowledgement of whatever part you played in all of this.

Jumi let out a big sigh as she started to feel emotional. She lowered her head as she realized once again the kind of person her father was. The person he had always been. A lone tear trickled down her cheek. As she wiped it away her motion caused her father to awake from his slumber.

Chapter 5: Jerri

Jerri opened his eyes slightly. He looked around, allowing his eyes to get accustomed to the bright lighting and unfamiliar surroundings. A figure to his right startled him. Bright-eyed Jumi gawked at him.

"Dang it Jumi. You scared the crap out of me."

"Sorry Dad. I didn't mean to startle you. How are you feeling?"

"I'm okay baby. Where's your brother?"

Given their rift, she was surprised by his question. "I don't know where your son is. I even went to his house after you came out of recovery."

"So, I guess he wasn't there?"

"Nope. But his female dog of a wife was there."

"Watch your mouth!"

"Yeah, yeah, whatever. She's such a pain."

"Well, what did she say?"

"Nothing much worth repeating really. Oh yeah, she did say she was looking for him too. I told her he probably out with some friends since he was off today."

"He took the day off work?" asked Jerri.

"All day. But yeah, I told her that he would probably turn up drunk somewhere. I even said, he probably at the strip club smacking some booty. Ha! But yeah she looking for him too."

"Why you always starting trouble with her?"

"Because I can't stand her. I don't like how controlling and selfish she is. She thinks that she is miss high and mighty and that the sun rises and sets on her funky behind."

"Hmm, if you ask me, I think you don't like how much your brother loves her. But hey what do I know?"

"Whatever. Anyways, Dad, since you seem like you are relatively yourself again, the nurse and doctor seemed a little alarmed at how you woke up from the anesthesia. Do you remember any of that? What happened?" Jumi prodded.

"Honestly, I'm scared to death. I had such a terrible dream. It was so vivid and seemed so real. So much so I really need to know he is okay."

Jerri started to envision his dream once again. And scowled as he relived some of it in his thoughts. He was clearly bothered by the thought of losing his son. Tears welled in his eyes. He tried his best to contain his emotions, but he couldn't. It was like something was ready to burst on the inside. He turned on his side to try to hide his tears, but the thought of Seven being in danger jolted him. He couldn't relax. He needed to see Seven.

"Dad, are you okay?" Jumi asked, her voice laden with

worry.

Jerri's lips quivered. He tried not to respond because he knew if he opened his mouth, he would no longer be able to control his emotions.

"Dad?" Jumi inched closer, a panic beginning to settle.

"No! It's all my fault! I'm so sorry!"

Jerri began to cry again—even more uncontrollably than when we awoke from anesthesia. He couldn't hold it in any longer. He had reached his limit. Jumi's eyes widened, quite taken back, as she had never seen her father show this level of emotion before.

"What's wrong Dad? Please tell me," Jumi stretched out her hand to console him.

"I've been a horrible father. I *am* a horrible father," he cried out, his voice laced with suppressed pain and guilt.

Jumi looked on in amazement hearing her father's words. Never had she heard her father sound so remorseful. Not for anything. Her mouth was slightly ajar as she was in utter disbelief of the words that were flooding out of her father's mouth. She tried to console him but really didn't know what to say.

"Dad, it's okay. Well it's not okay, but it will be all right… I dunno… What happened? Tell me please," she consoled. She knew there was no way of denying the truth. Their father had messed up, big time. But rehashing the past when he was in this state was a bad idea. So, she waited.

“I have failed my son. In so many ways have I failed my son. As a child, as a young man, and as an adult. I have failed him! Over and over again. I have failed him. The many times he has tried to make amends with me, I have been stubborn and blamed him. I blamed him because he would call me out on my crap and I hated that about him. It reminded me of his mother,” Jerri cried, putting his face in his hands.

“I could’ve been there for him, I could’ve made a difference. Instead, I allowed my son to go through so much pain, hardship, and abuse. Like that man his mom married. I remember him telling the story of how he first met that guy. I’m so sorry that I left him hanging.”

*****Summer of 1984*****

“Hey Mom?” Seven approached cautiously, knowing too well how his mom didn’t like to be disturbed when she was watching daytime TV on her day off.

“Yes, Seven?” She answered rather abruptly, but this didn’t prevent him from continuing.

“Can I go outside?” He waited, anticipating the next question.

"Where are you going?" She asked without taking her eyes away from the TV.

"I wanted to go to the store and then go up the street and play with my friends. Is that okay?" Seven asked in the sweetest voice he could muster. He waited with bated breath.

"Sure baby, go ahead. Make sure you are in by the time the street lights come on," she responded, oblivious to the sweaty mess that had formed underneath Seven's armpits. He was nervous, but after her reaction, he wondered why he had been.

"I know Momma, I will," he turned to leave, but he heard the sound from the TV lowered. He spun back around to face his mother.

"And I want you to meet someone when you come back too okay?" She looked at him, a smile on her lips.

"Okay. Who is it?" Seven asked, curious about his mother's request. Usually, she wouldn't announce her visitors. But this felt different and he didn't know why.

"Just a friend of mine. They'll be here by the time you get back in. I want you to be on your best behavior okay?" Her question was more of a command, but Seven understood what she meant.

"Okay Momma," he acquiesced, his mind diverting back to the mission at hand.

Seven's insides jumped with joy as he rushed to his room

and pulled out his Incredible Hulk change bank from behind his room door. He took twenty dollars to buy candy for himself and his friend.

"Bye Momma," he yelled as he left. He started to run down the steps so fast that he didn't even notice the man headed up.

"Hey watch it kid!"

Seven barreled into the man and knocked something out of his hand. In his anger, he pushed Seven to the ground and barked at him.

"That cost me money you stupid kid!" The corners' of the man's mouth formed as he shook a finger towards Seven.

"I'm sorry sir. I didn't see you. But you don't have to yell at me."

"Who do you think you're talking to twerp? I'll smack fire out ya behind! You best learn to respect your elders." The man inched closer.

"My grandpa says respect is earned not given. And if an adult disrespects a kid, then the kid has the right to stand up for himself. My grandpa is a boxer and I'll get him to beat you up, so go ahead and hit me."

The man stared at Seven. Seven stared back with his fists clutched.

"Hmm, you're pretty tough for a little kid. A good butt

whoopin' would soften you up a bit. You're lucky I have something to do. But I'll see you again. Twerp!"

Seven watched and wondered who the man was going to see. Seven and his mom lived in a rooming house on the corner of Straight Street and Hamilton Ave, so he literally could have been there to see anyone. The man turned and walked into the house.

Seven ran along and met his friend at the store. They bought candy fish, a bag of dipsey doodles, and some Now & Laters. Once they had their snacks, they headed off to play. With the earlier incident with the man a fleeting memory, Seven enjoyed his afternoon eating and playing to his heart's content. Before long, the street lights came on.

Seven then ran down the street, past the store, and back to his house. As he walked up the steps, he could hear someone laughing with his mother through the cracked window. The voice sounded familiar. Familiar enough that he paused before going into the house.

"Who is that?" Seven said aloud as he slowly walked up the steps. He listened to the voices as he went. He reached the door and hesitated to enter until he heard his mother.

"Seven should be in by now. I don't know where he is, but he should be in any minute."

"It's okay."

"So, how long have you worked for transit?" asked Sissy.

"Um, like 2 years now. It's been great for me. Shoot, I'll even retire there if they let me." he replied.

"That's great. Only thing better than a man with a job is a man planning to *keep* a job," Sissy retorted, pouting her mouth in the process.

"Oh *really*?"

"Anyways, what route do you drive?" Sissy asked, a slight chuckle lingering in her voice.

"I drive the 746. Goes all the way up to the Ridgewood train station which is not far from Valley Hospital. That's the only route I've been driving for the last 2 years. Drive it all day long," the man replied confidently.

"That's a lot of driving. How long it take you each way?"

"About 20 minutes or so."

"So, tell me. How much do bus drivers actually make?"

"You really going to ask me that?" The man asked, slightly taken aback by Sissy's forwardness.

"I'm just saying. Didn't mean to offend you."

"It's okay. But we make *enough*. Hey, can I use your bathroom?" he asked.

"Um, sure, go walk to the back. It's the room to the right of the hallway next to my son's room," Sissy said, pointing in the direction she was describing.

At that moment, Seven used his key to unlock the door and walked in. "Hey Momma. Sorry, I'm a few minutes late. I ran down the street as soon as the streetlights came on just like you told me to."

"Hey baby. It is okay you're not too late. Have a seat here. I would like to introduce you to someone."

Sissy patted the empty space beside her on the couch. Seven obliged her, and ran over. He made himself comfortable, as she nestled him in a shoulder-to-shoulder embrace.

"Who Momma?"

"Remember I told you before you left that I wanted to introduce you to a friend of mine?"

"Oh, yeah. Are they here already?" Seven's earlier memories came flooding back to him. He had forgotten about what his mom had told him.

"Yes, he's in the bathroom."

"Is this like, your boyfriend or something?"

"Um, I wouldn't say that quite yet, but I like him a little and he seems to like me, so I thought it would be fair to introduce you to him. Is that okay?"

"Okay Momma."

"So, did you have fun outside?"

"Yeah, we went to the store and then to the field and were

flipping on the mattresses. I'm a little tired now."

"I hope you didn't spend all of your money."

"No, I only spent like a dollar or two, so I still have change left."

Seven patted his pockets, looked up at her, and produced an ear-splitting smile. A faint jingling sound could be heard.

"That's my baby. Money doesn't grow on trees so always be careful with what you have. Always save some for a rainy day," Sissy smiled back, rubbing the top of his head in the process.

"I will."

"Are you hungry?" she asked.

"Yep. What's for dinner?"

"Corned beef and cabbage."

"Okay. Momma, is your friend eating dinner with us?"

"Um, I believe so."

"Well, what time are we going to eat?"

"Once he comes out the bathroom. Then, you can go wash your hands and we'll eat and talk."

"Okay. But he sure is taking a long time in the bathroom. I hope he ain't stinkin' it up in there," Seven teased, emitting a small chuckle.

When Seven heard the toilet flush, he said, "I guess he's done Momma. I'll go set the table."

"You're such a wonderful son," Sissy beamed with joy. She couldn't help but feel like the luckiest woman on the planet for having such a kind and thoughtful son like Seven.

Seven left the living room and went into the kitchen to set the table for dinner. After a few moments, he heard his mom speaking again to someone in the living room. The voice boomed throughout the room.

"Dang am I gonna' need to spray in there?" his mom asked.

"What do you mean?" asked the man.

"You were in there for a long time."

"Yeah it's not what you think."

"It better not be!"

"Oh, stop playing and introduce me to your son already."

"Mhmm. Come into the kitchen so I can introduce you."

"After you beautiful."

They went into the kitchen. As they walked in, Seven turned and couldn't believe his eyes.

"Hey baby. This is my friend Sam."

"Sam, this is my son, Seven."

They both looked at each other and had a similar sense of confusion. Seven couldn't believe it. This was the man that threatened him outside on the steps. His mom immediately knew something was off as the awkward silence was obvious.

"Seven? Where's your manners? Aren't you going to say hello?"

No one spoke. Not even Sam.

"Okay what's going on here?" she asked.

"Ask your friend, Momma."

"Sam? What's up? Do you know my son from somewhere or something?" Sissy turned her full attention on Sam, a questioning look on her face.

"Um… actually I do. We just met as I was coming in and he was headed out. I don't want to get him in trouble but, he damn near knocked me down when he was running down the steps. Didn't even apologize. And when I tried to tell him he needs to apologize, he said something about getting his grandfather to beat me up," Sam replied, shrugging his shoulders.

"Liar!" Seven shouted.

"Seven, hush your mouth," Sissy said, shocked by Seven's attitude.

"He's a liar, Momma."

"I'm sorry, like I said, I didn't want to get him in trouble, but he even cussed at me because he dropped all of his money on the ground. And to be honest, after he cussed at me, I was ready to put hands on him and he knew it. And he knew he was wrong, but refused to apologize still. I yelled at him that he needed to have respect for his elders, and he yelled back at me saying his grandpa is a boxer and that respect is earned not given. This young man right here, is truly something else," Sam's voice dripped with feigned honesty.

"Liar!" Seven couldn't believe what Sam was saying. He was twisting the story.

"Seven. Don't make me tell you again," Seven's mom hissed through gritted teeth.

"But Momma, it didn't go like that."

"So how did it go huh? I'm telling you to hush up and you not listening to me. Your mother. The only one that takes care of you. So, if you ain't listening to me, I can only imagine how you treated him with him being a stranger. I tell you all the time. What does the Bible say about strangers?"

"Be careful how you entertain strangers because they may be angels unawares."

"That's right. Now go wash your hands and get ready for dinner!" she hissed at Seven.

Seven's shoulders slumped and his head lowered, as he couldn't understand why his mom wouldn't believe him. He then became furious. His eyes bulged and his face frowned. He saw the look on his mom's face. She was very upset and embarrassed shaking her head at him. He could hear his heart beat in his ears, hard and fast as he walked past them heading for the bathroom. He stopped halfway and looked up.

"He ain't no angel. He's a liar!" Seven yelled.

"Go. Now!" she yelled back.

Seven turned again and walked into the bathroom. He initially held his breath, assuming that there would be a foul odor since Sam took so long in there. To his surprise there wasn't one. So, he reached for soap to wash his hands and noticed something on the sink.

"What is this? I guess someone spilled baby powder?"

He rinsed it off, grabbed the soap, and washed his hands. The whole time he was trapped in his own thoughts as he dried his hands and went into his room.

I guess I should clean up my room and watch TV.

Seven started to change his clothes, preparing for bed. He took off his jeans and then realized he still has change left over from the store. So, he went into his pockets and grabbed the change he had and walked over to his bank. He looked at it and he was confused. So, he opened it up from the bottom and was in disbelief.

Where is it? Where is my money? He thought to himself.

He frantically searched his room in a panic— looking under his bed, in the corner behind the door where the bank had sat. He looked everywhere. He sat on his bed and retraced his steps in his mind.

Where did I put it?

A tear trickled down his cheek and then he had a realization.

Him! He did this! He is the devil that Momma warns about all the time! It's him!

He became so furious that his hands started shaking as he heard his mother talking. "I'm sorry. I don't know what has gotten into my son today. I assure you I have never ever seen him act this way."

"Ah it's okay. He's a teenager." Sam replied in a tone excusing Seven's behavior.

"No, he's not. He's only nine."

"Really?"

"Yes."

"Wow, that's crazy. You have a big boned son. I just knew he was fourteen or fifteen by his size and how he spoke."

"Nope he's only nine. Anyway, I originally wanted you to stay for dinner. I understand if you didn't want to now. This totally didn't go as I expected."

"No, it's okay. Listen, I'm sorry. I didn't mean to put him on front street like that. But listen, I'll take a raincheck on dinner to give him some time for this to pass. I wanted to make a memorable first impression but I think this will be memorable for the wrong reasons."

"Again, I'm so sorry. I hope you give me the chance to make it up to you."

"Oh, you best believe sexy. You are going to definitely make it up to me!"

"Oh, is that *right*?" Seven's mom chuckled and teased.

At that moment, Seven ran into the living room, only in his underwear, and stopped in Sam's face as he was sitting on the couch.

"Where's my money!" Seven yelled as he stood in front of Sam.

"Money? What money baby?" his mom asked.

"The money that was in my hulk bank. He stole it!"

"I don't know what you're talkin' 'bout boy. But I know you better raise up off me." Sam gave an unconcerned response, as if Seven was a fly bothering his tranquility.

"Seven! Sam! Stop this!" Seven's mom begged, wondering what had gotten into him.

"No Momma. He's a liar and a thief!"

"You know what, I don't have to take this. I suggest you call me when you get your son in line."

"Excuse me?" she replied.

"You heard." Sam fired back.

"Don't talk to my momma like that!" Seven's angered

boiled.

"Listen, you clearly got something against me. Maybe I'm wearing the wrong jeans or you don't like my dreadlocks, or maybe you hate your dad so much that you hate all men, including yourself. But I'm not going to stand here, and take this from some child that is clearly spoiled and needs a good whoopin'," Sam's laidback aura belied the contempt in his voice.

"Sam wait. Let me walk you out." Sissy insisted.

Sam's words stung Seven like he touched a hot stove. When Sam and his mother walked outside, Seven ran to his room and cried. Tears ran down his face as he replayed Sam's words in his mind. From sadness, to anger, to feeling unworthy. He cried and punched his pillow repeatedly. His last swing missed the pillow, and hit the wall so hard that he put a hole in it.

What does he know about my dad? I wish my dad were here so he could kick your butt! But why isn't my dad even here? Does he even know about me? Momma never talks about him. Does he not even want to be my dad?

Seven cried and punched until he ultimately fell asleep. The exhaustion of it all put him in a restless state, tossing and turning as if having a bad dream.

Chapter 6: Hindsight

"Wow Dad. Seven never told me that story before. But I do know that Sam guy was something else," Jumi stated, her hands clutching her shoulders in comfort.

"Yeah. I always wondered if Seven was making some of it up to try to make me feel bad. That's why I resisted it for so long," Jerri stifled a sniff.

"I mean some of the stories he told me seem to be unrealistic. Like the time Sam beat Seven with an extension cord for changing the channel on the TV," Jumi shook her head, a sense of guilt settling in her bones.

"Yeah, he even told me that Sam whooped him for not being me…" Jerri's voice trailed away. His chest heaved slightly recollecting his blasé attitude when Seven had relayed the story.

"For not being you?" asked Jumi, her eyes widening.

"Yeah. He said one day Sam was drunk or high, which from what I hear he was consistently, he was stumbling home and some kids Seven's age were throwing rocks at him. So, he decided to go home and get Seven to fight the kids for him."

"Really? Did Seven do it?"

"No. He refused. Not only did he not fight the boys, when Sam asked him if he were his real father, would Seven fight the boys then. Seven said that he would. So, he ended up getting whooped really bad. I wished I were there for him," Jerri's eyes remained downcast as he stared into his hands shocked by his past attitude.

"Dang I didn't know that story either, Dad," Jumi shifted slightly, mimicking her dad's posture. *Did I really know my brother?* She couldn't help but think.

"Yeah Seven has so many stories. I didn't know most of them till the last year or so. But when did he tell you the story about the extension cord?" Jerri averted his eyes upwards, fixing attention on Jumi.

"Oh, when he came to live with us. He told me another story. One that really scared me," Jumi explained.

"Well, tell me," Jerri's voice was calm, belying the impatience that was growing within.

*****Spring of 1986*****

Seven woke to the sound of his mother calling his name. He turned over slowly, rubbed the sleep particles out of his eyes, and yawned. He stretched his limbs, reliving his muscles from the fixed and bound state he had been in while asleep.

"Is it 6:30 already, Mom?" He asked, mid-yawn.

"Yes, it is. So, you have to get ready for school," Sissy said, in a matter-of-factly sort of way.

"I hate school. You think I could go to another school next year?" There was no point in masking the truth. Seven did not like school. In fact, he wished he could skip the hustle altogether and graduate without needing to be physically present at school.

"Seven, we talked about this. We can't afford to move right now. Besides you'll make friends next year. I'm sure of it," Sissy assured.

"They don't want to be friends with me. Everyone in my class is a year older than me. They call me a nerd for being eleven in the seventh grade," Seven said, counting on his logical argument to convince his mom to let him stay at home and away from the bullies.

"Don't let them make fun of you just because your smart baby," Sissy's soothing and uplifting voice fell on deaf ears.

"It's too hard, Momma. I don't want to go there anymore." Seven pleaded.

"Come on, get up and get dressed and I'll make you some breakfast," the finality in her voice told Seven that she had had enough of his whining.

"Okay, what are you making for dinner?" Seven changed the subject. He wanted to make sure that even though he was going to school, he had something to look forward too after.

"You worried about dinner already?" Sissy chuckled.

"Just asking. I'll be hungry after school because the school food sucks bad," Seven punctuated the sentence with a 'bleurgh'.

"I understand. I think I'll make some rice, ground beef patties and gravy. How does that sound?" Sissy's tone elevated slightly.

"Sounds good to me."

Seven could already anticipate the feeling of fullness that accompanied a home cooked meal. His struggles in school would be well worth the dinner waiting for him.

"Okay, I'll make it before I go to work and you can warm it up when you get home."

"Thanks Momma. What time will you be home? Oh, and are the exterminators coming today?"

"Oh, it will definitely be after midnight tonight. Why do you ask me this all the time now?"

"I like to know when you will be home. I miss you, Momma."

"Aw, I miss you too baby. Especially since I don't get to see you when you come home from school since I changed schedules. And the exterminator will be out this weekend."

"Okay good. We have so many roaches I think we need bunkbeds so they don't have to sleep with me," Seven teased, a look of mischief on his face.

"Ha! That's funny," Sissy laughed. "Hopefully that won't be a problem anymore after they treat the house again."

"Do you think you're going to change your schedule back?"

"Hmm, not right now baby. Like I told you before, they pay me more to work late and we really need the money."

"I understand. I just wish we could go back to how things use to be."

"All we can do is move forward and let God do the rest."

"Doesn't seem like God is with us these days though, Momma. Especially not with me," Seven felt a tightness grow in his chest.

"Why do you say that?" Sissy asked, curiously.

"Because things are different and I'm sad. We moved away from my friends, the kids over here all hate me, all the girls in my class think I'm ugly, and other things too."

With things in school not going well, Seven felt the pang of loneliness more than he had ever felt.

"Okay, things will get better baby, trust me," Sissy tried to console him. She extended her hand to rub his shoulders as a sign of affection, but Seven shrugged it off.

"You always say that. But everything keeps getting worse. I hate it here; I hate my life!"

Seven stormed by his mom and headed to the bathroom. He opened and slammed the door so hard that the walls shook. He looked into the mirror, stared into his own eyes and cried at his reality.

No one understands what I'm going through. No one! Why did you let this happen to me? No one likes me. They all hate me. I even hate myself! I'm all alone. Why do I have to be by myself? Everyone else has an older brother or sister or even a cousin that protects them. Who is here to protect me? No one, that's who! Seven's mind was racing. Thoughts merged into each other, sending him on a spiral. He couldn't believe how things had turned out so horribly wrong. He couldn't believe how unfair life was.

Seven looked in the mirror again, then something happened. His sadness, and insecurity, turned to anger, better yet, rage. He washed his face and looked at himself again.

"Screw it. If no one wants to be there for me, or protect me, then I'll take care of myself!" he mumbled aloud.

He finished washing up and then went back to his room to get dressed for the day. He put on some slightly ripped jeans, an old t-shirt, and his play sneakers.

If they want war then it's war. I wish someone would say something to me today. Because today we all will be fighting! He thought while nodding in agreement with himself. He was determined to stake his ground. He had had enough.

Seven grabbed his bag and headed to the door.

"Seven... listen…Boy what are you wearing?" Sissy wanted to talk about what transpired between them, but his attire preceded the much-needed conversation.

Seven looked at his mom, eyes-narrowed and squinted, and walked out the front door without acknowledging her question—down the steps and out the door without a seconds thought. He walked up the street he lived on, North 4th Street, and headed to his school, School #12. Before long he was walking in a small crowd of other kids headed into the school.

"I must be running late. There's normally more kids out here," he muttered under his breath. The anger within him subsided slightly, but still lingered within his peripheral.

As he approached, he heard the bell ring to start class. Seven rushed into the building and up the stairs to class. All the other kids were already in their seats as Seven opened the classroom door. His heart was pumping hard, he was still angry, but nervous at this point as he walked through the front of the class.

"Yo, why you dressed like a bum?" one of the boys teased.

The anger surfaced, like a bull waiting to charge.

"Leon yo momma a bum." Seven spat, his mouth opening before any sense of logical thinking stopped him. He snarled and waited, patient like a cheetah after its prey.

"What? You gonna' let this punk talk to you like that?" another boy yelled.

"I ain't no punk. Your father a punk Brandon!" Seven replied, spitefully. He wasn't taking any prisoners today.

"Ugmug must've ate his spinach today. Y'all gonna' let him talk like that to y'all?" Another voice from the back piped up. The nonchalance in the voice fueled Seven's anger.

"Who you callin' Ugmug? *Baldilocks*! At least my mother ain't no crackhead!"

And just like that, Seven was going off on anyone who had something negative to say to him. The class erupted into laughter, and an air of commotion settled in the room.

"Seven calm down. I'm not sure why you're feeling the need to start trouble this morning. Please take your seat," the teacher quickly tried to calm the situation down.

"Me? I'm not the trouble maker. They always bothering me and you never say anything to them. But as soon as I defend myself then you yell at me? That's not fair. Y'all all against me and have always been but I'm not taking no more crap from none of y'all. Every single one of you can kiss my butt and go to hell. And if you don't like it then we can fight!" He raised his voice above the continued class chatter.

"Seven sit down before I send you to the office!"

Seven briefly stared at his teacher, walked to his desk, and sat down.

"And I meant it. Play me close if you wanna'!" Seven pulled out his books and smirked. It felt good to defend himself.

Yeah I told them. They know not to mess with me anymore. Yeah, I'll stand up for myself! Seven mentally patted himself on the back.

While he had never been a disrespectful kid, he had clearly had enough of the constant bullying by his older classmates. Every day, different kids would do all kinds of things to him. Like smack him in the back of the head, talk about his clothes, push him around, all while the girls laughed while he was ridiculed. But not anymore. Today was going to be the last day he would be bullied. Seven made it through the rest of the day without incident. No teasing, no bullying of any kind. Even the girls didn't bother him.

Finally, school was over and Seven was excited to go home and tell his mother how his day went. Seven started to pack up his things and noticed the rest of the kids were already headed out the door. Normally, he would be the first to leave because he always rushed to get away from the same three kids that bullied him the most. He threw his book bag over his shoulder and strutted out of the classroom, full of pride, with his head held high. He walked down the steps and onto the playground as he headed for the street that led to his house. He then noticed a huge crowd forming outside of the playground gate. He was almost through the crowd and then he heard someone shout out, “There he go!”

Seven turned to the voice and realized it was one of the boys from his class that he insulted earlier. He looked again and realized that all three of them were together and the crowd was around them waiting for him.

“You said you wanted to fight us right?”

“Yeah you called my father a punk, right punk?”

“Yeah, we all can go to hell right? Or we can fight, right?”

Seven took a step backwards as he was caught completely off guard. He never expected that the boys had planned to try to catch him after school. He started to get nervous and his heart begun to pound in his chest. But the morning pep talk flooded his mind. There was no turning back. He had no recourse other than standing his ground and showing them that he was not a coward.

Instead of running, Seven walked up into the middle of the crowd and got in their faces.

“I don’t hear you talking now punk!” Brandon snickered, squaring up with Seven.

“Like I said before, your father is a punk!”

Seven then reached back and punched Brandon in the face. Brandon staggered and fell to the ground.

“Ohhh,” screamed the crowd of kids.

He looked up at Seven in almost disbelief. "Get him!" he yelled to the other two kids.

They rushed Seven and tackled him. One was holding him and the other was kicking and pinning him next to the gate. Seven could barely move.

"Let me up punk! Y'all some girls! Gotta jump me?" Seven yelled.

"Let him up. Get off of him. Let him up!" Someone yelled.

They backed away and Seven returned to his feet, still swinging. This time he punched Leon in the face. The other kid grabbed him again and tackled him. Leon and Brandon both joined in, and the beat down started. Kicked and punched, Seven felt every impact, sensing bruises already forming under his skin. Some older high school kids started to break it up after a few minutes.

"That's it, y'all got yours. Let the kid up."

After it was broken up, Seven stood, head held high and stared down the three boys that had jumped him. His eye slightly swollen, jaw and ribs slightly hurting, blood trickling down his mouth, he wiped it away and stood tall. Despite the physical impingement, a sense of pride warmed Seven's chest.

"Y'all all some punks. Took three of y'all just for me. I'm gonna' see y'all again. And if I ever catch any of y'all by yourselves it's over for y'all. Y'all better stay together for the rest of y'all lives!" He spat, punctuating his declaration by spitting out a mouth full of blood and looking them dead in the eyes.

Oddly enough the three looked at each other and then walked away. While they clearly did not lose this fight, they recognized that Seven was no longer going to back down. Strangely enough, he had earned their respect.

"That's right walk away sissies. We can do this again tomorrow punks. I ain't scared of y'all no more. We can fight again right now!"

Seven continued to talk trash while the older boy held him back.

"Hey, little man. I think they get the point. You proved yourself, but you may want to be a little smarter next time. Truth be told, we saved you cause they was kicking your behind."

"That's okay, but I'll never go down without a fight again." Seven said, neither flinching or wavering in his admittance.

"I respect that fight in you lil man. I think you should go home now though."

Seven looked at him and nodded. He picked up his book bag, and headed home. All the while he walked like he was ten feet tall. He had regained his sense of pride and respect in himself.

I did it. I stood up to them. They know not to mess with me now. Man I dropped two of them too. If they were one on one fights I know I would've won. I'm the man! I can't wait to tell Momma! He thought to himself.

As Seven got to his house, he grinned. He pulled out his key and unlocked the door. Then he paused. His smile gradually dissipated and in moments he was sad again. He looked at his watch and had a thought.

Dang I only have two hours before the street lights come on and eight whole hours before Momma gets home. I'm just going to do my homework in the hallway.

Seven opened the door and sat on the steps in the hallway. He looked up the stairs to his door, on the second floor, and sighed as he pulled out his notebook to get his homework done. He was always good in class so he powered through most of it before his watch alarm went off.

Seven packed up his book bag with his notebook and school books and slowly walked up the stairs. The closer he got to the door, the more and more he could hear the reggae music that played in the background. He dropped his head, sighed again, and then used his key to open the door. Once the door opened, the blaring music filled the entire hallway, shaking the walls of the three-bedroom family house. He peeked down the hallway, but didn't see anyone. So, he closed the door, locked it, and then made a dash for his bedroom on the other end of the house.

Maybe he's asleep. Let me hurry up, he thought.

Seven rushed through the living room, through the den, but

stopped abruptly in the kitchen.

"Well don't just stand there looking stupid. What's up?" asked Sam.

"Hey."

Seven dropped his head and tried to maneuver past Sam without getting too close to him.

"And how was your day?" asked Sam.

"It was okay." Seven responded softly.

"Was it really?" Sam asked feigning interest.

"Yeah." Seven wanted to maintain some distance with Sam, especially today, but his insistence on carrying on with the conversation was putting a damper on those plans.

"I suppose it was. You seem to have lost track of time. You late."

Seven froze. His body shook slightly. He didn't know whether it was from the adrenaline washing away, and his body finally feeling the effects of earlier events, or the curtness in Sam's voice.

"Momma said I have till the street lights come on. And they don't come on till 6:30. It's only 6:10," Seven explained coherently. If anything, he thought mentioning his mom would keep him safe.

"I don't care what you momma told you. You little momma's boy. What time did I tell you to be in this house?" Sam asked, his voice tinged with malice.

"Right after school." Seven replied, his shoulders slumped.

"What?" Sam inched closer.

"Right after school." Seven responded, slightly hesitant.

"So then why are you late?" Sam asked between gritted teeth, towering over Seven.

"Well, because…"

Sam reached his hand back as Seven explained himself and smacked him so hard that he fell to the floor. He could feel that his face was swollen even more from that one hit alone.

"Seems I need to get that phone extension cord again for you, don't I?"

"No Sam, please." Seven realized his mistake too late.

"What did you just call me?"

"Dad, I called you Dad. Please Dad it won't happen again."

At that moment, Seven felt disappointed in himself. He had bravely fought the battle of his life against three kids in his class who constantly bullied him and won respect—three older kids at that. But at home, he could only whimper and beg for mercy—much like he had done for the past two years since his mom married Sam. One beating after another, and there was nothing he could do about it. If he told his mom then Sam would beat him harder the next time she wasn't around. But Sam wasn't a kid. He was a grown man and he hit like one too. Nevertheless, Seven was beginning to feel that same anger, that same rage build up on the inside of himself. Even more than what he felt this morning.

"I'm tired of this. Stop putting your hands on me!" Seven yelled.

"What was that, you little twerp?" Sam responded.

"I said, you are going to stop putting your hands on me."

"Oh yeah? And who is going to make me? You?" Sam let out a hearty uncontrollable laugh. He really thought that was funny. Sam then kicked him in the stomach as he was on the floor.

"You gonna' stop me? Huh? Get your behind up before I hit you again. Get up, do your work, eat your food, and get in your room. I don't want to see your face for the rest of the day."

Seven could barely breathe let alone get to his feet. Sam saw him struggling so he grabbed him by the back of his shirt and brought him to his feet. He then shoved him into his bedroom.

"Now get your work done and then come out to eat dinner after you get your mind right."

Seven winced in pain as he sat on his bed. He lifted up his shirt and saw that his side was bruised and had turned purple. When he took a deep breath, it hurt even worse.

"I hate him." he mumbled.

Seven quickly finished his work since he did most of it in the hallway. He then peeked out of his room to see if Sam was gone so that he could grab some food and then go back into his room.

Seven walked over to the stove and saw that the food his mother prepared did not have the lid on it.

Why didn't he put the top back on this? he thought.

He grabbed a plate and spoon and quickly started to closely inspect the food as he put some on his plate.

Okay, the rice is good to go. Let me check the gravy and meat. He thought as he continued to check the food.

As he picked through the ground beef and gravy, he was mortified. There were two adult roaches in the food. They were dead and not moving.

"Yuck. Why didn't he put the frickin' top back on the food? Now it's all ruined and I'm starving." he grumbled.

"What's ruined?" yelled Sam from his bedroom.

"There're roaches in the food," Seven responded in a somber tone.

"What?" Sam's voice boomed through the house.

"The food. It has roaches in it."

Sam came out of his room and walked into the kitchen.

"What's in the food?" He asked, an amused expression on his face.

"Roaches. So, I guess we need to throw it away," Seven

shrugged, extending his hand to put the plate down and prepare to empty the contents of the cooking pot.

"Throw it away? Nah we not wasting that food. What you think money grows on trees or something? You're gonna' eat that food."

Sam grabbed a spoon and filtered out the roaches and threw them in the trash. With the same spoon, he grabbed a huge helping to put over the rice on Seven's plate. Seven looked at Sam in disbelief that he actually wanted him to eat the food.

"It's okay, I'll just eat the rice."

"Either you eat it all or you eat nothing. You choose."

"Why can't I just have the plain rice?" Seven asked in confusion.

"Because I said so twerp. Now bring your plate over here."

"No. I'll just eat the rice."

Seven tried to turn away from Sam and walked as quick as he could with the rice he had already placed on his plate. He was starving after not eating the school lunch again today. Before he could take a bite of the rice Sam smacked the plate out of his hand.

"Why'd you do that?"

"You gotta problem with that?" Sam baited.

"Yeah I do. I'm hungry and my mom made that specifically for me."

"Oh yeah? Do something!" Sam walked up to his face. Seven didn't back away and glared at him. He really wanted to do something but he knew that it wouldn't end well for him.

"That's what I thought. Twerp."

Sam punched him in his stomach and Seven dropped to his knees. He gasped for air yet again. Desperately, he tried to catch his breath. Tears rolled down his face as he struggled to breathe.

"I'm telling my mother."

"What did you say?"

Seven dared not to repeat it. Sam grabbed a fistful of Seven's shirt and stood him up.

"What did you say? Answer me!"

Seven was so afraid that he shook and dared not say a word.

"Sounded like you said you were going to tell your mother. Is that what you said?" Sam snarled, white residue forming at the corners of his mouth.

Seven still refused to answer because he knew it would only get him hit even harder. So, he stayed quiet and whimpered again in pain. Sam looked at him face to face. Sam grabbed him by the throat. He lifted Seven in the air with one hand and choked him. Seven squirmed to try to get free and nearly did. Sam felt that he almost lost his grip so he added his second hand firming up his grip around his throat. Seven kicked and squirmed but Sam's grip around his neck was too tight. He couldn't scream, he couldn't breathe, and his movements slowed.

"You wanna' tell your mother, do you?"

Seven, with his back against the wall, unable to move, unable to breathe, started to black out. His limbs went limp, his eyes closed, and he could no longer resist. Sam then dropped him to the floor.

"The day you tell your mother anything is the day you die."

Sam walked away and left him sprawled out on the floor unconscious. He didn't even so much as turn around to see if Seven was okay. He walked into his room and closed the door. After a few moments, Seven opened his eyes. He could breathe. His body was so sore. The three boys jumped him from his class, and then he came home to be physically beaten and abused by his stepfather. He crawled into his room and closed the door. He started to tear up which quickly turned into a heartbroken weep.

"God why do you let this keep happening to me? I told my momma he was the devil when he stole the money out my bank and lied about how he talked to me when we first met. What else is there that she needs to see in order to know he's not right for us? I want to run away but where can I go? There is no one to protect me. My mom says you protect us all but where is my protection? Are you even real? You are a fake! Because if you was real you would help me!" he cried aloud.

Seven continued to cry and cry, lost in his thoughts about his life. How hard it had been. And how everything changed, the moment that his mom met Sam. It seemed like he had thought and cried for hours on end. And soon he felt he was ready to fall asleep.

No. I gotta stay up. I gotta stay up. Don't go to sleep.

He desperately fought off the heaviness of sleep that was cocooning him like a soft blanket. But he was drifting. Slowly, his body relaxed more and more, and before he realized it, his eyes were closed. He heard a slight noise that caused him to open his eyes once more. He thought he heard the front door close.

He waited in anticipation. He had hoped that this was the moment he long awaited. But he dared not move ahead of time as it would result in another beat down. So, he waited, patiently. He listened ever so closely. Then he heard Sam. He was now excited and couldn't wait.

"Hey honey. How was your day?" asked Sam.

"Hey. It was tiring. I'm so tired. I just want to eat some food and go to sleep," Sissy sighed, placing her car and house keys on the table adjacent to the door.

"Yeah I hear ya. Let me take your coat," Sam offered.

"Oh, aren't you such the gentleman," Sissy chuckled slightly.

"You know I love me some you," Sam replied, eyeing her up

and down as she twirled to remove her coat.

"Did Seven get in from school okay?"

"Yeah he got in all right. Just not on time as usual. I swear, that boy of yours never listens to a word I say."

"Really? I'll speak to him in the morning."

"Baby you spoil him too much. That's why he's soft. You need to toughen him up a bit and stop spoiling him," Sam's voice was laden with indignation, that for some reason Sissy could not detect.

"Yeah, yeah, yeah. Can we talk about this tomorrow? I'm really tired."

"Sure. You want me to make you a plate?"

"No. I can manage."

They both then walked into the kitchen.

"Actually, you know what you can do for me?" Sissy asked.

"Anything."

"Hmm, I bet. Anyway, can you run the tub for me. I think I want to soak in the tub for a while. My feet are killing me."

"Your wish is my command beautiful."

Sam walked out of the kitchen and into the bathroom. Seven could hear the water as it ran from his room. He gently cracked open his door and peeked out. Seven left his room light off so no one could tell his door had opened. He could see his mother in the kitchen making her a plate of food.

He didn't even tell her there were roaches in it. I hate him. He thought.

He was about to step out of the room, but then Sam walked back into the kitchen.

"Think we can go out this weekend beautiful? Just us? Maybe we can get someone to watch the kid?" Sam coaxed, a flirtatious tone in his voice.

"Did you hit the *lottery* or something?" Sissy asked, in between spoonsful of food.

"No, why you gotta say it like that?" Sam shrugged, his expression turning slightly sour.

"Because last I checked, you was broke." Sissy answered after a few seconds.

"Why you always have to be so negative? I told you the strike will be over soon at Transit," Sam coaxed.

"I'm not being negative. I'm being realistic. I'm not spending any money on anything that we don't absolutely need because it's really tight right now," Sissy sighed.

"Yeah I get it. I'll be making some more money soon," he chuckled lightly to reduce the tension in the room.

"Listen Sam. I don't wanna' be rude but I'm really *really* tired. Can you check and make sure the tub is not overflowing?"

Sissy looked at him, pleading to be reprieved from the situation they were in.

"Overflowing? I just came back out and it's only been a minute," Sam's voice dripped with confusion.

"I don't want to argue Sam. I'm simply tired," Sissy shook her head slightly, yearning to be left alone.

"Okay, sure. I guess you don't want to talk to me today. Fine, I'll check on the tub and then I'll go to bed… I guess," Sam put up his hands in frustration.

"Thanks. I'll be in soon."

"Promise?"

"Mhmm..." Sissy said as she brought another spoonful up to her mouth.

Sam walked back to the bathroom with a slight grin on his face. Seven watched him walk down the hall and waited for a second. He then swung his room door open and bolted to his mother. He grabbed her by the waist and hugged her so tight.

"Hey baby. What you still doing up? Aw, you miss me?"

Seven stayed quiet, but refused to let his mother go. He squeezed her tighter and tighter—so tight that she could feel how fast his heart was beating.

"Seven? What's wrong baby?"

He didn't answer. He just held her. She looked down at him

and saw that tears were streaming down his face. As she looked even closer, she noticed a bruise over his left cheek.

"Seven, what happened? Come on. Tell me what's wrong."

He looked up at her and all he could muster was a whisper.

"Sam."

"Sam? What about Sam? What happened?"

"Sam. He choked me, Momma. I couldn't breathe. And he threw me on the floor."

"What!"

She pulled back his shirt and the force of Sam's hands around Seven's neck had left welts where his fingers were. They were quite visible.

"He hurt me, Momma. He always hurts me when you're not home," Seven answered, his body beginning to shiver.

She looked Seven in his eyes and a tear rolled down her cheek. She was ashamed and disappointed.

"I'm so sorry baby. This is my fault. After today, you won't ever have to worry about Sam ever again." Sissy uttered, a sense of guilt filling her body.

******

Jerri's eyes widened in disbelief. He couldn't imagine that his son had gone through this type of abuse. And at the hands of his mother's husband.

"He actually told you that?" asked Jerri.

"Yes Dad," Jumi averted her eyes. Retelling the story had left her feeling empty. To-date, she couldn't believe the things that Seven had gone through.

"When did this happen?" Jerri prodded.

"He came to live with us during his freshman year of high school and this was in the seventh grade he said. So, 2 years before he came to live with us," Jumi responded, digging deep within her to remember the exact dates.

"Wow Jumi. He's been through all of this?" Jerri looked at his hands, a mixture of shame and guilt weighing heavily on his mind.

"Yeah. We talk about stuff every so often since we are adults now. He specifically said that this was a moment that altered the trajectory of his life, for the second time."

At that moment, Faith walked into Jerri's room. She clearly looked worried, but sat in the chair positioned by the door without saying a word not to interrupt their conversation.

"It makes me feel even worse. The whole time I felt like he had no respect and needed discipline, but the truth is I wanted him to respect me because I felt like he had no respect for me as his father.

All the beatings I gave him. And that last one? I'm so ashamed," Jerri heaved.

"I mean, I don't want to add insult to injury, but you really did do him wrong when he lived with us for those few months, Dad," Jumi shuddered at the memories.

Chapter 7: Off the Porch

****Summer of 1988*****

Sissy hurried to finish preparing for her shift, packing up her things in her night bag. She searched around for her house keys, looked at herself in the mirror to make sure everything was in place and walked towards the door. She slipped on comfortable work shoes while simultaneously patting herself down to make sure she had everything she needed. She sighed, mentally preparing for the long shift that awaited her.

"Seven?"

"Yeah Momma?"

"Are you going to be okay while I'm at work?"

"Yeah I'll be fine."

"*Yeah*? And when did you start answering me with *yeah?*"

"Sorry. *Yes*. Momma," Seven replied.

"That's more like it. Just because you're 13 and starting high school in September, that doesn't mean you're grown."

"I know momma. Sorry."

"Now listen, I left the number to my cottage at the nursing home on the fridge. So, if you need me for something you call right away okay?"

"Yes Momma, I will."

"And what time do I get off?"

"At 7 a.m.," Seven replied, stifling an eye-roll. He couldn't understand why his mom insisted on having this conversation every day.

"That's right. It would probably take me a little over an hour or so to get home."

"Okay."

"All right. Its 10:30 p.m. and my bus comes in about 15 minutes so I need to leave. Remember don't open the door for anyone okay?"

"Okay Momma. See you later. And have a good day. Or night at work."

Sissy gave Seven a hug and kissed him on the cheek. She left out the door and closed it behind her.

"Make sure you put all the locks on the door," she said through the closed door.

"Okay Momma."

Seven did as instructed and locked the door behind his mother after she left out. He went into the living room, turned on the TV, and smiled. He was happy. It had been a little over a year since his mom left Sam and they moved to Harrison Street. His eighth-grade year went by relatively quickly. He had done well in school and was looking forward to the summer. While he watched TV, he heard the glaring sounds of a siren from outside. The piercing noise rung high above the TV sound, accompanied by flashing red and blue lights that illuminated the living room walls and ceiling. Seven's attention was drawn and he walked over to the window and peeked outside but couldn't see what was going on. But he heard what sounded like crowds of people yelling. He desperately wanted to see the action, so he decided to take a look.

Seven walked outside and sat on the porch of the multi-family house. He watched as the police arrested someone and had many other people laying on the ground with their hands behind their heads.

"What did you do?" a lady yelled to her son who was in cuffs.

"They hit me mom. I didn't do anything. Look at my face mom!" her son yelled back.

"Officer, why are you arresting him?" his mom asked.

"Ma'am get back." The officer responded.

"My son is only 15 and as his parent I have a right to question you. Now what is he being arrested for?"

"Ma'am if you don't get out my face then you will be arrested too. Now back up!"

The lady backed off as the officer got in her face. This

seemed wrong to Seven who had no previous interaction with the police. As he watched the officers place the kid in the back of the car, he couldn't help but feel something. His heart started to pound. His mouth dried. He felt anxious. It was all of the excitement. The police had the street blocked off and because it was a one-way, traffic started to back up. People blew their horns, more people walked onto the street to see what had happened, another car stuck in the jam blasted music. As he looked around, he watched everyone interacting differently. Some were laughing and joking while others had a look of concern for the kid. He watched in amazement at all the people who had gathered around.

Man, it's poppin' out here, he thought to himself.

He had never been outside this late at night because he still needed to be in the house by the time the street lights came on. But with his mother now working late at night, he decided to venture out. His eyes widened as he walked down the street. People were everywhere due to the commotion. His head swiveled as he walked by the crowds of people. He walked a little further and ended up at the small grocery store in the middle of the block. The outside had the steel gate pulled down around it, but the doorway was open. Seven checked his pocket and as expected he had five bucks so he decided to walk inside.

As he walked in, he looked around and noticed how small the store was. In the front was a rack where the chips and popcorn and cakes were kept, to the right was the counter, and below it was the freezer that had the ice cream and ice pops. He seen an older man sitting behind the counter as he walked by. But something from the back caught his attention.

Wow. He thought to himself.

There were arcade games in the back. That sat on what looked like a small stage. He quickly walked to the back of the store and up the 4 steps that led to the game room. Amazed he looked at the three games. There was Mrs. Packman, Galaga, and a pin ball machine.

"I need change", he mumbled.

After he examined them all he quickly rushed to the counter to get change because he was excited and wanted to play them.

"Can I have four quarters please?"

"Sure."

The person behind the counter examined the five-dollar bill Seven had given him and then gave him four quarters.

"Where's the rest?" asked Seven.

"The rest of what?" the man behind the counter retorted.

"What do you mean the rest of what? My *change*," Seven's voice dripped with agitation.

"Hmm. Calm down young blood. I was only playing with you." The man chuckled, suppressing the urge to laugh out loud.

"You shouldn't play with people's money sir," Seven huffed and sighed.

"Yeah I suppose you right. You new around here?" asked the man.

"Yeah, how you know?" Seven asked quizzically.

"Because I've never seen you in here before," the man sounded irritated, but gave the boy the benefit of doubt.

"So?" Seven shrugged, wondering what the man's point was.

"So, everyone comes to my store. And the fact that I've never seen you around here means you are new here." The man replied, none-the-wiser about Seven's attitude.

"Okay, I guess I see your point," Seven nodded.

"Well here's your change. Go and enjoy the games young man," the man stretched out his hand, studying the boy in front of him.

"Thanks," Seven took the money and turned on his heels. His attention was somewhere else at that point.

Seven took his change and walked to the back to play the games. As he walked away, a guy and girl walked in the store as well.

"Aye what's up Pops?" said the girl.

"Aint nothing to it. What's goin' on out there?" Pops inquired.

"They just locked up lil' man. He gave em' a run for they money though. But they beat the breaks off him man. His mom is out there right now arguing with the cops."

"Dang that's too bad." Pops responded.

"Aye Pops, can I get some change?" asked the girl.

"Sure, but somebody beat you to Mrs. Packman." He replied.

"For real? Aight, I'll go wait."

The girl got her change and walked to the back where Seven was playing Mrs. Packman. She leaned next the machine and waited for Seven to finish. Seven occasionally looked over at the girl as she waited but she didn't look back and more so paid attention to the game. He looked over once more and their eyes met. He smiled at her and she smiled back.

"You live around here?" She asked.

"Yeah up the block." He replied.

"How come I've never seen you in here before?"

Seven shrugged his shoulders and continued to play. About fifteen minutes passed and he got closer to the high score.

"Oh, you think you good huh?" she asked.

"What you mean?" he asked in return.

"You getting close to the high score. You think you gonna' break it?"

"Oh, most definitely!" He mused.

"You do know whose score that is don't you?"

"Nope, but its 'bout to be mine."

"Oh really? That's my score, and nobody breaks my scores. I have the high score on all these games in here," she teased, eyeing his dexterity in the game.

"Seriously? Are you like the only one that plays them then?" he said in a sarcastic tone.

"Oh, you got jokes."

"So, what's your name?" Seven asked.

"Lola. What's your name?"

"Seven."

"Lola, that's a pretty name."

"Thank you. Well Seven is a weird name."

Seven was about to reply when he ran into the red ghost and the sound of death was initiated. Lola had managed to distract him enough to lose.

"Whatever. Oh Dang! You made me die," Seven cried out in frustration.

"No, you made yourself die. Move over, and let me show you how it's done." Lola purred, a sense of determination lingering in her voice.

Seven moved to the side to let Lola have the controls. They continued to talk as they took turns and played Mrs. Pacman. After a while, the guy who walked in with her called her.

"Lola!" he yelled.

"What?"

"You sounding really friendly up there. Who is that you talking to?"

"Whatever. None of your business."

The guy walked to the back where Lola and Seven were. He walked up to Seven and looked him in dead the eye. Seven's instincts intensified.

"Who the hell are you?" he asked.

"Who are you?" Seven shot back.

"I'm June and why you talkin' to my little sister?"

"Well June, I'm Seven. And your little sister is talkin' to me."

"Oh, you think you tough or somethin'?"

"Nah, I'm just tellin' you what it is."

"You must be new around here 'cause you obviously don't know where you at and who you talkin' to."

"Actually, I'm right here, you're right there, and I'm talkin' to you, *June*."

Their back-and-forth caused tension to rise. You could cut straight through it with a sharp knife. They both stood in each other's faces, neither takin a step backwards. They stared, unflinching and unbothered. Lola remained oblivious to the situation that was unfolding beside her.

"June, leave that boy alone," yelled Pops. "He's new around here but I know his peoples. He's good."

"Oh really?" June asked.

"Yeah."

"You lucky Pops know your peoples. Or it was 'bout to be a problem."

"'Bout to be a problem *indeed*," Seven responded.

"Can you believe this kid?" June chuckled. "How old are you man?"

"Thirteen why?"

"Thirteen? Man you play football or something? I would've thought you was at least fifteen or sixteen."

Seven shrugged and looked away. He had been hearing how he looked older all his life—especially since he started growing facial hair.

"Anyways, I'm out. *Nice meeting you Seven."* He said in a sarcastic tone. "Lola, let's go. I got things to do and you need to go in. It's passed midnight."

"Why I gotta' go in, and you get to stay out till three in the morning?" Lola fired back.

"Because I'm sixteen and you're only fourteen."

"Come one June, I want to stay out too. Please?"

"Hmm, okay, but you gotta' stay on the porch. So, let's go. Right now!"

"Bet," Lola responded, a smile etching its way onto her lips.

Seven watched them both as they walked out of the store. He slowly walked back to the counter because he wanted to get four more quarters to keep playing the games.

"Um, thanks Pops."

"Thanks for what?" Pops replied.

"You know for sticking up for me. I don't ever have anyone to stick up for me. So, thank you," Seven smiled appreciatively.

"Oh, well you're welcome. Besides I don't need the cops coming in my joint over some kid getting beat up for acting tough."

"Yeah aight. Thanks anyways," Seven nodded, seeing the sense in his words.

Seven got the change from Pops and turned to go back up the steps. He had a thought that stopped him in his tracks.

"Aye Pops, you said you know my peoples?"

"What?"

"You told June that you know my peoples."

"Yeah, and?"

"Who do you know?"

"I know you father."

Seven's heart pounded hard in his chest. Other than his mother, he had not even met anyone who knew his father, let alone mention him. He stood there shocked by Pops words.

"*What*? How do you know *him*? And what makes you think whoever you *claim* you know, is *my* father?"

"Your father name is Jerri, right?"

Seven's mouth slightly dropped. His mind filled with questions.

"Yeah that's his name. But I don't know you. So, how do you know me?"

"You kidding me? You look exactly like him. Y'all could be twins. But yeah, I know your dad from way back. I haven't seen him since before you were born. Matter of fact he was standing right where you are standing telling me about how he was about to be a father."

"Really?" Seven replied sheepishly.

"Yeah man. I thought you looked familiar but didn't really think nothing of it until you said your name. Seven. Your father was so happy about having a son, but he was pissed that your mom wanted to name you Seven. He hated that name for some reason."

"Really? Why?"

"I have no idea, he never told me that. But yeah that was the last day I seen him. Had to be over ten years ago."

"Thirteen to be exact," Seven corrected.

"Oh, I guess you're right. So anyways how is old Jerri doing?" The man chuckled, scratching the side of his head.

Seven's facial expression changed. He dropped his head and became sad. The thought of not even knowing how his father was doing, if he was dead, or alive, if he loved him or not, quickly made him angry.

"Honestly, I don't know. But if you see him someday, tell him I said what's up."

Seven quickly walked out of the store and slammed the door behind him. He was enraged at the thought of looking exactly like his dad, but have no knowledge of the man. He couldn't even remember the last time he saw his father. His mom didn't even have any pictures of his father anywhere. He marched up the street headed for his house when he heard a voice calling his name.

"Yo Seven. Wait up!"

Seven turned around to see where the voice was coming from. It was June. He slowed down and allowed June to catch up to him.

"Seven where you going?"

"*Why*?" Seven responded.

"Take it easy man, I'm not trying to bother you."

"I'm going in the house."

"Oh, to do what?" June asked, his tone suggesting that Seven's action was a dumb idea.

"Nothing."

"Nothing? Man, you should hang with me and my boys."

"Why? What are y'all gettin' into?"

"Who knows but the night is young. We got some drank and we got a car, so we 'bout to go ridin' around the hood."

Seven looked at June and paused. The thought of the boredom that was waiting for him in house didn't seem appealing—not when he was just presented with an alternative. Besides, his mother wouldn't be home 'till around eight in the morning she said.

"Hmm, okay. I'm down." Seven replied.

"Bet. Let me introduce you to my guys. But listen, don't tell nobody how old you are okay?" June said, a serious expression placating his face.

Seven nodded and followed June up the block to where his friends were sitting on the steps of one of the abandoned houses.

"Yo' fellas. What's shakin'. I want to introduce y'all to my lil' man Seven. Seven this is Rick, and Leo."

"Whaddup." Seven replied as he was introduced.

"June, what's the move man? We been waiting for like an hour for you." Rick yelled.

"Yeah man. We ain't got all night." Snarked Leo.

"Chill fellas. Who got the drank?" asked June.

Rick reached in the bushes behind the steps and pulled out a forty ounce of Colt 45. He handed everyone a cup and filled each of them to the brim.

"Here's to some fun tonight." June said as he raised his cup.

The others did the same. But Seven looked down at the cup and hesitated. He had never drank any alcohol before. He only knew what it smelled like because it reminded him of Sam. He was always drunk, so his breath always smelled like beer.

"Come on new guy lift your cup." Leo yelled.

Seven slowly lifted his cup with the rest of the boys and they all quickly drank from them. As soon as they were done, they refilled their cups and emptied them until the forty ounce of beer was gone. They walked up to the beginning of the block and jumped into a black Honda Prelude.

"Seven, come on man. Hurry up we out." June yelled.

Seven was nervous, but excited at the same time. He followed the rest of his newly made friends and jumped into the car and they were off. It was live everywhere they rode through—Governor St, Carrol St, 12th Ave, 10th Ave, everywhere. The entire time they blasted music and laughed and joked with each other.

"Hey whose car is this anyways?" Seven asked from the back seat.

"It's your *mother's* car. What difference does it make?" Rick joked.

"Yo' Leo, you got that?" asked June.

"Yeah. You want to spark it up now?" asked Leo.

"Yeah fire that thang up man." June yelled.

Leo reached in his top pocket and pulled out a jay and lit it. He took a few pulls and passed it to Rick. Rick in turn did the same while he drove. He took another hit, letting the rush fill his body.

"Hey man. You can't hit it twice. Pass it back here," yelled June.

"Stop being a baby. Take it." Rick joked.

He handed the jay back to June and June snatched it from him. After a few more pulls, the scent from it lingered in the car. Seven thought it had an earthy smell to it. As June smoked, Seven watched him closely as he took pulls. He watched how he held it and also how he inhaled after taking a puff.

"Here man. Hit that." June said as he passed the jay to Seven.

Seven had taken it from him and held it with his thumb, pointer, and middle fingers. He'd taken a quick pull and inhaled.

"Man hit that thang and stop acting scared!" June teased.

Seven looked at June and sighed. He had taken another pull, but this time he had taken a long pull and tried to inhale. He coughed uncontrollably while the rest of them all laughed.

"Virgin lungs!" June screamed.

They all laughed. Even Seven laughed after he recovered from his coughing.

"Aye Rick, where the chicks at man? Let's find some girls." June said.

"Two steps ahead of you man." Rick replied.

They rode past a small club at the corner of 12th Ave and E 18th St. There were so many people outside. Seven had never seen so many people congregated in one place. All outside partying and having fun. Cars blasted music while people walked around, smoking weed, enjoying themselves.

"Yo. Pull over. Next to that group of girls. Hurry up." June yelled.

"Okay, okay. Dang. You act like you never seen a girl before." Rick teased.

Rick pulled the car over as instructed. There were a group of attractive girls standing off to the side of the club, whispering and giggling to each other. They bumped along to the music, while enjoying the attention that they were receiving. From a distance, you could tell that they were confident and sassy, and they knew it. Seven didn't know if it was the haziness of the weed, but something about the girls drew him in.

As soon as the ignition was off, the boys huddled outside the car, trying to look cool. Seven mimicked June's stance— displaying a blasé but confident look. Their actions seemed to attract some attention, especially from the girls.

"Hey *light skin*. What's *your* name?" asked one of the girls.

"Hey now. The name's June. And yours?"

"Kisha," she replied, blushing coyly.

"Okay Kisha. Well, let me introduce you to my boys. That's Rick, that's Leo, and he's Seven," June nodded to each of them, his eyes travelling Kisha's body.

"Okay now. Well, these are my girls. China, Nikki, and Tameka," replied Kisha.

"Nice to meet you guys. Aye Kisha, come over here so we can talk."

Kisha walked over to June and they struck up a conversation. Nikki and Tameka gravitated to Rick and Leo. Seven was nervous. He had never been in a situation like this before. He was barely off the porch as this was his first time hanging out. He thought to himself, *I may never have this moment again, so I'm not going to waste it*. He got up enough nerve to go over and strike up a conversation.

"Hey there," Seven said nervously and then cleared his throat.

"Hey," China replied.

"You having fun?" Seven asked, trying to sound calm.

"Yeah, it's been a dope night so far. You?" China asked, shrugging slightly, a lop-sided smile on her face.

"Yeah it's been cool. So, what you drinkin' on over there?" Seven peered over at her cup.

"Henny. You want some?" she asked, lifting her cup.

"Yeah thanks," Seven replied giddily.

"There's a liquor store up the block on the right." China replied, a mischievous smile forming on her face.

They stared at each other for a minute, and then erupted into laughter. The connection between them crackled.

"Oh, little Miss China got jokes! That was funny. Girl give me your cup," Seven replied in between bouts of laughter.

She passed him her cup and he took a swig. He wondered if she had known how nervous he was. Because that joke served as bit of an ice breaker and calmed him down a little.

"Thanks, I needed that," he said, releasing an audible gratification at the soothing effects of the drink.

"Anything *else* I can do for you?"

"Nah I'm good," he replied without realizing she was flirting with him. China scrunched up her nose a little, but shrugged off his reaction.

"So, where you from?" Seven asked.

"Da' pound."

"True."

"And you?" she asked.

"The fourth. Not too far from here."

Seven looked around, taking in where he was. The vibrancy of the atmosphere intoxicated him. He had never felt this way before. He was buzzed from the alcohol and high from the weed. As he kicked it with China, he felt like he finally arrived. *This is what I've been missing out on,* he thought. As he soaked it all in, he noticed that June and Kisha were hugged up together as they talked. She seemed to slide him a huge wad of money. As he took it from her, June looked up and they made eye contact. Seven quickly looked away and turned his attention back to China.

"So, what you doing after this?" asked China.

"Going back to the crib. How 'bout you?" Seven asked.

"Same. But I don't wanna' hear my mom's mouth. She always on me for coming in too late on the weekends. Last week, she didn't even let me in. I had to go to Kisha's house and stay the night there," China sighed, rolling her eyes in the process.

"Oh wow," Seven exclaimed.

"So, I guess you don't have those problems huh?" She asked, looking him straight in the eyes. *Such pretty eyes,* Seven couldn't help but to think like that. He didn't know whether it was the alcohol or the weed, or both, but he found himself staring a bit too long. He shook his head slightly to reengage in the conversation.

"Um, not really. Not because my mom won't get mad, 'cause she would. But because she works nights, she won't even know that I was out so late."

"Yo' June. You gotta' drive yourself back kid. Me and Leo 'bout to make moves," yelled Rick, interrupting the conversation that had been flowing between Seven and China.

"Really? Y'all leaving already?" June yelled back.

"Aye man. When it's time, its time. Besides we get up with you tomorrow." Yelled Leo.

"Aight bet." June replied.

Rick and Leo both gave a head nod as they walked off. Suddenly, Nikki and Tameka were saying their good byes as well to Kisha and China.

"See y'all tomorrow." Said Nikki.

"*Ohh*, now y'all leaving too?" teased Kisha.

"Whatever." Laughed Tameka.

"Y'all hoes ain't slick. I see y'all." Said China in a teasing tone.

Nikki and Tameka chuckled as they walked off headed in the same direction as Leo and Rick. Out of nowhere, gun shots rang in the air, piercing through the veil of enjoyment that settled amongst them. Everyone ran. Some ducked behind cars, others ran in the opposite direction, but Seven froze. He had never heard a gunshot before.

"Seven. Seven come on!" June yelled.

When Seven turned around he saw that June, China, and Kisha were running together towards the car. He was so scared and ran as fast as he could to catch up to them. They all jumped in the car, and June drove them away.

"Man, that was close," June said, struggling to catch his breathe. His eyes darted towards the side and rear-view mirror to see if they had left the trouble behind and no one was following them.

"Yeah, it was only a matter of time before someone messed it up. I was having fun," Kisha remarked, wiping at her forehead and taking in deep breaths.

"Oh, the fun doesn't have to end," June gave her a side-eye, pouting his lips suggestively.

"Oh yeah? Well what about them?" Kisha motioned her head to the back seat where Seven and China sat.

"*Ohh, umm*, yeah. Aye Seven. Where can I drop you at man? Back to the block?"

"Dang. Okay yeah just drop me on the block."

He felt cool saying that. *Yeah*, d*rop me on the block*, he thought to himself.

"China anywhere close I could take you? Cuz I'm not tryna' go all the way to Da Pound."

"What? Where am I supposed to go? If I would've known that you wasn't taking me home, I could've started walking."

"My bad China. Aye I can give you money for a cab. Yeah, I'll give you money for a cab and Seven can wait with you until it comes. Right Seven?" June said. It felt more like a statement than a suggestion.

"Um, yeah. Oh yeah definitely. We can wait in my house until the cab comes," Seven replied.

"Is that okay with you?" asked June.

"Yeah I guess," China shrugged, slumping her shoulders in the process.

June dropped them off on the block in front of where Seven lived.

"Yo' Seven. I'll get at you tomorrow."

"Aight, I'll be out."

"Bet."

Seven and China got out of the car. And for the first time Seven noticed that there was a screw driver in the ignition. *Maybe the key broke some kind of way,* he thought to himself. They walked to his house and went inside.

"Hey, the phone is right there. Did you want me to call you a cab?" Seven asked.

"Do you know any cab numbers?" she responded.

"Umm, no I don't. But you can call 411."

China did just that. She called 411 and got the phone number for a cab and then called them. Seven went to the kitchen and poured himself some water while China used the phone. He soon heard that China had hung up the phone.

"How long before they get here?" he asked after gulping down the water.

"No one picked up," China replied a defeated look on her face.

"Oh. Well so what you going to do?" Seven asked blatantly.

"I don't know. What time is it?" China's eyes glanced around searching for the clock.

Seven looked at the clock in the living room.

"It's 2:30."

"Dang. It's too late for me to go home anyways. My mom not going to let me in. I was planning to stay with Kisha. But I didn't get a chance to ask her," China sighed, her eyes downcast.

"Oh, umm, you could stay here. Well… only if it was okay with you," Seven replied, raising his shoulders in the process.

"Oh, that's right. You did say your mom didn't get home 'till like eight right?"

"Yeah something like that. Probably would be best if you left around seven just to be sure. No need for us both getting in trouble."

"Okay sounds good," she replied.

"Can I have something to drink?"

"Sure."

Seven walked to the kitchen once more and China followed. He grabbed a cup and opened the fridge to get the pitcher of water and pour her some.

"Dang good thing I'm not hungry. You don't have anything in your fridge."

Seven was embarrassed because they seldom had food since his mom left Sam. "Yeah, my mom needs to go shopping," he said a tinge of sadness laced in his tone.

"Yeah, it looks like the fridge at my house," she chuckled. "Well I'm tired now. Where am I sleepin' at?"

"Um, wherever you want. You want to sleep on the couch?"

"I don't want to sleep on no *couch.* We may not have much food but I *do* have a bed at home," China replied rather curtly.

"Oh okay, I was just sayin'. You can sleep in my room. But I'm not sleepin' on that couch either," Seven raised his hands defensively.

"Oh really?"

"Yeah that couch hurts."

"And you was going to make me sleep on it? You foul," she teased.

Seven walked her into his room and he changed into some basketball shorts. He was tired. It had been an eventful night. He had experienced more excitement in the last four hours than he had experienced in all his life. China walked into his room, looked around briefly, and sat on his bed.

"Your room is nice," she said.

"You think so?"

"Yeah. It's only you?"

"Yeah, I'm the only child. From my mom anyways."

"That must be nice. I have to share my room with my little sisters. It's a pain. I never have any privacy."

"Well being the only one isn't the greatest. I be lonely. I wish at times I had a bigger brother or somethin'."

"I guess I can dig it. Hey, can you give me a t-shirt or something I can sleep in?" she asked sheepishly.

"Sure, take this."

Seven gave her a shirt and showed her where the bathroom was. She went in and he heard the water start to run. *Wow this was a great night. I can't wait till tomorrow night*, he thought to himself. He felt tired, better yet, fulfilled. He grabbed a movie and put it in the VCR his mom bought from The Salvation Army, and turned off the light. He felt tired. His eyes were heavy until China walked back in the room and got in the bed. She laid next to him as they watched the movie together. She snuggled up against him which made his heart pound.

"Seven, you're nice," her voice pierced through the television noise.

"Oh, thanks. What made you say that?" Seven asked, reaching around to reduce the volume of the television.

"Well, most boys would be trying to get in my pants as soon as I walked through the door. You've been pretty cool and not stressing me to have sex just because I'm staying at your house."

Seven looked at her, shrugged his shoulders, and smiled.

"Wait, do you think I'm pretty" she asked.

"Um, why do you ask?"

"Because maybe you didn't try anything because you don't think I'm pretty."

"No, I think you are very pretty. It's just that. Um, well…." Seven took a deep breath and blurted out his truth. "I've never actually did it before."

"Oh, so you're a *virgin*?" she asked.

Seven was embarrassed again as he nodded his head in agreement.

"Are you?" he asked.

"No. I'm surprised that you are. I don't know anyone sixteen who hasn't had sex," China displayed a look of shock, scrunching her eyes slightly.

"Yeah, I'm a little shy I guess. So, what do you think about me?"

"What about you?"

"Do you think I'm handsome?" he asked.

China didn't answer. Instead she looked him in his eyes, leaned in, and kissed him very passionately. Seven could feel a sudden warmth engulfing his chest. Her lips felt soft to the touch, and their kiss lingered for a while.

"You cute or whatever," she chuckled. "Not only do I think you are handsome, you seem to be really nice, and gentle. I think I like you."

She laid her head on his shoulder and he leaned in and kissed her. He couldn't contain the smile that consumed his face. She kissed him back and then laid on top of him. He was so excited and she could tell. China took complete control and soon undressed herself.

"You sure?" He asked hesitantly.

"Mhmm…" she replied, removing the t-shirt that he had given her.

Seven undressed himself and laid on top of her, feeling the softness of her body pressed against his. He explored her body hesitantly, waiting for cues from her. It was the most sensual thing he had ever experienced. As they kissed and touched, their passion transformed into a blur of activity leading up to the best ten minutes of Seven's entire life. Once they were done, they simply fell asleep holding each other until the next morning.

"Hey. Hey China...." Seven nudged her gently as he called her name. "It's time to get up. It's 7:00 a.m."

"Hmm? What?" she answered sleepily.

"Hey. Yeah. Remember? My mom will be home soon."

"Oh, okay. Do I have time to take a shower?" she asked.

"Yeah, but hurry up okay? I don't want to get in trouble."

"Okay," she got up, went to the bathroom, and took a quick shower. She walked back in Seven's room wearing only a towel.

"Hey can you hand me my clothes? They are on the side of your bed," she asked, clutching the towel.

"Sure," he responded and handed her the things she asked for. "Do you need to call a cab?"

"No. I'll walk. Besides I'll use this $20 June gave me and go buy me some breakfast."

"Oh okay."

"Too bad he ain't around. I would ask him to take me

home."

"Nah, but then you might have to give him his money back. It's not worth losing breakfast," Seven chuckled.

"Yeah you right. Hey. Do you know where he stashed the car? Maybe you can take me home?"

"The car? The car he was driving? Nah. I don't know where his car is," Seven answered.

"You are so innocent, aren't you? That wasn't *his* car. It's a stolee'," China chuckled while dressing.

"A stolee'?" Seven looked at her, confused.

"Yeah, meaning it's stolen. It's everybody's car until the cops get it," China answered in a nonchalant sort of way.

Seven was taken a back. He hadn't realized that the car was stolen. The more he had thought about it, the more it made sense. He remembered the screw driver in the ignition when they were dropped off. It was as if a light bulb had lit in his head. He couldn't believe how relaxed June and Rick had behaved while driving the car as if it was theirs.

"So, you mean anybody can drive those cars and he wouldn't be mad?" Seven asked, scratching his temple.

"Why would he be mad? It's not *his* car," China chuckled.

"Yeah, but I don't know where the car is. So, sorry that I can't take you home."

"It's okay. I guess I'll see you around?" China shrugged on the last of her clothes and gave him a smile.

"Um, yeah I guess. Hey before you leave, what's your number?" Seven asked hesitantly. He had never done this before and wasn't sure how China would respond. But for some reason, he felt compelled to ask.

"You're cute. I left it on your dresser. Call me."

Seven nodded and he walked China to the door. They kissed once more and she left to go home. He went back to bed and he slept.

"Seven. Seven?" Sissy's voice broke through his peaceful sleep.

Seven rubbed his eyes and stretched, remembering the blissful sensations that had run through him hours before. He got out of bed and stumbled out of his room.

"Yes Momma?" He responded, in between yawns.

"Hey sleepy head," Sissy greeted the minute Seven entered the living room. She seemed relaxed and had stretched out on the couch watching a show on TV.

"Hey Momma."

"Did you stay up late watching movies again? You were knocked out when I came in. I opened your door and you sounded like you were cutting down trees in there," Sissy smirked.

"Really?"

"Yep," she laughed.

"What time is it?" Seven asked.

"It's 1:30 p.m."

"Wow. I must've really been tired."

"That's what I said. Anyways, I just woke up myself so I made you some food. But I'm tired and will go back to bed."

Seven's eyes perked open. The mention of food jolted him fully awake. "Really? You went shopping Momma? What did you make?" he asked.

"I made you eggs, grits, and toast," she said, smirking her lips and clearing the plate that she had in her hands.

"Oh yummy. Let me wash my hands."

Seven darted into the bathroom and washed his hands. He rushed into the kitchen and grabbed his plate.

"God thank you so much for this food. Please help my mom make more money so I don't have to be hungry all the time. In your name I pray, Amen!"

"Okay kiddo. I'm going back to bed. If you go outside make sure you lock the door," Sissy smiled and dragged her tired body to her room.

"Okay Momma I will. Oh Momma? Do you have to work again tonight?" Seven called out.

"No, I'm off on Saturday nights but I do have to go back to work tomorrow night. They were offering overtime so I'm not going to miss out."

"Oh okay. Well get some sleep Momma."

"Love you baby."

"Love you too," he replied.

Seven took his time while he ate. He wanted to savor every bite since he hadn't eaten in about two days. His stomach was filled, his body was relaxed, but his mind was busy. *What a night*, he thought. He wanted to see what this day had in store for him as well. So, he showered, got dressed, and went outside. There were many people hanging out, chatting and laughing. Seven smiled as if he had never observed people in such a mood. For the first time in a while, he felt alive. He walked down towards Pops' store.

"Seven, wait up!" Screamed June.

"Aye what up." Seven replied.

"Where you going?"

"I was going to Pops' store to play the games."

"Games? You're such a kid man." Joked June.

"So, what I like the games…" Seven replied defensively.

"I see. Anyways, last night was crazy right?"

"Yeah it was."

"It had a good *ending* though. How about you?" June raised

his eyebrows suggestively.

"What you mean?" Seven asked as he was confused by June's question.

"Last night? You and *China*? How did it go? Did you get the skins or what?"

"Oh? Yeah. I did actually," Seven boasted, a sense of pride tinged in his tone. He had a good time with China, and wanted to see her again. He wasn't sure when, but she was definitely on his mind.

"My man. Did you use a condom? I hope so because I know a few people that tapped that," June high-fived Seven, nodding his head in approval.

"Um, yeah… Sure… I used one," Seven stammered, his pride stifled slightly.

"Yeah right. Anyways, be careful if you hit that again. Unless you want to be a daddy. Or worse, take a trip to the clinic."

Seven became nervous. He knew what condoms were, but never had to use them before. He never had anyone even talk to him about sex. So many thoughts rushed his mind at that time. *What if she is pregnant? That would make me somebody's dad. I don't want to be a dad. But I'll make a great dad. Better than my dad that's for sure.*

"Hey. Snap out of it. You look like you seen a damn ghost. Don't worry about it, I'm sure you still shooting blanks anyways.

You can't get no body pregnant till you at least fifteen," joked June, lightly smacking Seven on his shoulder.

"Really?" asked Seven.

"Boy. Just come on."

"Where we going?"

"I'm hungry. I'm going to Torpedo Base to get me and my sister something to eat."

"Well, if you want me to come with you, then you need to get me something to."

"*What*?" asked June.

"You heard."

"Yeah okay I got you. Come on."

"Wait are we walking over there?"

"*Walkin'*? Nah. If nobody found the car we gonna' take that."

"Where did you stash it at?" asked Seven.

"All the way down the hill on the other end of the block."

Seven and June walked down the hill and found the black prelude still parked where it was left. They jumped in and headed to get food.

"Yo, you gotta' drive back so I can eat my sandwich. I'm starving." Said June.

"Um, nah. You drive." Replied Seven.

"Why can't you drive? I'm already buying you food. The least you could do is drive back punk."

"Who you callin' a punk?" Seven responded sternly.

"You always walk on edge? I'm kidding with you dang. Wait, do you even know how to drive?"

"Whatever, and no I don't so you need to drive."

"Word? You want to learn?" asked June.

"Um, I guess. Um, yeah actually." Seven responded.

"Bet. I know the perfect place. It's where everybody go to learn how to drive. Bunker Hill," June nodded, his mind already made up. Seven mimicked him, already looking forward to learning how to drive.

Seven and June picked up their food from Torpedo Base, hopped back in the car, and June drove them to Bunker Hill. Once there, he pulled over and turned off the car and they both switched seats.

"Why you turn the car off?" asked Seven, settling into the driver's seat.

"So, I can show you how to start it. Now you take the screw driver and put it into the ignition. You can see a little ridge there and that's where the flat part of the screw driver goes. Just turn it and the car should start."

"Okay."

Seven did as instructed and the car engine came alive. June directed Seven on the basics of driving as they drove multiple laps around the few blocks that Bunker Hill consisted of. He quickly started to get the hang of it. June sat back as he watched Seven cut the corners as if he had been driving for years. A smirk appeared on his lips, confident about his teaching ability.

"Okay, you did good. So now let's go back to the block." Said June.

"You mean, drive in traffic with other cars?" asked Seven.

"Yeah, come on. Just go."

Seven was nervous, but he managed to drive them back to the block. They drove through once and then went back around to park the car back down the hill.

"See? Piece of cake right?" joked June.

"Yeah it wasn't so bad." Laughed Seven.

"Aight, well I see you later man. I'll be out when the sun goes down. It's too hot out here."

"Aight, see you later."

Seven and June walked up the block together. They separated paths when they reached Seven's building. After a quick nod, June walked on. *Man, why am I going in the house? There's nothing to do in there. I know, I'll go riding around,* he thought.

Seven went in the house and put the Torpedo sandwich in the

fridge and then walked back outside. He walked back to Fulton, then down the hill, and took off in the Prelude. He had driven all over. He had even taken a trip to his old neighborhood on North 4th St. He drove around and blasted music without a care in the world. *Wow, this is the life,* he thought. After riding around for a few hours, he decided to go home. He made it back to Rosa Parks Blvd without a problem. He slowed down to make a right on Fulton St. so that he could park the car back down the hill next to the warehouse. As he hit the break, he saw a cop car headed in his direction. He panicked. He hit the gas pedal too hard and the car jerked and the tires squealed a little. He quickly made the right turn down Harrison St. He was beyond frightened as he drove by Pops' store.

"Yo, Seven. What you doing in my car?" yelled June.

Seven didn't even look in his direction. All he could see was the cop car that turned on the block. Being halfway through, he hit the gas and quickly went around the round about which turned into Fulton St. He made it halfway around and then quickly parked the car on the corner next to the field. He turned off the car, and was so nervous he dropped the screw driver. As he looked back, he could see that the cop car had reached Pops' store so he walked faster up Fulton. June then appeared in front of him somehow. He walked out of one of the driveways, a few houses ahead of him.

"Seven. Come on hurry up," yelled June.

Seven then ran to the driveway that June was in. But before

he could make it to the driveway, the police car had cut in front of him and he froze.

“Get over here,” the cop yelled, his voice cutting through the panic that had settled in Seven.

“Get your hands up and don’t you move!”

Seven didn’t move at all and kept his hands high in the air. The cop grabbed Seven and threw him on the hood of the car. The heat from the cop car burned his hands so he jumped back.

“Stop resisting. Get your hands on the car and don’t move!” The cop screamed. “You people love taking things that don’t belong to you don’t you. Frickin’ animals. When will you all learn? Do you have anything on you?” the cop yelled as he patted him down.

“No, I don’t,” Seven replied in a soft voice.

“No weapons, no drugs?”

“No sir. I don’t do nothing like that sir.”

“Oh, so you’re just a thief then. Put your hands behind your back.”

Seven did as ordered. A crowd quickly formed and they all watched Seven being arrested. The cop threw Seven in the back of his car and walked away to inspect the stolen car. Seven glanced at the crowd from the back seat of the cop car, a deep-seeded regret and embarrassment co-mingling within him. They looked and pointed while he was in the cop car as if he was a circus freak.

Seven hung his head. *My mom is going to kill me*, he thought.

The cop walked back as another cop car pulled up. He jumped on the car radio and pulled off. They arrived at the police station where he sat in a cell and waited. After an hour or so, a cop walked in twiddling a pen and notebook in one hand, and cup in the other. The smell of coffee wafted in the room, suppressing the stench that had been the signature scent of the room. The cop took his time settling on a seat opposite Seven. He flipped through his notebook and sipped on his coffee slowly. Seven's nerves were on edge. He wanted to say something, but a feeling in his gut told him to remain quiet.

"How old are you? Sixteen? Seventeen?" asked the cop.

"No sir. I'm only thirteen." Seven shook his head, trembling at the situation he had put himself in.

"So, you're a thief, and a liar now, aren't you?" The cop's eyes shot up, a sneer on his face.

"I'm not telling a lie sir. I can call my mother and she'll tell you I'm only thirteen," Seven replied in one breath.

The cop looked at him, his eyes squinted. He sucked his teeth and jotted down something on the notepad.

"What's your phone number boy?" He asked, a tinge of impatience in his voice.

Seven gave the cop his phone number. He sat in the holding

cell for what seemed like hours. Before long, his mother showed up and spoke to the police. He was processed, and then released with the understanding that he would need to see a judge for this arrest. He and his mother walked to her station wagon and they both got in.

"Well? What do you have to say for yourself?" Sissy asked.

"I didn't steal that car. I only drove it," he pouted.

"If you didn't steal the car then who did?" Sissy asked, her hands gripping the steering wheel.

"Um, I don't know," Seven bit the side of his lip. He could sense that he was in a lot of trouble.

"You don't know?" Sissy asked, her voice trembling. Seven could almost smell the anger emitting from her.

"Really Momma I don't," Seven answered, trying to reassure her.

"Really? You gonna' lie to me now? Don't talk to me for the rest of the ride home. Sound just like your father. Telling lies instead of *owning* what you did," there was a sense of finality in her voice that told Seven that she meant business.

Seven remained silent for the rest of the ride. *How am I like him? I don't even know him*, he thought to himself. They parked the car at their house and walked in. He went straight to his room and barely came out until later that evening.

"Seven?"

"Yes Momma?"

"Where did you get this sandwich from?"

"Oh, from Torpedo Base. I got it for you."

"And how did you get to Torpedo Base? Did you use that car?"

"Yes Momma."

"And where did you get the money from?"

"My friend June bought it."

"Hmm. Well, thank you. Do you want half?"

"Yes please. Momma?"

"Yes baby?" Sissy sighed.

"I'm sorry I got into trouble."

"Well, I appreciate your apology. But something like this doesn't just go away. It's more than my forgiveness you need. You have to go see a judge and he has the power to let you go with a light punishment or even send you to juvenile detention. This was a bad mistake. You understand that?" Sissy looked at him to emphasize her point.

"I do now Momma." Seven replied, his eyes downcast.

He couldn't believe how things had become so bad. One minute, he was in blissful heaven, the next he was being detained. After a brief moment, his mother replied.

"Good. I'm going back to bed. But before I do, I want you to know one thing."

"What's that?"

"That I love you so much. You are the most precious thing in this world to me. No matter what. Okay?"

"Okay. I love you too Momma."

Seven went in his room and watched movies until he fell asleep. He woke up the next day and dared not ask if he could go outside. He had caused too much trouble already. He stayed in his room for most of the day. He heard his mother as she played her church music like she did each and every Sunday. Out of habit, he sang along to the songs that he knew while he sat on his bed.

"Hey Momma?" asked Seven.

"Good to see you finally came out of that room of yours. But what's up?" she answered.

"Did you buy bread, peanut butter, and jelly?"

"You know I did. I also bought some Raman noodles. Should be enough to hold us over this time until I get paid in two weeks."

"Okay. Yeah last week I was pretty hungry."

"Yeah, so was I baby. Things will get better. I'll work as much overtime as I can to take care of us. But the more I work, the less I will be here. Do you think you'll be okay?"

"Yeah, I'm a big boy now. Do you think I could get a job?"

"Hmm, I honestly don't know. We can talk about it more tomorrow okay? I need to get some more rest before I go back to work tonight. Okay?"

"Okay Momma."

Seven made himself a peanut butter and jelly sandwich and went back into his room. His mother did the same. There, they stayed until it was time for her to leave for work.

"Seven, its 10 o'clock. It's time for me to leave baby."

"Okay Momma."

"Make sure you lock the door okay?"

"I will."

Seven and his mother hugged each other before she left and he locked the door behind her. *I wonder what June is doing*, he thought. Sitting in his room, he wondered how he could make some money to help his mother. After about thirty minutes, he made the decision to get dressed and go outside. Seven walked out his building and headed to his new favorite place: Pops' store.

"Aye, Seven. Back for the games huh?" asked Pops.

"You know it," Seven replied.

"How many quarters you need?"

"Just four please."

"Hey, I heard you got into some trouble yesterday. You okay?"

"Yeah, I'm good."

"Be careful out there man. The cops don't play around out here. Especially with *us*."

"Yeah I will. But what you mean especially us?" Seven asked, a confused expression on his face.

"With us black folks."

"Oh. Yeah. That cop was really mean to me. He called me an animal and a thief."

"Yeah, they really racist out here. But to be honest, you put yourself in that situation. It doesn't excuse how the cop treated you, but you were the one driving a stolen car."

"Yeah you right. I was bored and didn't have anything else to do. I'm tired of staying in the house by myself."

"By yourself? Where's your mother?"

"She works *all* the time, so she's hardly there."

"Yeah, I know what that's like. It's hard out here for us all you know? Parents trying to provide the best way we can for our children."

"Yeah, I understand it. I miss her but we need the money."

"Don't we all," Pops exclaimed, shaking his head slightly.

Just then an idea came to Seven.

"Hey. Pops. Do you think I could work for you? I could maybe help clean up from time to time or something like that. Do you need any help?" asked Seven.

"I'm sorry kid. I'm only making enough to keep myself afloat." Responded Pops.

"Okay thanks anyways."

Pops gave Seven his change. He then paused and thought, *why am I about to waste this dollar on the games? I should keep it instead.* Seven put the change in his pocket and turned to leave the store.

"Change your mind?" asked Pops.

"Yeah. I need to keep this money and not waste it," Seven replied.

Seven walked out of the store with his head down as Pops watched. *He's a good kid*, Pops thought to himself. Seven walked out the store and saw June. He had handed something to this guy who looked dirty and homeless. The guy had handed him what looked to be money. Seven watched closely as he walked to June.

"June what up man?" asked Seven.

"Ain't nothin'. What's good with you?" June asked in return as they dapped each other. "Yo, you good? I seen the cops bagged you the other day."

"Yeah I'm good. I have to go to court though. And mom was pissed."

"Have you ever been in trouble with the cops before?" June

asked, his eyes darting around.

"No."

"Oh, so you should be okay. You'll get probation or have to pay a fine or something. Nothing hard because it's your first offense."

"Pay a fine? I don't have no money. And my mom is strugglin' as it is. Man, I need a job." Seven was frustrated at the realization that he needed to help his mother in some way.

"Yo, what your mom don't have a job or somethin'?" asked June.

"What you say about my momma?" Seven fired back.

"Aye, chill out man. I'm not tryna' be no kinda' way. I'm just askin'."

"Yeah she got a job. But it's not enough money."

"Yeah, at least your moms have a job. Not my mother. She strung out and ain't doin' nothing but gettin' high."

"Dang. My bad," Seven replied, averting his eyes.

"It's cool. But that's why I have to look out for me and my little sis. Anything we got is because I make it happen. Can't sit around waiting for a hand out cuz ain't none comin'."

"Yeah I hear ya. Speakin' of that. Yo, how you get all that money you be havin'?" asked Seven.

"You really wanna' know?" he asked.

"Yeah."

"I hustle."

"Hustle? Hustle what?"

"Crack, stupid. I swear you don't know nothin'."

"I ain't stupid!" Seven exclaimed. Though June had been nice to him, Seven wasn't going to allow anybody to down him.

"And you so sensitive. Always walkin' around with a chip on your shoulder. You need to relax." June took a step back raising his hands defensively.

"Relax? Relax? All I know is people tryin' to hurt me. I may be younger than you, but I been through a lot. I know that at times family ain't family. I know they will hurt you just like a regular person in the streets. I've been bullied and beaten and I ain't takin' it no more from nobody. So yeah, I'm on edge. I'm down to fight for everything, because I've lost everything I've ever known to be good. All I have left is my mom. And she going through it right now. So, I need to make some money. Now, can you help me or nah?"

"You serious?" June looked at Seven, searching his expression.

"Yeah I'm serious."

June paused for a moment and thought. He shook his head and sighed.

"This is hard for me. I wanna' help you because I like you.

You're a good dude. But that's the same reason why I don't wanna' help you. Cause you a good dude. This drug game, once you in it, it changes you lil' man."

"Changes you how?" Seven prodded.

"In every way. Now think about this. You are much younger than anyone else out here hustlin'. The older dudes out here will try to punk you and take your sells or even rob you for your money. They even try me sometimes which is why I stay with this." June lifted his shirt and revealed the handle of a gun.

Seven took a step back, stunned by June's reveal. Seven had never seen a gun up close, but knew they were never to be played with. Guns always brought issues, and deep within him, Seven knew he should leave and run. But something else tugged at him. He was tired of the poverty they were in. Struggling to make ends meet was not something he enjoyed. He needed to help his mother somehow. They needed a way out.

"Now do you really think you 'bout this life?" asked June.

"There's only one way to find out because, all I know is, I need to get some money," Seven replied, determined to make things work.

June nodded in slow-motion, the wheels turning in his mind.

"Okay. So, this is what I'm gonna' do. I'm gonna' give you a 50 pack of red tops. These sell for ten dollars a vial. So, I will give you two dollars for everyone you sell. But first you need to watch me. It's Sunday so it will be a little slower today on the block which is good so I can school you a bit."

"Okay. So, what do I need to do?"

"For starters, never keep these on you. Stash them somewhere close by, but not in too much of an obvious place. So, if the cops roll up they won't find nothing on you. What I do is roll it up in a paper bag and put it next to a car tire so it looks like regular trash. But you gotta' do it slick like because if someone sees your stash, they can try to take it from you if you not payin' attention. You getting all this?" asked June.

"Okay so look. Here come a fiend now. Sit back and watch." June continued after Seven nodded to the affirmative.

The fiend walked up the block towards June. He flashed two fingers and June nodded. June walked to the stash and grabbed what he needed while the fiend slowed his pace.

"Aye what up June?" He asked as he shook his hand.

"Same ole same ole." June responded.

"These good like last time?"

"You already know."

"Okay bet I'll get at you then."

"True."

June shook his hand once more. "Yo, you see shorty sittin' on the steps right there?" asked June.

"Yeah. What about him?" the fiend asked.

"That's my little man. From now on you see him okay? If you don't see him then come to me. But he gonna' be out here."

"Okay bet."

The fiend nodded at Seven and then walked off.

"You see that?" asked June.

"Yeah. It looked like a regular conversation and y'all dapped each other up." Seven replied.

"Exactly. That's how they all go down. It's very important that you get the money first. Once you get the money then you dap them back with the product."

"Okay I got it."

"You sure?" June prodded.

"Yeah."

"Okay, well here comes another one. Your turn."

Another fiend came down the block and head nodded to June.

"See my lil' man." June said to the fiend. He then flashed two fingers to Seven.

Seven was nervous. He had never sold a drug, but he was determined to make some money to help out his mom. Seven walked up to the stash, grabbed two vials, walked over to the guy, and shook his hand. He felt the guy put money in his hand and when he looked down he saw it was twenty dollars.

"Okay I got you," said Seven, flashing a pearly smile.

He shook the guys hand again and placed the two vials of crack in his hand. The guy nodded his head and walked away.

"Yo, see my lil' man from now on ya heard?" asked June.

"Yeah, I got you," replied the man.

Seven looked in his hand and thought, *wow I made my first twenty dollars.* A smile on his lips, he felt slightly giddy with joy. He couldn't believe his luck. He finally felt as if things were looking up. He turned and walked back over to the steps and sat next to June.

"That wasn't too hard," Seven remarked.

"Yeah, that's the easiest part of this game. The hardest part is to keep from gettin' beat, robbed' or locked up," June responded.

"So, what you want me to do with this money?"

"Hold it until the end of each night or whenever you are done with your pack—whichever comes first."

"Okay bet."

Seven continued to sell the vials of crack for the next three hours while June watched closely and instructed him as he went. He managed to sell the entire 50 pack.

"Yo. We done," Seven whispered to June after his last sell.

He did the math in his mind, *wow I literally made $500 and*

$100 of it is mine. "So now what?" he asked.

"We go to my house and re-up." Said June.

Seven and June walked up the block to June's house. They walked through the alley that led to the backdoor. He opened the door and they both walked in.

"Aight. How much you got?" asked June.

"$500 total." Replied Seven.

Seven handed June the money and he counted it out.

"Okay, here's your cut."

June handed Seven $100 and made good on the promise of two dollars per sell. Seven's eyes widened as he held the money in his hand. His mind raced with the endless possibilities that were in front of him. He felt like this was the beginning of a new life for him and his mom.

"Thanks man. I can't wait to give this to my mom."

"Where you gonna' say you got it from?"

"Huh?" Seven asked, confused.

"You can't just walk up to your mom and give her $100. The first thing she will ask you is where you got it from. So, what you gonna' say?"

"I'll say I found it and give it to her. Do you have a better idea?" asked Seven.

"Nope, only wanted to make sure you had a plan."

"Yep. Okay well I'm going home to get some sleep. I'm pretty tired."

"Okay. You back out tomorrow night?"

"Yep."

Seven walked up the block and went home. He was tired. He made himself some Raman noodles for dinner and went to bed.

"Seven. I'm home baby," his mom called out a few hours later.

"Hey Momma. What time is it?"

"It's 8:30. You sure look tired. Were you up all night again?"

"Um, yeah. There's nothing to do, but watch movies until I fall asleep."

"Yeah, I suppose you right. Hey can you do me a favor?"

"Sure Momma."

"Go to the little store down the street. I need some change for the laundry. They don't take twenties so see how many singles they will give you."

"Oow… Can I have a few quarters to play the video games in the laundry mat?"

"Sure baby. I'll give you fifty cents. We not going till Saturday though."

"That's okay."

Sissy gave Seven a twenty-dollar bill. He went into his room, grabbed the $100, and he quickly scurried off to the store.

"You here early today. I thought you were saving your money?" asked Pops.

"Yeah I am. My mom wanted to know if you could give me some singles for this twenty." Seven responded.

"Oh, sure thing."

Seven reached in his pocket and pulled out all of his money and gave Pops the twenty.

"That's a lot of money you got there." Said Pops.

Seven shrugged his shoulders without providing an explanation. Pops sighed and shook his head as he handed Seven back the twenty singles.

"Thanks Pops."

"You're welcome. Seven make sure you don't get into trouble out there. These streets will chew you up and spit you out," Pops said, a disturbed expression on his face. Unfortunately, it was an expression that he had too often.

"Thanks Pops," Seven replied without even looking up.

Seven was excited to go back into the house to give his mother the money he had made for her. He rushed in the house screaming, a plan in his head.

"Momma, Momma!" he screamed.

"Yes baby? What's wrong?" she asked.

"Look what I found on the way back from the store?"

Seven pulled out the money from his pocket and handed it all to his mother.

"Wait what? You found this money?"

"Yeah it was sitting on the sidewalk as I walked back home."

"Really?"

"Yeah. How much is it? Count it Momma."

"It's $100. Wow. This is wonderful. I told you things would be okay."

Sissy handed twenty back to Seven. "Here. This is for you," she said.

"Really Momma? No, you keep it. Maybe you can go buy more food for us," Seven feigned shock.

"Awe you're so sweet. But listen, you take it. I couldn't look at myself if I ever had any money or good fortune if I didn't share it with you. We are a team Seven. You and me. Okay?"

"Thanks Momma. I understand."

Seven was happy that he was able to help his mom. He went in his room, a smile was on his face for the rest of the day. His mom also felt lighter with the little extra cash. He could tell the difference immediately in her mood. It was as if all the worries of that day had disappeared. From that moment he made the decision that he would keep selling drugs in order to help his mother.

For the rest of the summer, he continued to sell crack. Seven came up with different ways to give his mother the money. He left money in the hallway of their building. Close enough to their door that she would find it on her own. The rest he put in a shoe box in his room. By the time the summer ended he saved close to $2000. It all seemed too good to be true, until something happened.

"Aye Seven. I'm 'bout to go to the chicken store. You want somethin'? Or do you want to just ride?" asked June.

"Nah. It's too much money out here right now. So, get me a center breast and some fries," Seven responded.

"Aight. I'll be back in a minute."

June walked down the block and grabbed one of the stolen cars that they had parked in the usual spot. Seven sat on the steps and made sells as usual. The block was particularly live since it was one of the few remaining Fridays left in August. The summer was drawing to an end and going back to school was on the horizon. It seemed like a party outside that night.

About an hour passed since June had left. *Where is he at? I'm starving*, he thought to himself. Since his mom worked a triple shift, he was out grinding all day on Friday. He had to re-up with June four times throughout the day, and now he was ready to be done. He only had a handful of vials left so he hid them in his mouth.

While he waited two guys walked up the block. The one

looked like a fiend, but the other looked regular. One guy held up three fingers and the other held up two.

Great. This ends my night, Seven thought.

He spat out the five vials of crack into his hand and waited for the guys to reach him.

"What up lil' man?" asked one of the guys.

"What up. Wasn't you here earlier today?" Seven asked.

"Yeah man. Y'all got that fire. I told my man here that he needed to come try y'all rock for himself man. This that same cut you had earlier right?"

"Yeah you know."

"Hey it's live out here. Walk in the alley," said the other man, jutting his chin in the direction of the alley.

Seven led the way to the alley next to the building where he sat and turned and faced them both. The fiend gave Seven fifty dollars, so Seven, passed him the drugs.

"Aye man. Where's June? I don't see him out here like that no more. You shuttin' it down huh lil' man?"

"He around. Why what's up? You need something else?" asked Seven.

"Nah we good lil' man." He replied.

"Okay." Said Seven.

"Aye. You gonna' be around later in case we come back?"

asked the other man.

"Nah. I'm done. Look for June. He'll be out soon."

The two men looked at each other and a brief silence settled among them. Seven looked at them in confusion, wondering what was going on.

"Oh, you done for the night? You sold out?" asked the other man.

"Why you asking so many questions. I served your boy now keep it moving. You know what it is," replied Seven.

Seven turned to walk out of the alley and he felt a hard punch to the side of the head. It staggered him and his back hit the wall. They both pressed him.

"What you got punk? What you got for us?" they asked, both foaming at the mouth in excitement.

Seven swung back, but he missed. The other man punched him again. This time he fell to the ground.

"We can do this the easy way or the hard way. The choice is yours. Now give it up. Yeah run dem' pockets!" they both yelled.

Seven didn't budge. That was until one of the guys pulled out a gun. Seven immediately put his hands up in the air.

"Give it up. Now." The man with the gun demanded.

"I ain't got nothing I told you. You want your fifty dollars back? Because that's all I got."

Seven pulled the money out his right pocket and held it in the air.

"We'll start with that."

At that moment, a lady fiend walked passed the alleyway and seen the three of them standing there.

"What y'all doin' in here? Lil' man can I get one?" she asked.

Her presence startled the two men and they both turned towards her direction when they heard her voice. The lady took a few steps back, clearly noticing that she had walked in on a delicate situation.

"Get out of here!" The man with the gun yelled. The other man grabbed her and pushed her out of the alley.

When the man with the gun turned back around, Seven kicked him in the groin and ran. He ran as fast as he could out the alley, and up the block. The man with the gun fired two shots at him while he ran and it caused everyone to scatter. People ran in all directions as they attempted to get away from the shots.

Seven made it to Pops' store and ran in.

"Pops! Help me. They trying to get me," Seven screamed.

"Come back here!" Pops responded.

Pops opened the door that led behind the counter and Seven ran in.

"Go back to the storeroom in case anyone comes in." Pops said.

Seven did as told. *This is my last night hustlin' God. I promise. Please get me out of this*, he thought to himself. He waited and waited. But no one ever came in the store. About a half an hour passed, and not one person came in the store.

"I think you can come out now." Said Pops.

Seven came out of the store room and stood next to Pops' chair behind the counter.

"Now didn't I tell you a few months ago to be careful out there?" Pops reprimanded.

"Yeah you did," Seven shook his head, remembering clearly what Pops had told him.

"And I know what you been doing out there. You been selling that poison. You hard-headed, but you learned today didn't you?" he asked.

"Yeah. That guy tried to shoot me. I can't believe he tried to shoot me," Seven responded, his voice shaking.

"These streets ain't got no love for you. I told you that didn't I?

"Yeah. You did. But how else was I supposed to make money to help my mom, Pops. I even came in here asking to work for you and you shut me down. What else was I supposed to do?"

"Look somewhere else Seven. That's what."

"I did. And this is the door that opened."

Pops shook his head in disapproval. "You know I see you out there late night. Drinking, getting high, driving those stolen cars, and peddlin' your little rocks. You got family that love you man. You're a good kid and you're getting sucked into the street life."

"How you know who I got? I ain't got *nobody*. It's only me and my mom. And she work so hard that I barely see her. She worked a double of overtime this week. So, I haven't seen her since Wednesday. And it's always like that. So, I'm out here by myself," Seven cried out. He didn't understand why Pops was coming down on him like that. He was just a young man trying to help his mom.

"You don't have to be alone," Pops reached out to place his hand on Seven's shoulder.

"What? You acting like I have a choice in this. Did you not hear me when I said all I have is me and my mother?"

"But that's not all you have."

Seven took a step back, shrugging off the hand that was on his shoulder. He squinted his eyes and focused on Pops.

"*What*? What you know about it? You don't know nothing about me."

"Now that's where you're wrong. I know a lot about you. You know how? Because I know your *father*. And he loves you man."

"What? Man get out of here with that. He loves me so much that he ain't around. What is this? Why you coming at me like this?" Seven spat, feeling the anger rippling through his body.

"Sorry to lay this on you like this man but, I've been meaning to tell you. I spoke to your dad. Remember when I asked you how he was doing when we first met? And you told me to tell him what up?"

"Yeah. And?" Seven took deep breathes, trying to dissipate his anger.

"Well, let's say I did just that. We have some mutual friends that I reached out to and I was able to get his number. I spoke to him and he told me to give you his number."

"You ain't speak to him. If you spoke to him then why he ain't come through or call me?"

"He said he doesn't have your number. I think him and your moms not on good terms, but hey that's on them. How I see it, shouldn't have nothing to do with you and him."

Seven sighed and thought for a moment.

"Man. I'm out. I'm goin' home," he uttered a few moments later.

"Hey. Seven. Here."

"What's that?" asked Seven.

"It's his number. He asked me to give it to you. And from the sounds of it, he may even have a spot for you with him. You right. I don't know you like that, but I do know these streets. And it's best for you to get out while you can. Wouldn't you want the opportunity to do right as opposed to runnin' around these streets duckin' bullets and police?"

Pops had Seven really thinking.

The fog in Seven's mind lifted. He took the paper that had his father's number written on it and went home. He put it in the same box where he kept his money stashed in his room. He looked in the mirror at his face. It was swollen and bloody. *Being punched by a grown man ain't no joke. That crackhead punched harder than Sam*, he thought. He looked at the mirror and wondered, what it would be like to live with his dad.

He immediately thought of all the fun he had since moving to Harrison St. But he also realized, it was the most trouble he had ever been in at the same time. Stolen cars, drinking, smoking weed, and selling drugs were all common place throughout his summer. He looked down again at his dresser. He noticed blood from his nose had dripped on the top. But when he went to wipe it, he recognized something else. The old burn mark in the middle of the dresser. This used to be his mother's dresser before they moved. She had brought another one from Salvation Army and had given him this one. It brought back memories. Bad memories.

He remembered how he would bite the skin off the sides of his fingers until they bled. He remembered how he used to start fires in the house and how he had developed a weird fascination for fire. He liked to watch the dancing flames turn from blue to red and then stare at it until he had to put it out. Sissy could never understand why he did these things or even where he would get the matches to start the fires in the first place.

******

"Now if you touch that TV again, I promise you will regret it." Sam yelled.

Seven cried in his room. *I hate him,* he thought.

"Now I'm going out and you better not mess up anything. You hear me?" screamed Sam.

"Yes." Seven's voice was weak.

Seven cried in his room as Sam slammed the front door as he left. Seven sat and cried for a while until, once again, he became angry. He was so angry that he wanted to do something. Seven went his mother and Sam's room and rummaged through their drawers. What he found in the bottom drawer, tucked all the way in back, was a plastic bag. In the bag was a pipe, a small baggie that had some kind of powder in it, a lighter, and two books of matches. Without hesitation he reached for the matches. He set one book of matches directly in the center of the dresser, and the other, he used to light a single match

He held the match and curiously stared into the small flame that it produced. He held it until the flame moved down closer and closer to his fingertips, and then he blew it out. He pulled another match from the book and lit that one as well, staring into the tiny flame. Again, watching it until it got close to his fingertips. He didn't blow this one out. Instead used it to light the entire book that sat in the middle of the dresser. He stared into the bigger flame with amazement. His eyes glistened as he watched the fire. He could feel the heat of the flame burn hotter as he watched. He then put the book that he was holding on top of the book of matches that burned on the dresser.

Within seconds, both books were engulfed in flames. The more the fire burned, the wider the smirk on Seven's face grew. A few moments later, the middle of the dresser had caught fire. His body was intoxicated with the sensory overload. It sparked an inner excitement. Seven watched. With a full smile on his face. He didn't even budge when he heard the front door open. He stayed and watched, smiling, now giggling at the fire he created. When Sam came into the house, he could see that the hallway was smoky and smelled of something burning.

"Seven? What's that smell?" asked Sam.

But Seven didn't answer. Sam quickly followed the smell and found the source. His bedroom, and Seven, giggled as he watched the flames closely. Sam rushed into the room and looked for something to smother the flames, but it started to grow. He needed to extinguish it fast or the whole dresser and maybe even the wall would go up next.

"Seven, come on, grab some water!"

But Seven didn't budge. Amazed at his creation, he held still studying the flames as they continued to spread. He was in a trance, refusing to make any movements. At that point, he hadn't registered that Sam was home, and hadn't really noticed him. Seven was in a different headspace, as if his soul was floating above his body.

Sam, grabbed a big bucket from the closet, filled it with water, and rushed back into the room.

"Get out of the way!"

But again, Seven did not move. Sam grabbed him by the shoulder and threw him out of the way—so hard that he fell and banged his back against the bedframe behind him. Sam threw the water onto the fire. He ran back to the kitchen and filled the bucket again. Sam returned to the bedroom and threw it on the flames once more. More of the flames went out. He had to fill up that bucket one more time to completely put out the fire. Once he was sure the flames were completely out, he turned to Seven, who sat on the floor exactly where he fell. He had a satisfied look on his face.

“Are you crazy?”

Seven looked at him and then looked at the charred dresser and laughed so hard. So much so, that Sam actually felt nervous. Seven looked up at him again with a huge smile.

“Maybe I am!”

Sam quickly took off his belt and began to beat Seven. This was no ordinary beating. Sam didn’t beat him out of anger, but out of fear. Seven realized this and laughed.

“You scared? That’s right, I’m crazy.” Seven laughed.

Sam beat him even harder. He could see that Seven continued to smile and was happy with what he had done.

“Oh, you think this is funny?”

Then Sam struck him again with the belt. At this point Seven hadn’t even shed a tear.

“Oh, it doesn’t hurt? I’ll show you.” Yelled Sam.

Sam grabbed the telephone. He unplugged the cord from the wall, he wrapped it around his hand and swung at Seven with all of his might.

Seven dropped to the floor where he squirmed, rolled, and desperately tried to get out of the way. The initial fog had dissipated as a warm rush of fear took its place.

“No! Please no! I’m sorry!” Seven cried out, feeling the welts form under his skin.

"Oh, now you sorry? Not as sorry as you're going to be!"

By the time Sam had finished, Seven's entire body was covered with welts. Most of them bled and were visible through his shirt.

"Now go to your room!"

Seven slowly hobbled to his room. Each movement caused the welts on his body to burn. So, he gingerly went to his room sobbing profusely. *I hate him*, he thought to himself.

******

It was after he burned the dresser that his mom decided to take him to see a therapist. Seven went, but he never explained to the therapist or his mom what he had gone through. As he looked back, there was no doubt in his mind that his anxiety was caused by the trauma Sam brought into his life.

That vicious beating caused Seven to stay in fear of Sam. He couldn't even sleep regularly afterwards. He stayed in constant fear that Sam would find a reason to beat or hurt him in some way. The only way he could ever get rest was by self-gratification. This became one of his coping mechanisms. He did it so often it would cause him pain to release, but it was the only way he felt relaxed enough to go to sleep. That curious exploration of his body was a bad seed planted during his childhood by his Aunt Ivey. And much like biting his fingers until they bled, he used these methods to cope when he felt anxious. So, he used them interchangeably all the time to escape his reality. He went from an innocent little boy, to one who started using pain and self-gratification, as a drug to cope with the many pains of his young life.

Chapter 8: Freshman Year

It was the first day of school. Seven was so excited when he woke up. He had looked forward to this day for a couple of weeks. Somehow, he had missed the structured way of things. Deep inside, he welcomed the discipline of going to school; a juxtaposition to his summer of recklessness. His mother had spoken to him the night before about making sure he stayed out of trouble and to focus on his studies.

Seven showered and put on one of his best outfits and rushed out the door. Giddy with excitement, he almost forgot to lock the door properly. He did a double take, climbed back up the stairs two-by-two and closed the door—making sure he had done it right this time. Without catching a breath, he ran back down the steps to the street. June was on the block waiting for him.

"Seven what up man." Said June.

Seven walked over and they dapped each other.

"What up man." Seven replied.

"Yo, you ready?"

"For what?"

"It's your first day of high school."

"Yeah. I'm a little excited," a smile crept on Seven's lips.

"I can tell. Cause boy you *fresh*. Head to toe huh?" June

remarked, sizing Seven up and nodding in acknowledgment.

Seven felt a sense of pride wash over him. He adjusted his sleeves and held his head high, upturning his nose in a boastful manner.

"Yeah you know. If you gonna' do it, you might as well do it right."

They both laughed and started the thirty-minute walk to John F Kennedy High. They went their separate ways once they got to school.

It seemed like a lifetime ago since Seven was in school. The school colors—red and black—seemed vibrant, and the mascot—a knight—appeared majestic. It was as if Seven was looking through a different set of eyes. *That summer must have messed up my mental*, he thought. He shrugged and walked ahead, happy because being here made him feel part of something bigger than himself.

He walked into his homeroom and felt like a superstar. Fresh haircut and fresh clothes all sponsored by his summer time hustlin'. For the first time, he didn't feel shy. He felt like he belonged. He looked around at all the different faces as he searched for a seat in the middle of the class room.

"Hey what's up? My name is Seven. What's your name?"

"Hey. I'm Kim."

"Anyone sitting in this desk next to you?"

"Nah you got it."

"Bet."

Seven sat next to Kim. She was pretty, which is why he sat next to her. He figured he would try to get her number at some point, but for now he simply made small talk.

"So, where you from?" asked Seven.

"I live in the Towers. How 'bout you?" she asked.

"I'm in the fourth. Harrison St."

"Oh, you from *up the hill*."

Kim snickered slightly, which Seven picked up on. He cocked his head to the side, adjusting his position to face Kim.

"Oh, is that a problem?"

"Nah but *down the hill* is where it's at."

"You say that because you ain't never chill in my hood. It's a party every night. You should come through some time."

"Oh, you gonna' be my tour guide or somethin'?"

"Or somethin'," Seven winked, chuckling in the process. Kim turned away, a slight blush appearing on her face. She had caught on, on what he meant.

They continued to talk until the bell rang for them to switch classes. Seven pulled out his paper schedule to look at what class was next. The hallways were packed. People laughing and catching up as they all switched classes. He watched in awe as he maneuvered through the hallways. All the doors had numbers on them based on the wing that they were in. He headed to his first class which was Science—Room 201

Here it is, he thought. He walked into the class and found an empty desk. He waited and watched as other kids started to fill in the class. Once the bell rang, the teacher began her introduction.

"Hey everyone. Settle down now. My name is Mrs. Brown I will be your teacher for the year. Now, I have a stack of books sitting on the front desk of each row. Everyone be sure to grab your book before you leave class."

Seven looked at the stack of books while Mrs. Brown went over her expectations of the class. They were old and worn. *So this is high school education in the hood huh*, he thought to himself as Mrs. Brown gave a detailed overview of what they would learn for the first marking period. Before long, the bell rang and it was time for Seven to make it to his next class. The rest of the day played out the same way—meeting new kids and getting his books from the teachers. The first day went by and the sound of the last bell initiated the mass exodus of students. Seven walked to the front entrance and looked around.

"Seven. Over here man." Waived June.

"What up bro." Seven answered.

"Yo you ready to head back to the block?"

"Yeah let's do it. I need to put all these books down."

"Why didn't you put them in your locker?"

"Nah. I don't really like using the lockers."

"Oh, I get it. Too cheap to buy a lock huh?"

Seven looked at June and they both laughed.

"Yeah you right," Seven chuckled.

"All the money we made together and you still super cheap man. I was surprised to see you go shopping," June joked.

"Aye man. Like my mother says all the time. Money doesn't grow on trees."

They continued to laugh and joke around as they walked back to the block. Seven went in the house and went directly to his room. He took off the clothes he bought for himself so that his mom wouldn't see them. He did not want any questions that he had no answers for. He folded the clothes neatly and stashed them with the rest at the back of his closet.

"Seven?" his mom called from the living room.

Seven looked around his room to make sure everything was hidden before heading to the living room.

"Hey Momma."

"How was your first day of school?"

"It was good. I met all my teachers and met some new people."

"That's good baby. I was worried."

"Yeah? You worry about everything Momma. Like you said, things will be okay."

"Well now… look at you quoting your momma," she joked.

"Aye I learn from the best."

Seven smiled wide and gave his mother a hug. She looked at him and placed her hand on his face.

"You look so much like your father. Especially with that haircut."

Seven dropped his head. Any mention of his dad poked an open wound in his heart. He yearned for a man who didn't seem to be interested in him. Seven couldn't understand why. It's not like he had done something wrong.

"Mom. Can I ask you something?" Seven asked in a soft voice, after a few minutes of sad contemplation.

"Sure baby. What's wrong? Why you look so sad?"

"What happened between you and my dad? Why hasn't he ever been around?"

Sissy sighed. "Truth is. He didn't want to be a man. He rather run around with different women than to be faithful to me. So, because of that, I decided to end it because I wanted more. More out of life, more out of him, and more for you."

Seven was angered by her explanation and yelled. "Is that why he is not here for me? He's mad at you for leaving him. Why would you do that to me?"

"Now hold on a second. I never kept you away from him. If he really wanted to be in your life, he could've. He not being around is his choice and not mine," Sissy responded, her arms folded.

"Why would he not want me Momma?" asked Seven as he started to cry. "Does he miss me? Does he even care?"

"I'm sorry baby. I don't want you to hurt. Hey, listen I have enough love in my heart for you for both me and him combined. I will *always* be here for you. I will *never* leave you. You hear me?"

Seven nodded his head. He hugged his mother again and went in his room and cried again. He reached under his bed and grabbed the box where he stashed his hustle money. He opened it and picked up the paper that had his dad's number on it. He stared at it for a few moments, and tears dropped from his eyes. *Should I call him? What if he doesn't want to hear from me? He don't care about me*, he thought.

He placed the number back into the box and put it back under his bed. He cried himself to sleep. He woke up when he heard a knock on his door.

"Seven. It's time for me to leave for work." Said Sissy.

"Okay Momma. I'll come lock the door."

Seven walked out and met his mother at the front door. She hugged and kissed him and then left. He locked the door as he always did in the past. The more his mind raced, the sadder he got. He couldn't focus on anything. He couldn't stop thinking about his father. He went back to sleep with a heavy heart.

The sound of his alarm filled the air and woke him from his slumber. He felt heavy and burdened—similarly to the way he felt when he went to sleep. He didn't have the same energy as he had just a day before. He showered and got dressed in his old clothes and met June outside.

"Dang bro. What's wrong with you?" asked June.

"Nothing. Just don't feel like going to school today." Seven replied.

"Did you not sleep at all? You look like trash man."

"Nah it was a bad night."

"Well, why don't you leave school early?"

"Early? What do you mean?"

"It's simple. Leave when you had enough and go home."

"What? You can't just leave school."

"Yes, you can. It's high school. You can cut a class if you want. All they do is charge it as an absence from class."

"Really?" asked Seven.

"Absolutely. Listen I'll meet you after lunch and we can walk home together. That cool with you?"

"Okay. Yeah because I don't really even want to go at all but it's only the second day. My mom would be mad at me."

"Well we can go to my house until school lets out and then you go home."

Seven nodded his head as they walked to school. They did as planned and left school after lunch and went to June's house until school let out.

"Aye what's up man. You sure you don't want to talk about it?" asked June.

"Nah. I'm good." Responded Seven.

"You just so quiet. You really gonna' sit there and watch TV without saying anything at all?"

"I don't want to talk about it man."

"Okay bet. You can stay here, but I'm going outside to see if I can make some money. You coming?"

"Nah. I don't want to get caught by my mother," Seven sighed, unable to lift the fog that had settled in his mind.

"Aight well I'll be back in a couple hours. You can stay in my room. I got some smoke on the dresser so light up and get your mind right."

"Thanks June."

"You got it."

June left and Seven watched TV in his room. His mind was a blur. If anyone was to ask Seven what he was watching, he would stammer his way through the response. The TV served as background noise until it was regular time for school to let out. He then walked out and saw June up the block.

"Aye yo!" he yelled.

"Be right there." June yelled back.

June came up the block so that he could lock his door while Seven went home.

"You good man?" Asked June.

"Yeah. I'm going home now."

"You coming out after your mom leaves for work?"

"Nah. I'll see you tomorrow man."

"Aight."

Seven went home. He quietly entered the house as he didn't want to wake his mom. He didn't want to talk about his day and he was also high, so he crept into his room and closed the door.

And for the first time, Seven had cut class. For the rest of the month, he had cut classes often for different reasons. Sometimes he did not got to school at all for a whole day. Whether it was the classes that he didn't like or didn't feel like staying the whole day, he would leave early and go hang out at June's—whenever June was down to cut. On the days June didn't cut with him or if he decided to not go to school at all, he would play the block until it was time for him to go home. He learned quickly that his mom rarely came out after work because she needed to sleep. He continued this for the rest of September and early October.

The cloud that hung over Seven was heavy and dark, and he couldn't shake it off for some reason. By this time, he was so used to coming and going whenever he pleased, it felt normal. Oddly it made him feel completely free. But at his core, he was sad and disappointed in himself and his life as a whole.

"June what up?" asked Seven.

"What up Seven." June replied.

"Ready to take this walk to school?"

"It's Friday, so you know it."

They walked to school as they had been for the past month and a half. They went their separate ways as Seven walked to his homeroom. He sat next to Kim as he did on the days he showed up for school.

"Hey stranger. How are you today?" asked Kim.

"Hey Kim. I'm okay. How are you?" Seven asked.

"I'm good. Haven't seen much of you lately. I thought we were going to be friends."

"Yeah I know. But hey we are friends. Right?"

"We can't be friends if we don't see each other. Right?"

Seven smirked. "So, you want to see me do you?"

"Whatever. I'm just saying."

She blushed as they smiled at each other.

"Seven? Seven come here please sir." The teacher called.

"Yes?"

"Your guidance counselor wants to see you. So, you need to report to her office. She'll give you a pass if you are late for your first period."

"Okay thanks."

Seven walked to his desk and grabbed his things. He winked flirtatiously at Kim and left the class.

Seven's sneakers made a squelching sound as he walked down the empty hallway to the counselor's office. As the sound reverberated on the walls, he thought about why the counselor requested to meet him. He had never been called to the school administration office before. He shrugged and reasoned it out to the counselor doing a routine check.

When he reached the office, he knocked on the door. After hearing a brief response, he entered and sat down opposite the counselor—a stocky lady with a head full of hair, brown-rimmed glasses and a stern look on her face.

"Mr. Bradford. How are you?" asked his counselor, as she fixed her glasses.

"Hi Mrs. Greene. I'm doing okay."

"Do you know why I asked you here today?"

"No."

"Your attendance, or should I say, the *lack* thereof. Do you know how many days you have missed?"

"Umm, no I don't."

"It's the middle of October and between cutting classes and full day absences you currently have twenty days of total absence. Now, do you know how many days you are allowed to miss for the entire school year before you lose credit and need to repeat the year?"

"No, I don't."

"Twenty-one. On the twenty-second day, you lose all credit for the year and need to repeat the year."

"Oh, I didn't know that," Seven could feel the weight of the world on his shoulders. *How could I have been so stupid,* he thought.

"So, I called you up here so that you would understand the situation that you are in. Now, I don't have all of your grades, but I would assume that you are not doing well since you have missed so much time. Do you think that's a realistic assumption?"

Seven nodded his head realizing that he had been in a funk. At first, he didn't care too much. His blasé attitude was quickly squelched as his counselor continued to speak to him. The thought of telling his mom that he failed out of his freshman year of high school within the first couple of months disappointed him. His mother was the only person who believed in him at all. He always felt her love even though they didn't see each other much. She left him little notes on the dining room table or on the refrigerator daily. Always encouraging him to do well and to stay out of trouble.

"So, Mr. Bradford. What are you going to do about this sir?" asked his counselor.

"I'm not totally sure Mrs. Greene. I need to really think about what I need to do."

"Well okay. I suggest that you talk to your parents because I'm sure they wouldn't approve of you failing for the year. Am I right?"

"Yes, you are."

"Okay. Well that is all I needed to speak with you about. You can go to class now."

Seven went on to attend his next class, but he was far from present. His mind occupied with the news that he received, wondering how he was going to tell his mother. *This is going to break her heart*, he thought.

At that moment, he knew that he needed to do something different. Throughout the day, he reflected on all summer events and weighed the good versus the bad in its entirety. He decided he needed a change of scenery. *But where would I go? Could I go and live with my dad? I'm going to call him*, he thought.

The thought of living with his father, his actual father, excited him like nothing ever did in his life. He made up his mind and knew he needed to get home and convince his mother. He needed her buy-in before he called his father. At the end of the school day, he didn't even wait for June. He immediately headed home after the last bell rang. He took a deep breath as he entered his house. He placed his things in his room and then knocked on his mother's door.

"Mom." Seven called.

"Come in baby," Sissy replied, her voice heavy with sleep.

Seven opened the door to find her tucked in neatly underneath the covers. She looked so peaceful, and he hated himself for disturbing her tranquility. But deep inside, he knew he had to do this. There was no other recourse.

"Hey Momma."

"Hey baby. What's up?" Sissy replied, in between yawns.

"Can I talk to you about something?"

"Of course. What is it?"

"It's something bad. But I don't want you to get mad."

"Whatever it is, we will figure it out together like we always do."

Seven sighed, "Mom, I'm failing in school."

"What?" The bed covers that had cocooned her, now

remained wrinkled and forgotten as Sissy sprung up from a laying position.

"Yeah. I spoke to my counselor today and she told me that if I miss another day of school that I would need to repeat the whole year."

"Wait. You haven't been going to school?" She asked sternly.

"No…" Seven replied, his eyes downcast.

"If you haven't been at school, then where have you been, because you ain't been in here?"

"I was hanging around outside. I'm so sorry Mom."

"Sorry? You're sorry? Sorry enough to get your act together?"

"Yes. But I don't think I can do that here. It's too much to get into living here. And you aren't here enough. I know you're doing what you need to do to take care of us, but I'm lonely. That's why after you leave for work, I go hang out with my friends every night. And I don't want to do that anymore because I'm scared I will keep getting in trouble."

Sissy dropped her head as she listened. Seven was verbalizing pent-up emotions that he had suppressed for a very long time. She was saddened and knew she was responsible. But she didn't know what she could do differently to better support him.

"So, what are you getting at?" asked Sissy.

"I think I need to move."

"Move? Move where? There isn't anyone that you can move with. It's only us son."

Seven hesitated while his mother waited for an answer.

"I thought maybe I could move in with Dad."

"Your *dad*?" asked Sissy. "And why do you think you would be able to do that?"

"I think he might agree. Do you know Pops who owns the store down the street?"

"No. I know the store that is there, but I never went in that store. I don't like the crowd that hangs around of there."

"Anyways. The owner's name is Pops. And he knows my dad. My dad told Pops to give me his number. But I never called because, I didn't think he wanted to talk to me or know me…" his voice trailed off.

He looked up to catch a glimpse of his mother's grief-stricken face. Sissy looked as if she had lost her son forever, to life's cruel nature. She stifled a cry, wanting to hear Seven's solution.

"I'm listening."

"So, I think it may be better to go live with him while I get myself together and get back on track. So, what do you think?"

"Baby. You know that I will support you in anything that

you do. But I don't think this is going to work out the way you think. But if you are really serious, then go ahead and call and we will see how it goes. Okay?"

"Okay. I'm going to call him now."

Seven hesitated slightly, but walked to the phone and dialed the number. He waited while the phone rang, leaving Sissy in her room, her mind in a daze.

"Hello?" a young girl's voice answered the phone.

"Hello. Um... Can I speak to Jerri?" Seven asked.

"Hold on. Dad somebody on the phone for you."

A smile landed on Seven's lips. The girl must be his sister. He wanted to talk to her, but knew the timing wasn't right. So, Seven waited patiently for his father to come to the phone.

"Hello, Jerri speaking," a low voice boomed through the phone.

"Hey. Um… Hey Dad. It's…um… Seven."

"*Seven*? Like my son Seven?" Jerri's voice broke a few times.

"Yeah. Dad. It's me."

"Hey… um… son. This is random. I'm sorry I don't know what to say. How are you?"

"Um, I'm doing okay. I guess. Well. Not really. That's why I'm calling."

"Well, what's wrong?"

"I'm in a little trouble and I need your help."

Seven cried as he spoke to his father. He explained his situation. They spoke for a little over an hour.

"Son, this is not what I expected to hear. I'm caught a little off guard here. Because you are asking to come and stay with me right away. And you're sure your mother is okay with this?" asked Jerri.

"Yeah. She's sitting here. Did you want to speak to her?"

"No. I have nothing to say to her. And now look. What kind of mother leaves her son all hours of the night to get into all kinds of trouble? I've lost all respect for her in how she's raised you."

"Dad, this is not about Mom. She has done everything that she could for us. Where have you been through all of this? Sitting pretty with your new life and new family and left me hanging. So, don't talk about my mom because you don't know what we have been through," yelled Seven.

"I'll call you back." A click reverberated through the phone.

"Hello? Hello? Dad?" Seven yelled, his voice breaking up as tears streamed down his cheeks.

"What happened?" asked Sissy.

"He hung up on me." Replied Seven.

Sissy shook her head and hugged Seven tight. He didn't

know what that meant. *Why did he hang up on me? Was he going to let me stay with him? I guess he doesn't care*, he thought.

The rest of the night was a blur as Seven's mind revolved around the conversation that he had with his father. He stayed by the phone and waited for his father to call him back. But he didn't call that night.

"Seven. I'm going to work. Come lock the door baby. I'm off tomorrow so I'll be home all day so we can talk okay?"

"Okay Momma."

"Listen, no matter what happens. We will figure this out together okay. We are a team no matter where you live alright?" Sissy assured him, rubbing the sides of his shoulders in a comforting manner.

"Thanks Momma. I love you so much."

"It's going to be alright. Don't you worry okay?"

Sissy gave Seven a hug and kissed him on the cheek before she left out. He locked the door but couldn't sleep. He had bitten his fingers as he was stressing about the conversation with his dad.

"Owe!"

He had bitten too much and his finger started to bleed. He was extremely anxious. *Calm down*, he thought to himself. He went to his box and pulled out half a jay he had saved and lit it. After a few puffs, he felt the rush slowly take over his body. He closed his eyes and laid back on his bed. He smoked it all and duded the clip in a cup he kept by his bed. Seven closed his eyes and took a couple of deep breaths. Before he realized it, he had fallen asleep. The jay had hit the spot, sending him to snooze land where problems were a distant memory.

The sound of the front door opening woke Seven.

"Seven? Where's mommy's pumpkin?" Sissy yelled.

Seven got out the bed, walked out his room and greeted his mother.

"I'm here Momma." Seven replied.

"I have a surprise for you."

"Oh yeah? What you got?"

"Your favorite. I got you a cheesecake."

"Awe thanks Momma. This is the perfect Saturday morning treat."

Sissy placed the shopping bags on the table. Seven sat down and spoke with his mom while he opened the cheesecake.

"How was your night at work Momma?"

"It was okay. I'm getting used to the time now, but I'm still tired."

As they spoke, the phone rang. They both looked at each other, frozen in place. Neither of them expected a call.

"Well you know it ain't for me. I hardly ever get any phone

calls," Sissy said, settling into the couch.

Seven shrugged his shoulders, walked over to the phone and slowly picked up the receiver.

"Hello?" asked Seven.

"Hello? Seven?" the voice on the other end of the phone queried in a hush tone.

"Yeah?" Seven responded.

"It's your dad." Said Jerri.

"Oh. Hey. What's up Dad?"

"I was calling to finish our conversation from yesterday."

"Oh, you mean the one we were having before you *hung up* on me?"

"Yeah well, you were being disrespectful."

"I wasn't being disrespectful. You were talking trash about my mom, and you have no idea what you are saying."

"Listen, I didn't call you to argue."

"Then why did you call?"

"I called to say that I talked it over with my family and we all agree that you would be better off here. With us. So, if you still want to come, we would be more than happy to help you out."

"Um, yeah sure. When would you be able to come get me?"

"When were you thinking?"

"Actually, I was thinking as soon as you can. Maybe

sometime this weekend?"

"Wow. That's soon. Didn't realize it had gotten *that bad* living with your mom. Okay I can come get you tomorrow if you want."

Jerri's tone didn't sit well with Seven, but there was nothing much he could do. Seven was determined to change the tide. After everything he had been through, he wasn't going to fail at school. If this was the only solution available, then he would make it work. Although, he couldn't help but feel unsettled inside.

"Yeah that um… sounds good. I'll… uh start packing my stuff."

"Okay that's great. We'll be through in the morning tomorrow. See you soon son."

"Okay."

Seven hung up the phone and felt conflicted about the conversation with his dad. On one hand, he was happy to finally be able to be with his father—the man he envisioned as his savior and superhero. But on the other hand, he didn't want to leave his mom by herself. But he needed to make the decision for his own life.

"That was your dad?" asked Sissy.

"Yeah. They will be here tomorrow morning so I need to start packing." Replied Seven.

"Okay. Now you're sure you want to do this baby?"

"Yeah. I think so Momma. Will you be okay though?"

"Now, you know I'm going to be okay. I will miss you but I will be fine baby."

"I will miss you to Momma," Seven cried. "I'm sorry Momma. But I feel like this is a chance for me to be with my dad and get myself together at the same time."

"I understand baby. You're only thirteen and look at you making an adult type of decision. I'm proud of you for taking a step in the direction that you think would be good for you. Like I always say, we are a team no matter what and I will always be there to support and guide you."

"Thanks Momma. You are the greatest!"

Seven walked into his room and began to pack his things. His heart seemed heavy as he packed. He quickly threw the clothes that he bought himself into the suitcase and added his other clothes on top. After an hour of packing, he was almost done.

He packed the last of his things and looked around his room. He was going to miss everything about this place. They had moved here after his mom left Sam. So, it was where he gained his sense of freedom—too much freedom. Yeah, he would miss this place. He made his first real friend, lost his virginity, drove his first car, and financially helped his mother for the first time. He looked around his room once more, and noticed the blood stain on his dresser from the night when he almost got robbed. He remembered his introduction into it all. Overall, it was the most exciting three months of his life. He pulled his stash box from under his bed and counted the money that he had left. $1000 was what remained. So, he took $200 out and placed the rest back in the box and put it back under his bed. He didn't push it all the way under the bed so it was slightly visible. *Just in case Momma need something maybe she will find it*, he thought.

He looked around his room one final time. He was really anxious about seeing his dad. Now all he needed to do was wait for tomorrow to come. He anxiously waited. Most of the day went by quickly, but he couldn't sleep. So, he stayed up and watched movies like he always had done. Before long, he fell asleep.

He woke up the next morning even more anxious. He showered and dressed. He placed his suitcase by the front door and then paced. He paced between the kitchen and his room continually, his body frantic with thoughts.

"Stop biting your nails baby. He'll be here soon." Said Sissy.

Seven looked down at his fingers and noticed his thumb was bleeding. *Dang, I did it again*, he thought. Then, he heard a horn blowing outside. He looked out the window and a man as he stood outside the car. *That must be him*, he thought.

"Momma, I think they are here."

"Okay baby. You have all of your stuff?"

"Yes ma'am."

“You excited huh?”

“Mhmm...”

“I can tell. Okay, well don’t keep them waiting baby.”

“Okay I love you, Momma.”

“I love you too baby.”

Seven hugged his mother really tight and a tear rolled down his face. She looked him in his eyes and kissed him on the cheek.

“Remember, you can come home whenever you want okay?” she said as she choked back her own emotions.

“Okay Momma.”

Seven grabbed his things and ran out to the car. For the first time in his life, he felt like he had a chance to be a part of a family—a real family.

He had his dad, his hero, his savior that he’d dreamt about for years.

“Hey Dad!”

Seven called out as Jerri walked from his car to the steps of the building.

“Hey son. You have all of your stuff?” He asked, as he ushered Seven to the trunk of the car.

“Yeah.”

“Yeah? That’s no way to respond.”

“Huh? What do you mean?” Seven asked, pushing his luggage into the trunk and closing it.

Jerri's demeanor belied someone who was eager to meet his son. He shifted impatiently, fidgeting with his car keys.

"You should say yes. Not yeah."

"Oh." Seven scratched the side of his head.

"Yo Seven." Yelled June.

"Hey Dad. Can you give me a quick second to say bye to my friend?" asked Seven.

"I shouldn't. He probably one of the reasons I need to bail you out of trouble now. Yeah whatever, make it quick." Jerri responded, snickering in the process.

Seven brushed off his dad's attitude and walked up the block towards June. After a courteous dap, he faced June, a sad smile on his face.

"What you doing man? You going somewhere? I see you put a big suitcase in that car. You leaving?" asked June.

"Yeah man. I'm going to stay with my dad for a while. Trying to get my act together you know." Seven responded.

"Yeah I can dig it. That's dope your dad is around man. You think you gonna' be good though?"

"Yeah I think so. Aye if it don't work out then I'll be right back here."

"Yep right back in Pops store playin' the games."

"Word."

"Well aight lil' man. I'll let you do your thang. You be safe out there ya heard."

"I got you."

They dapped each other once more and Seven walked back to his father's car.

"Thanks Dad. And yes, I have all of my stuff. So where are we going? Are we going home?"

"Yes we will get there eventually. I have a few errands to run," Jerri answered, putting the key in the ignition.

"Okay. So, what we have to do? We going to the store? And where is Jumi and her mom?"

"Not quite. And they are at home. You'll see them later."

"Okay. So, where are we going?"

Seven's excitement got the better of him. He was eager to experience life with his Dad for the first time.

"Boy if you don't stop asking so many questions," Jerri responded, widening his eyes at the sudden onslaught of teenage angst.

"Um, okay."

"So, here are the rules. You have to bring your grades up, you have to stay out of trouble, you have to respect my house and my rules, and you need to be honest at all times. I don't want no playing, no breaking things, no arguing with Jumi, none of that. You only get one shot and *one shot only*! You got that?'

Seven nodded. He didn't really know what to make of his dad's tone and the rules, but he was happy to be with him finally. They went to the grocery store, to the post office, and stopped to see one of Jerri's chess buddies. With each stop, he noticed his father had a particular glow about him—especially as they ran into people that he knew. He seemed proud to introduce him as his son. Afterwards, they left and headed to what was now Seven's new home. He was ecstatic.

They pulled up to the apartment building and parked. They gathered the groceries and Seven's belongings and got into the elevator. Seven was full of energy and anticipation to see his new surroundings. They exited the elevator and walked down the hall to their apartment. Jerri opened the door and Seven followed.

"Wow this is nice, Dad."

"Yeah, you like it?"

"Mhmm…" Seven took in the new surroundings, gawking in pleasure. Unlike his mom's house, his dad's house had a certain air of affluence to it. Beige-colored walls sprinkled with pictures of his dad's family, complimented the soft lighting that cascaded around them. Seven could tell, even from the wooden coat hanger stand, that the rest of the house was equally stylish.

"A whole lot better than that hole in a wall your mother had you living in huh?"

Seven was slightly taken back by what his dad said. But he didn't respond. *Why does he always have to talk trash about my mom?* he thought to himself.

"So where is my room?"

"Your room? Oh no you don't have a room. You'll be sleeping on the pullout couch in the living room. You got a problem with that?"

"Um, no. I guess that's okay. At least the TV is out here."

His sister came out of her room and spoke. "Hey Seven."

"Hey Jumi."

"Ew… you look even more like Dad than the last time I saw you."

"Do I really?"

He looked at his dad and realized that they actually could pass as twins. That's how much he favored his dad. He was always told that he looked like his mother, which he did, but after seeing his dad up close, he realized that he looked like him too.

"I guess I do then huh?"

"Boy it ain't even a compliment. Y'all both ugly."

"Yeah whatever. The girls don't think so."

"Hood rats never do."

"Does that mean your mom is a hood rat?"

"Hey now! That's enough you two. I explained to both of

you what I expect. So, none of that. We're going out to eat tonight so get ready."

Jumi glared at Seven, turned around, walked in her room, and slammed her door. Seven went to the bathroom and washed his hands as he got ready to leave. As he walked out from the bathroom, he was greeted by Jumi's mother.

"Hey Seven. Shall I say, welcome home?"

"Hey Rehi. Thank you. I'm happy to be here with you all."

She leaned in and gave Seven a hug and he embraced her. He felt relief as all he had known for the last few years was pain, disappointment, and loneliness. He quickly opened his mind and heart to the thought of being in this family—something he forever longed for. Even the thought of Jumi, no matter how annoying, spoiled, and bothersome she would be, he was happy to have someone to go through life with on his level.

"Come on Seven. While Rehi and Jumi get ready, I want to take you upstairs to see your grandmother." Said Jerri.

"Okay."

They walked out of the apartment and went to the elevator down the hall. "Dad, have y'all lived here long?"

"For a few years."

"You like it?"

"It's okay for now. I want to buy a house eventually though."

"That sounds nice. How much does it cost to buy a house?"

"It depends on the house. They are all different prices."

"Oh okay."

"I have to say, I'm surprised you called me."

"Me too actually. Pops gave me your number a little bit ago. I guess I wasn't sure if you really wanted me to call. Despite him urging me to do so.

Jerri looked at Seven and smirked. Not really acknowledging his comment. They made idle chit-chat for a few minutes more until the elevator bell made a loud 'ping' sound.

"This is our stop."

Seven followed Jerri down the hall until they reached his grandmother's apartment. Jerri used his key and opened the door.

"Jerri? Is that you?" she yelled from the kitchen.

"Yeah Ma. Who else would it be?"

"Could've been the delivery man."

"And why would a delivery man have a key to your house?"

"In case he wanted to surprise me with a delivery."

"And what would he be delivering?"

"Hmm, he'll be delivering something."

"Better not be no delivery man delivering anything up in here!"

"Whatever boy, I'm grown."

They both laughed and Jerri gave his mom a hug. Seven smiled at their banter, chuckling slightly at their easy-going nature.

"Ma, I have a surprise for you. Look who is behind me," said Jerri.

She came into the living room where Seven had stood and her face instantly lit up. "Oh my God. Seven?" she asked.

"Hey Grandma." Seven replied.

"Boy, how are you? Last time I saw you in person was when you were a little baby."

Seven walked up to his grandma for an embrace. She took him in her arms and retreated back to grab a hold of his cheeks. Seven could see her eyes roaming his face as if capturing every inch.

"Yeah I guess that was a long time ago huh?"

"I would guess right. It was after you had that surgery. You still got that scar on your little booty? It looked like a little dimple," she produced a hearty laugh.

Seven blushed, embarrassed that she even knew about that, let alone, willingly bringing it up in conversation.

"Yeah, I guess it's with me forever."

Jerri's phone rang. He looked to see who had called and started to turn toward the door. "Ma, I need to run downstairs really quick. I'll be back in a minute." Said Jerri.

"Okay baby." She replied.

"Seven stay here with your grandma. I'll be back in a few. And don't you go anywhere." Jerri said sternly. Jerri let himself out of the apartment and walked down the hall.

"Your father is something else. Anyways, have a seat. Are you hungry baby?" his grandmother asked.

"Actually, I am but Dad is taking us out to eat so I don't want to ruin my appetite."

"Fair enough. It's nice that you came to visit. Will I get to see you more often?"

"Yes, I'm moving in with my dad."

"Really?"

"Yep, I brought my stuff today."

"Oh, that's beautiful. So, when did you guys decide that?"

"Oh, just today. I called Dad yesterday and asked if I could come live with them."

"Really?"

"Yep."

"How does your mom feel about it?"

"She's okay. My mom supports me in everything."

"Hmm. That's good."

"It was good timing because honestly I was getting in all kinds of trouble."

"Yeah I heard."

"Well I think it's for the best. Plus, I get a chance to get to know my dad which is something I've always wanted."

Seven beamed, his mind racing with thoughts. He couldn't wait to get to do some father-son bonding activities. Seven would finally be able to get some alone time with his hero.

"Is that right?"

"Yes ma'am."

"You're a sweet kid."

"That's what my mom says all the time."

"Come with me, I want to show you something."

Seven walked into the kitchen and his grandma pointed at a picture that hung on her refrigerator by a magnet. It was a picture of him and his father when he was still a toddler.

"Wow, I don't even remember this."

"You were too young baby."

"Wow. Hey Grandma something smells good in here."

"Oh, that's the zucchini cake in the oven."

"Zucchini? Yuck."

"You always this honest?"

"My mom always says that you might as well tell the truth the first time. That way people always know where you stand on something. No point in telling a lie when you can be honest."

"Make sense. Anyway, you haven't tried *my* zucchini cake.

I'll send you down a piece once it's done."

"Um okay. I'll try it."

"If you don't like it you can share it. They all like it down there."

"Okay, I will. Are you making more or something?"

"Yes. I'm making a second one for my friend. But I couldn't reach the sugar on the top shelf. Your father put it up there and he knows I can't reach it. Can you grab the sugar for me?"

"Sure Grandma."

Seven reached up to the top of the cabinet, pulled down the sugar, and handed it to her.

"Here you go. But it feels light Grandma."

"Actually, it does. Let's see how much is in here. Dang, it's only a cup and a half."

"How much do you need?"

"Another two cups. Dang it. Hey, you think you have time to run to the store for me."

"Um, I'm not sure. You think it would be okay?"

"Um, yeah it should be fine. The store is up the street. You'll be back in ten minutes tops. But hurry so you don't hold your father up."

Seven didn't think twice. Once he was given the money to buy the sugar, he left—happy to help his grandma. Once he made it out of the building, he power-walked to the corner store, filled with anticipation to go out for dinner with his dad and new family. There was only one person in line so he quickly grabbed the sugar, paid for it, and swiftly headed back.

Seven hurried to make sure he made it back to his grandma's apartment as quickly as possible.

Seven knocked on his grandmother's door and his father opened it. He looked angry. His grandmother thanked him for getting the sugar and commented that he moved much faster than his dad.

Seven set the sugar on the counter and walked back to the living room where his dad sat.

"So, Dad, is everyone ready to go?"

"Yeah but um, where did you go?"

Seven looked confused as he was sure that his dad overheard the conversation that he had with his grandma about going to the store to get her some sugar.

"Um, I went to the store for—"

And before he could finish his statement his father had smacked him really hard in the face. The force made him stumble.

"Didn't I tell you before I left to not go anywhere? Why did you leave this house when I specifically told you not to leave?" shouted Jerri.

Seven caught his balance and was extremely confused by what just happened.

“Well? What do you have to say to this?” his father yelled.

“Jerri, why did you hit that boy. I told him to go.” Seven’s grandmother interjected.

“Stay out of this Ma, this is between me and my son.”

Jerri turned his attention from his mother back to Seven and waited for an answer.

“Um, grandma asked me to go to the—”

Once again, before he was able to finish his statement, his father smacked him. This time with even more force then the first smack. His face felt like it was on fire from the heat that built up under his skin.

“I don’t care what your grandmother asked you to do. What I say goes. Only what I say. You got it?”

“But, how was I supposed to know that?”

“You know now, don’t you?”

Seven looked at his grandma with some discontent. He felt like she had set him up to get in trouble. Clearly this was a major misstep, but he desperately wanted to make it up.

“I’m sorry, Dad. It won’t happen again.”

“You right it won’t. So, as of right now, you are being punished.”

"Punished?"

"That's right! And for two weeks."

"Two weeks? But Dad."

"But Dad my behind! When you go back to school on Monday, I want you coming straight home from school. Do you understand?"

Seven shook his head in disbelief that the result of him going to the store for his grandma had caused this reaction from his father. So many thoughts were running through his mind. He couldn't believe he'd been hit on his first day. It was similar to living with Sam. He wanted to call his mom, but he didn't want to make his dad angrier. *Why does this keep happening to me?* The thought fleeted through his mind.

With a tear in his eye, he looked at his father and nodded.

"I want to hear you say it!"

"Yes Dad. I understand."

"Now let's go."

Seven followed his dad down to the car where Rehi and Jumi were waiting. Jumi made eye contact with Seven, and he quickly looked away and put his head down.

"What took y'all so long?" asked Jumi.

"Just be quiet Jumi and get in the car okay?" Jerri replied.

"Dang Dad what's wrong with you?"

"Nothing just get in the car."

"Why are you shouting at me? Don't take whatever is wrong with you out on me because I ain't do nothing to you."

"Jumi, listen to him and get in the car." Said Rehi.

"Hmm…" Jumi listened to her mom and slammed the car door once she got in. Seven also got into the car, but was quiet for most of the ride. Even when Jumi would try to provoke him, he remained quiet. All the while, he could see his father looking at him occasionally through the rear-view mirror.

"You okay punk?" Jumi asked Seven when they got to the restaurant.

"Mhmm…" Responded Seven.

"So, why are you so quiet?"

Seven shrugged but kept walking without saying a word.

"Well forget you then *punk*." Jumi taunted.

Jumi walked ahead of him and bumped him slightly as she entered the restaurant. He continued to be very selective in how he responded to both Jumi and Rehi while at dinner in an effort to keep from angering his father. He had no idea what was the right or wrong thing to say or do so he sat there, and did nothing. Though the food was appetizing, and the most delicious meal that Seven had eaten in a while, earlier events lessened the joy of eating such food. After a few hours, they eventually went home for the evening.

After parking the car, they all walked through the door. It seemed like it had been a long day, or maybe it was that Sunday dinner that had everyone slightly sluggish. Jumi and Rehi walked down the hall, headed to their rooms, while Seven sat on the couch waiting for instructions from Jerri.

"Seven?" his father said.

"Yes Dad?"

"You will sleep on the couch. So, let me show you how to pull it out."

Jerri pulled the cushions from the sofa and placed them in the corner. He pulled the middle handle that opened up the bed. He also brought a blanket and some pillows for Seven to use.

"Now listen. Make sure you keep this area clean at all times. Even though you are sleeping here, this is not *your* personal space. This is *our* living room and it needs to remain respectable." Said Jerri.

"Okay Dad."

"Now, remember what I said. Straight home from school tomorrow. No detours. You understand?" Jerri turned to walk away. Just as he did, Seven stopped him.

"Dad?"

"What?"

Seven grabbed his dad and hugged him. Jerri wasn't sure

what to make of the sudden act of affection so he barely embraced him in return.

"I love you, Dad."

"Okay. I love you too. Have a good night. I'll wake you in the morning."

Seven lowered his head and turned to walk away. As he did, a tear rolled down his face. He placed his bags in the hall closet as instructed and changed into his basketball shorts and a t-shirt to sleep in. All the lights were out, it was quiet, and his stomach was full. Seven was about to stay his first night with his dad. He smiled to himself.

Wow, I'm actually here. With my dad. And I do look just like him, he thought to himself. He couldn't help but to think about how his dad had smacked him though. He was happy to be with him, but he was so nervous. Nervous because he didn't want to mess things up. All Seven wanted was to be happy. He'd dreamt of this moment for as long as he could remember. His dad was his superhero. The answer to all of his troubles as a kid. He wanted to be on his best behavior. As he lay in bed, he looked at his fingers. He inspected them closely. They were bruised and bitten—not yet healed from the last time he chewed the skin away piece by piece.

I'm okay. It's okay, he thought.

He laid on his back and became aroused. For so long, his routine to reduce his anxiety, was by self-gratification. He rubbed his thighs as they ached. His body had made a request. He rubbed his thighs and looked at his fingers once more.

"God, please help me." He said aloud.

He rolled over, closed his eyes, and before long, he was asleep. He slept the night away until he was awakened by the faint sound of an alarm.

What time is it, he thought.

He looked out the living room window and saw that it was still dark. He stretched, yawned, and then got on his feet. He felt good. He realized that he actually had a good night of sleep. No fear, no cold sweat, no repeated self-gratification, none of that.

Wow. I did it! Thank you God, he thought to himself.

Seven sprung to his feet, turned on the lamp next to the couch, and begun to figure out what he was going to wear for school today. He was nervous and excited. It was like the first day of school all over again. He pulled out his best outfit without hesitation. He laid it across his bed, and went into the bathroom to take a shower.

"Today is going to be a great day," he told himself while he looked in the mirror.

Seven showered, brushed his teeth, moisturized with some cocoa butter lotion he found on the sink, and headed out of the bathroom. He opened the door and Jumi stood there. With her hand on her hip, she tapped her foot.

"You better not have used *my* stuff!" she squealed.

"Like what?" he asked.

"Like *my* lotion."

"The cocoa butter one? Is that yours?"

"Yes. Did you use it?"

"Sure did. Doesn't it smell good? I love how smooth it makes my skin feel. Thanks sis. You're the *best*." He mused.

"Jerk! Don't touch my stuff. I'm not sharing with you so you need to get your own."

"Didn't know it was yours. But now that I do, I'll be sure to use it every morning" he teased.

"Mom! Seven used my lotion!" She yelled.

Jumi complained to her mom about Seven using her lotion while he went into the living room to iron his clothes. He quickly pressed them and got dressed.

"Seven?" asked Rehi.

"Yes Rehi?" he replied.

"Did you use your sister's lotion?"

"Yes ma'am. I'm sorry I didn't know it was hers."

"Okay, after school we'll take you shopping to get you some stuff. Okay?"

Seven was overjoyed with the thought of it all. "Shopping? Me? Wow. Today is already a great day." He cheered.

Seven finished getting ready, and it was time for him to leave for school. It was also time for Jumi to leave to get dropped off to her private school. Seven thought it was funny to watch her transform and pose as this pompous person with such proper etiquette. It was so interesting to see how someone else chose to live their life every day. He was appreciative to get a closer look at someone else's life other than his own.

"Seven did you want to ride with us?" asked Jumi.

"No thanks. I'd rather walk, *private school girl*." He teased.

"Suit yourself ugly."

"Actually, maybe I'll ride with you, so I can see some of your friends. Bet they don't think I'm ugly."

"Too late, you said no. Mom, Seven said he'd rather walk."

Jumi stuck her tongue out at Seven and taunted him. Seven thought nothing of it as he grabbed his jacket and book bag to begin his walk to school. Jumi was fixing her hair in the big mirror opposite the front door. Seven walked by her and headed to the door.

"Hey Jumi?" asked Seven.

"What?" she replied.

He quickly stuck up his middle finger at her and then walked out the door. As the door closed, he could hear Jumi telling her mother what he had done. He chuckled to himself and decided to take the stairs rather than the elevator. *Having a little sister is so much fun already*, he thought. Seven was anxious to get to school. As he walked the twenty-minutes to school, he often chuckled as he thought about his new family.

I'm glad to not be alone anymore. Jumi's funny. Rehi has been so nice to me, he thought to himself as he walked to school.

Seven was full of joy and anticipation as he walked through the school entrance. He took a deep breath and went to his counselor's office before going to homeroom. As he walked in, he saw another student already speaking with her so he sat on the bench and waited patiently.

As he continued to wait, the other student came out of the office and his counselor waved him to come in. He walked in and sat on the chair in front of her desk. She barely looked at him, her glasses slipping off the bridge of her nose.

"Mr. Bradford. What can I do for you?" Asked Mrs. Greene.

"Hi Mrs. Greene. I wanted to come in and speak to you today to let you know of my intentions." He replied.

This caught her attention. She looked up and studied the young man sitting in front of her. She placed her pen down and crossed her arms, sitting back to listen.

"Uh, okay. And what are your intentions? Are you dropping out for the year?"

"Absolutely not. I wanted you to know that I thought over the weekend about what you said, and from here on out I will be in school, all day, every day."

"Well glad that you intend on being here. But your presence is not nearly enough for you to not repeat the ninth grade. You need to pass all of your classes as well."

"Yes, ma'am I know, and I intend on doing that as well."

"And how do you expect to do that?"

"Um, it's quite simple actually. I need to do all my homework and pass my tests and I'll be good."

"Simple huh?"

"Seems simple to me. So yeah."

"You have some tough classes that you're failing. It'll take a lot of hard work to get the grades you need to pass them all."

Seven felt like his counselor didn't believe he could do it. He originally thought that she would be pleased with his change in behavior and approach, but she doubted him.

"I understand that, and despite your disbelief, I will do this," he said.

"Can I ask you something young man?" asked Mrs. Greene.

"Sure."

"What changed?"

"Well, a couple of things. Um... I moved in with my dad

recently, so I know things will be better for me at his house. And I also *want* to pass. Before, it didn't really matter to me."

"Hmm, okay. Well I sure hope these changes in mindset are consistent."

"I know myself so I know that they will be."

Seven reassured, readjusting his position in the chair. He was determined to make things better. The way he saw it is that if he was willing to sacrifice his life to make some money for his mother and him, why not work twice as hard to do well in school. School was a win-win situation, selling crack on the streets was not.

"Great. If you are serious then you need to speak to your teachers to make sure that you get all of the work that you have missed."

"Okay."

"You also need to ask about any extra credit that you can get done that could bring your grades up."

"Thanks for that and I will definitely do that."

"Sure thing. Anything else?"

"Yes, one last thing. Can you give me a hall pass for homeroom?"

"Absolutely. Have a good day."

"I already am. Thanks!"

Seven took the hall pass and headed to his homeroom. He

almost skipped through the halls because he was so happy. He made it to his homeroom and handed his teacher the pass.

"Hey Seven, I thought we weren't going to see you today." Asked Kim.

"I know. But I'm here, and I'll be here going forward." He replied.

"Okay, well, welcome back handsome."

Seven winked at her and sat in his seat until the bell rang. It was time for his first period class. He participated and answered questions asked by his teacher. And at the end of class, he did as suggested by his counselor. He asked for all of the work he missed throughout the month, and also asked for extra credit work.

And so went the rest of his day. Each class was similar—focused and engaged. Some teachers decided to oblige both requests, some gave him either the chance to make up the work or do extra credit, and a couple gave him neither and allowed him to lay in the bed that he had made. Either way, he was off to a great start with his first day. Soon, the end of the school day approached. The bell had rung and he headed out of class. As he walked by, he observed the various crowds of students that hung out in front of the school. Music was playing; kids were smoking, laughing and joking around with each other. He even saw June.

"Seven. What up lil' man." said June.

"Yo, what up." Seven replied.

"Haven't seen you all weekend. How are things at your dad's?"

"Yeah man. Things are going okay so far."

"Oh, that's what's up. So, you down to hang out?"

"Nah I can't man. I have to focus on getting my grades back up. So, I need to chill with the hanging for a bit."

"Well look at you. Turnin' into a nerd now huh?" teased June.

"Whatever. I'm the coolest nerd you'll ever meet." He replied.

They both laughed and dapped each other.

"Well, try to come through one of these weekends whenever you can man. Okay?" asked June.

"Yeah it's a bet. I'll get up with man. I gotta' roll." He replied.

Seven turned and headed home. He walked down the hill and noticed a girl ahead of him had dropped something. As he approached it, he could see it was a schoolbook. So, he grabbed it and jogged a little and caught up with her.

"Excuse me. I think you dropped something. Is this yours?" asked Seven.

"Thank you so much. I've been dropping things all day." She replied.

"No problem at all. My name is Seven. What's yours?"

"Seven?"

"Yeah, Seven."

"Do you live in the buildings at the bottom of the hill?" she asked.

Seven was puzzled. He looked at her face again trying to remember if he knew her from somewhere.

"Um, yeah I do. Do we know each other from somewhere?" he asked.

"Oh, sorry. No, we don't. I've heard of you though." She responded.

"Oh really? What have you heard?"

"Only that you were Jumi's brother and you recently moved here."

"Oh, so you know my sister?"

"Yeah. Y'all live in building one, right?'

"Yep. Do you live there too?"

"No, I live in building four."

"Oh, okay so we actually close to each other."

She nodded, but her demeanor soon changed. She squinted her eyes as if deep in thought and wondering if she should share what was on her mind.

"I also heard one other thing about you, but I wasn't sure it was true until now."

"Oh yeah? Well what is that?" he asked.

"That you were cute," she answered.

"Thanks. You're actually pretty nice on the eyes yourself. What's your name?"

"Monica."

Seven and Monica walked and talked the entire way home. They discussed all sorts of things such as school, hobbies, relationship status. The twenty minutes it took to get down the hill seemed like five minutes as they got to know each other a little better. Before they even realized it, they were walking up to his building.

"Oh wow, looks like this is my stop." Said Seven.

"Really Seven? You not going to walk me down to my building?" asked Monica.

"Um, I suppose I can. It's only down the block."

Seven and Monica walked a little farther until they reached her building. The conversation went so well that she ended up giving him her phone number. He would have liked to give her his, but he didn't know his dad's number by heart yet.

"Thanks for walking me home. See you tomorrow after school?" asked Monica.

"Absolutely. I'll call you later okay?" he answered.

It was almost prophecy. Seven had a great day! He skipped all the way back up the block to his building. He ran through the door and headed up the stairs.

Thank you God! I can't wait to tell my dad, he thought.

He knocked on his apartment door and Jerri let him in. Seven sensed immediately that something was wrong. Jerri moved to the side and allowed Seven to walk into the house.

"Um hey Dad. How was your day?" asked Seven.

"Mhmm..." Jerri responded.

"Everything okay?"

"You tell me."

"Um, I think it should be."

"And why should everything be okay?"

"Um, I had a really good day at school. I didn't get into any trouble. I spoke to my counselor and all of my teachers so I have a plan to catch up and bring my grades up. Also, I met—"

Before he finished his last statement, Jerri hauled off and smacked him. Seven saw stars as heat flooded his cheeks.

"Go ahead finish your story. You met someone right?" asked Jerri.

"Dad what's the problem?" asked Seven.

He hit Seven again. "Tell me who you met." Jerri yelled.

"A girl named Monica and we walked home from school

together."

"And what did I tell you to do?"

"I did come straight home. I didn't hang out with anyone. I even told my friend from school that I couldn't hang out."

"No, you didn't. Once again you disrespect me by doing what you want to do rather than doing what I told you to do. You are so disrespectful. You don't ever listen." He struck his son again.

"Dad I did come straight home!"

Seven responded, confusion and anger co-mingling inside of him.

"First off, lower your damn voice when you speak to me. Now, you gonna' lie to my face? So, you mean to tell me that you didn't walk past this building and keep on walking down the street?"

"Dad, I was trying to be nice and walk Monica to her building. I wasn't defying you. It took me like three extra minutes to go down there and come back."

"Shut up! Don't you talk back to me. When I say come straight home that's exactly what I mean. Now take off your pants. This is why you in the situation you are in. Because you run all over your mother. But you ain't gonna' run over me. She's too soft on you, and now I gotta' come and clean up her mess. I said take your pants off."

Seven couldn't believe what he had heard. He was in shock

that his father told him to undress so that he could be whooped for walking up the street. His father took off his belt and waited for Seven to pull down his jeans. As soon as he did, Jerri swung as hard as he could and struck him on the back of the legs repeatedly.

"You are going to respect me. What I say goes! Do… you… under… stand... me?"

Seven winced in pain with each strike. But he did not let go of a tear. He did not cry. He was angry and wanted to defend himself, but held back. He took the strikes and tried to remain respectful to his father. His hero, his savior from his dreams. At that moment, Jumi and Rehi walked in the room.

"Jerri. What are you doing?" Rehi asked.

"The boy doesn't listen. I told him to he is being punished and he needed to come straight home from school. But he blatantly disregarded what I said."

"Really Jerri? The kid has only been here for two days. Give him some time to adjust."

"Damn that. He had enough time to adjust when he was with his mother. She let him run all over her. Getting into all kinds of trouble, stealing cars and smoking weed. He probably sold drugs too. And I bet she ain't even care. I told her he wouldn't amount to be anything without me in his life. And look. She ruined him. And now I gotta' deal with all this crap. Well, not in my house. Not on my watch." he yelled.

"Jerri, come in the room. We need to talk."

"Rehi, you don't understand."

"Just come in the room so we can talk."

As they walked into their bedroom, Seven quickly pulled up his pants. His legs burned and eyes watered. But he refused to cry. So, he sat on the couch as Jumi stood there in disbelief.

"You okay Seven?" she asked.

He didn't respond. He didn't even look in her direction. He sat there, trapped in his own thoughts. She continued to speak to him, but he drowned her out. All he could hear was himself.

I get away from Sam just to come to my dad who wants to beat me too. Why is this happening, God? Does anyone love me? What did I do? Did I do something really that wrong? I should go back to my mom. But I'm trying to do better, and I was in trouble all the time at my mom's. God, what am I to do? He thought to himself.

"Well I can see you don't want to talk. I'll leave you alone." Said Jumi. She patted his shoulder and walked away.

"Wait…" Seven put his hands over his face and cried. "I really don't know what to do. And I don't have anywhere else to go. So, I have to stay to make this work. Dad can't be this bad, is he? He's the person that I always wanted to live with, this can't be all there is. He has to love me. Right?" asked Seven.

Jumi sat there speechless. She didn't know what to say that

would make him feel better.

"Yeah he loves you. He talked about you all the time before you came." She replied.

"Does he beat you?"

"*No*. Besides I'm a girl and my mother ain't having that anyways. I don't know what happened, but, it will be okay."

Seven nodded as he was committed to make things work with his new family. Despite the pain that Jerri had inflicted, Seven knew that this was the only chance he had to start a new life—free from hardships.

Over the next couple months, he strived to be on his best behavior. As his behavior improved, his grades improved. He had failing grades in all of his classes prior to when Seven moved in. So, his final grades for the marking period were either average or barely passing. But Jerri took exception to a report card that had only Cs and Ds. Seven even tried out for the football team so that he could have something to do after school which also required him to keep a passing grade in order for him to play. But when his report card came in, not only did he get whooped again, Jerri forced Seven to quit the team. Seven was embarrassed so he didn't even go to the coaches to explain why. He simply came home and never went back to practice. He didn't know what to do to make his dad happy. So, he sat on the couch. Defeated.

"What's wrong with you ugly?" asked Jumi.

"I can't get anything right. How am I supposed to have all A's when I was failing all of my classes to begin with?" Seven shook his head, face in hand, and cried some more.

"Yeah, I don't know." Responded Jumi.

"And he won't listen to reason. It's like he's purposely ignoring what I'm saying and he wants to have a reason to be mad at me. No matter what I do." Seven walked away and Jumi heard him cry in the bathroom.

A couple months passed, and whenever it seemed like Seven had taken a step forward something would happen that would set him back. There was always something that kept him from getting closer to his father.

So, when the second marking period came, Seven was ready. He put his head down and went to work. As time went by, his grades greatly improved—still not an A student, but a mixture A's, B's, and a C or two. Seven had changed his trajectory around and was half way there to passing all his classes for the year. He simply needed to stay focused for two more marking periods, then he would have erased his self-inflicted issues from the beginning of the year.

At the same time, Jerri, had created a chess club and Seven was proud to be one of his students. He took pride is honing his chess skills just to impress his father. Truthfully, Seven didn't like chess, but he desperately wanted to connect with his dad. He figured as long as he stayed focused things would work out with his dad.

Seven took it as a personal challenge to himself to succeed to spite anyone who doubted him—even his father. The more he thought on it, the more he wanted to rub it in the faces of the people who abused and hurt him. He was driven, but at the same time he wanted to be loved. Especially by Jerri. The harder he tried, the more he failed. And the more he failed the more he was punished. A vicious cycle that repeated itself without fail. Despite desperately wanting the love and approval of his father, he was close to giving up on it.

Saturday Morning

"Seven! Don't make me come out there. Stop making all of that noise," Jerri's deep voiced vibrated through the walls.

"It's not me, Dad, its Jumi! Tell her to stop playing and give me my hoodie," Seven yelled back, breathlessly.

"Such a tattler. You can't catch me, you can't catch me," Jumi teased.

Seven chased Jumi from the living room, to the dining room, through the hallway, and finally to the kitchen. Her love for sports made her unsuspectingly elusive as Jumi ran and dodged all the while with his hoodie in tow. The breeze from her running had the hoodie flailing behind her and gave Seven a chance to grab it. So, he extended as far as he could and lunged for it as she turned the corner from the hallway into the kitchen. The kitchen floor was ceramic which made his footing unsure.

"Gimmie that!" he yelled.

With his lunge he grabbed his hoodie, but slipped on the floor and fell on his back. He looked up at her, she looked back down at him, both in shock that he actually fell. And he didn't just fall, he fell hard. Like he really busted his behind on the floor. So much so that the dishes in the cabinet shook. Then they both started laughing uncontrollably. Despite the constant bickering and taunting one another, they really enjoyed each other's company.

They both heard a creaking sound coming from the back of the apartment. It came from their parents' bedroom door. Jumi heard it first. Seven wondered why Jumi stopped laughing. She transformed from being full of joy and laughter to that of worry, concern, and regret. Followed were the familiar sounds of the heavy footsteps coming down the hallway. Seven knew those steps ever so well. Jumi looked at Seven in a way that suggested she pitied him. She did not speak it, but rather, mouthed to him.

"I'm so sorry." She mouthed.

Seven lowered his head, saddened by what he knew was coming.

"Seven!" Jerri yelled.

Before he could even respond, Jerri whooped him with his belt. He struck him all over. His legs, his arms, his back.

Seven fell to the floor squirming in pain. Jerri swung the belt so hard and so fast that all he could do was ball up in the corner. He covered his head with his arms and hands.

Seven screamed and desperately tried to get away, but he was pinned in the kitchen corner. The sound of Seven screaming was not like a typical whooping and it concerned Rehi. She ran out the bedroom to see what had happened.

"Jerri stop!" Rehi yelled.

"No, he don't listen!" Jerri yelled back.

"What did he do that was so terrible?"

"He doesn't respect me. He will respect me."

"Respect you? They are kids. Kids play around."

"Not in my house."

"It's not only your house."

Seven, balled up in the corner, was relieved that Rehi came to save him. She saved him many times from being whooped by merely being home. Regardless of how he felt, Jerri did have respect for Rehi and her opinion so he stopped despite really wanting to hit Seven again.

"Come here Seven," Rehi said.

Seven tried to get up to go to Rehi, but his back was killing him. He had to turn over on his knees and then stand up from there.

"Come sit on the couch, baby."

Seven, cried and winced from the pain, as he did as he was told.

"My back really hurts Rehi. It really hurts." Said Seven.

"Okay let me take a look."

Rehi lifted his shirt to inspect his back and screamed.

"Oh my God. Jerri, what have you done?"

Jumi looked at his back and tears welled up in her eyes until she cried.

"Why did you do that to him? We were just having fun." Jumi cried.

It wasn't till that moment that Jerri realized what happened. He was so upset that he hadn't realized that he had whooped Seven with the buckle of the belt. Seven cried and winced again as Rehi patted the blood from his back with a cloth.

"How could you do that?" asked Rehi.

"I didn't know Rehi," Jerri answered.

As the back and forth ensued, Seven stood from the couch and limped to the long mirror opposite the front door. He turned around and lifted his shirt. He could now see the blood running down his back from multiple areas. He hung his head and cried—not from the pain but from the thought that his father, his hero, the man he dreamt would save him from all the horrors of his life, would be inflicting this kind of abuse on him. His back stung with pain. He could barely stand. He had to slouch to be able to withstand the pain. But no matter how much pain his back was in, his heart hurt ten times more. His dream had been shattered. He went to the couch and sat down. He was so choked up that he could barely talk.

"I don't want to live here anymore." Whispered Seven.

"What did you say?" Jumi asked.

"I want to go back to my mom's house."

Jerri scowled. "You what?"

"I want to leave."

"So ungrateful!"

"Ungrateful? Wow."

Seven stood and went to the closet. He pulled out his suitcase and began to pack his things. Jumi and Rehi tried to convince him to stay.

"No. Let that ingrate leave. He doesn't deserve to be here!" yelled Jerri. "Go ahead. Leave. Just like your mother did."

"Ingrate? That's what you call me?"

"That's right."

"I'm supposed to be grateful for this?"

Seven lifted his shirt exposing the bloody mess inflicted upon him by Jerri. "Can I ask you something, *Dad*? Did you ever love me? Why did you even agree to let me live here? So you could save face with Jumi and Rehi? And you always bring up my mother when she has nothing to do with you. Is that the problem? My mom left you and so you treat me like trash to get back at her?"

Jerri looked at his son, paused, and then walked away. Everyone in the building probably heard the door slam.

"Yeah. Figures you would walk away and not answer me." Seven yelled at the door, anger seething within him.

Jumi looked really sad as she watched Seven pack his things.

Seven flung his clothes into his suitcase and looked at his sister. "Yeah I have to go. I can't keep going through this sis. I've been hurt too much. I'm doing everything I can do. My grades are much better, I do my chores, and I've only been in any real trouble once. The time I stole $200 from that lady at the supermarket. I know I was wrong for that one for sure but I haven't done anything else even remotely close to that. I've been on punishment since my first night here for going to the store for Grandma. It's just too much. It was already too much. And now this?"

"I'm sorry you've been going through this." Jumi replied.

"It's okay. The one thing that I was able to do was focus on what I wanted to do. I wanted to get my act together, stay out of trouble, and do better in school. I know it's only been a few months, but I know I will stick with it," Seven replied, slumping his shoulders. Much like everything else, he knew that he wasn't going to give up trying to better himself.

"I love you big bro."

Seven looked at Jumi almost in shock to hear what she said. Jumi realized what she said and quickly back peddled a little.

"Well, you know what I mean. You were okay to live with, but at least now I don't have to worry about my lotion disappearing." She snarked.

"That's funny. Yeah, I guess. But hey, I love you too sis." Seven replied.

They exchanged a hug and Seven prepared to leave the house. Just then, Rehi and Jerri walked in. Jerri's eyes were downcast as Rehi pulled at his arm.

"Wait Seven. Your father wants to say something to you." Said Rehi.

Seven paused at the door, looked at Rehi, and then looked at his father.

"I'll take you back to your mom's. We can talk in the car."

Rehi looked at Jerri in a way to show her displeasure to move the conversation out of the house. She gave Seven a hug and kissed him on the cheek.

"We love you baby. Please know that." Rehi said.

Jerri grabbed Seven's suitcase and headed out the door first. Seven followed. They walked down the hall and to the elevator without a word spoken between them. As they drove, Seven waited for his father to speak. The silence engulfed them, causing his nerves to be frayed. Jerri pulled over in front of the chicken spot.

"Get out." Jerri yelled.

"What?" asked Seven.

"You heard me. Get your suitcase and get out."

How can this man who helped birth me, who looks just like me, my hero, the man I dreamt would be my savior, do this to me? What have I ever done to him? Why does he hate me so much? He never wanted me, he thought.

Jerri looked at Seven, and without any remorse, he reached over him and opened the passenger door.

"What are you waiting for? Get out I said."

"Why are you doing this to me?" asked Seven.

"Get out."

"Did you ever even want me to move in with you?"

"I said, get out."

Seven looked at his dad, sad and disappointed at the shell of the man that was kicking him out of the car. Seven's ideas of his dad fell away like shattered glass, and what sat beside him was the true reflection of what his mother had warned him about. Her words rung in his mind.

"So, did you ever want me? I guess not." Seven spat.

"For the last time get out of my damn car!"

"Fine! I see why my mom left you. You're an idiot. A real

lowlife. I hate you."

Seven got out of the car and grabbed his suitcase from the backseat. As soon as he closed the back door, Jerri sped off. He pulled off so fast that the wheels screeched and the gravel from the ground flew in Seven's face. He walked to his mom's house. It was about an hour walk because he had that very heavy suitcase to carry with him. Sad, defeated, bruised, and beaten, he reached his mom's house. He walked up the stairs of the building and walked into the apartment. He figured his mother was asleep so he knocked on her door.

His mom opened her bedroom door as quick as she could. The door swung open and his mom stood there in her robe.

"Hey baby. This is a pleasant surprise." Seven walked into his mother's room and grabbed her. He held her tight and cried.

"He don't love me Momma. Why don't he love me?" he cried.

"Aw baby. What happened?"

Seven let go of their embrace, and walked toward his room.

"Seven? Seven baby. Please tell me. What happened?" Sissy called after him, her body shivering in regret.

"I'm fatherless Momma. Fatherless." Seven said, slamming the door to punctuate his disdain.

Chapter 9: Genesis 2:24

"Therefore, shall a man leave his father and his mother, and shall cleave unto his wife: and they shall be one flesh."

As Jumi and Jerri continued talking about Seven, Faith just watched and listened not wanting to interrupt their moment. She patiently waited to ask if anyone had even heard from Seven. She was beyond nervous as this was totally out of character for him. Not one text reply from him. No return phone calls. Nothing. He had completely dropped off the radar. Finally, she couldn't take it any longer so she decided to clear her throat and speak up.

"Um, excuse me guys." Jumi and Jerri continued to talk not hearing Faith initially. "Guys. Hello."

They stopped mid-conversation and turned their heads toward Faith.

"Hey Faith. Are you okay, sweetie?" Jerri asked.

"Hey Jerri, I'm sorry. Um… I should be asking you that. How are you doing? I would've come sooner but I didn't know you were in the hospital."

"Yeah, I'm fine now. I was in a lot of pain. Wait, Seven didn't tell you I was in the hospital?" Jerri sat up, alarmed.

Faith stood and slowly paced the small area between his bed and the chair that she had sat in.

"No, I had no idea until Jumi told me at our house a little while ago. Jumi said she had spoken to him and he was preparing to leave right away to come to the hospital. But Jumi said he never made it here. I'm so nervous because I can't get a hold of him. Do you think something has happened?'

Jumi rolled her eyes and looked out the window as Faith talked. Jerri noticed that as well and tried to offer a suggestion.

"Maybe he changed his mind about coming to the hospital? It's not like we've been the best of friends before this happened. I mean we are making progress but…"

Jerri then turned away, his dream still lingering on his mind and what he said was a hope that Seven was okay. But he felt something was wrong as well but didn't want to say anything in Faith's presence.

"Yeah, maybe he got wind of your, um… *lunch meeting* and decided not to show," said Jumi, snickering in the process.

"You know what Jumi, I'm tired of your attitude. I'm so sick and tired of your constant judging and questioning me and the relationship with *my* husband!"

"Whatever. I still don't see what *my brother* sees in you."

"And you know what? Maybe you never will. And you know why? Because if you ain't ever had what we have, then you will never understand."

"Whatever. Quiet as it's kept my dad never seen it either and he and my mom been married since we were kids. So, if he ain't see it then something really has to be wrong."

"Really? Are you kidding me? Being married and being soulmates are not the same thing. Just like loving someone and being *in love* with someone is totally different things. But I wouldn't expect either of you to understand that because y'all don't know the difference. You've never had that feeling or even someone to feel that way about. So how can you understand? Jerri you didn't even love your son enough to support him when we were married. All these years all he ever wanted was your love and approval only to get rejected over and over again."

"Shut your mouth! I know everything about being in love and having a soulmate. So, you don't know what you are talking about" Jerri objected.

"Actually, I do. Whose shoulder you think Seven cries on every time y'all hurt him? Whose ear you think he talks off about wanting to have been an actual family? It sure as hell ain't yours," Faith crossed her arms, ready for a challenge.

For once, Jumi stood silent. She knew some of the pain her brother went through when it came to their dad. Just based off of some of their conversations, it was clear how hurt he had been.

"Now, I understand that my brother has been through a lot here, but that doesn't give you the right to sit here and lecture us on love and marriage."

"I'm not lecturing you, all I'm saying is that I understand how you don't understand our relationship. We are perfect for one another."

"Girl you are *far* from perfect." said Jumi.

"I never said that I was perfect, but I am *perfect* for him. And he is perfect for me. God put us together. He himself selected us for one another."

"Yeah right."

"You don't have to believe it, but it's true. And maybe if you invested as much energy to understand our story, then maybe you would have someone for yourself and not always criticizing everyone else's relationship while you sit home alone and miserable without a man."

"Please. I don't need no man. Besides I'm married to my career. I don't need no one distracting me from my work. Anyways. Your story you say? Okay well let's hear it?" asked Jerri, stepping in to defend Jumi, like he usually does.

The Prayer

Seven had hoped that his dad was the person who would love him and save him from the tragedies of life. He was wrong. But he continued to desire a companion. Someone who would be able to go through life with.

At one point, he thought his sister would have adequately filled the role. He had looked forward to living with them for a few years to solidify a bond that would be unbreakable. He enjoyed not being alone. Despite the typical sibling rivalry, he rather enjoyed having someone around. But that came to an end when he realized his father wasn't who he had hoped he would be.

As he continued to grow up and mature, he continued to long for someone to be there for him. His mother was definitely his number one fan; however, due to her work schedule, they very seldom were in each other's company. He wanted a wife. Up to this point Seven had been in multiple relationships, however something didn't sit right with him in each of them. Either they were not driven enough, not passionate enough, not polished enough, not interested in a long-term relationship, or just didn't sync with him spiritually. He didn't just want anyone, he wanted the only one. The only one that was made for him, much like how Eve was created from Adam. This is what he wanted and prayed for continually.

"Lord, I haven't been the greatest follower of your word or your principles," he prayed aloud. "I have had many struggles during my walk with you. I have been hurt more times than I can count and I have been responsible for the pain of others. What I am looking for now is balance. The perfect balance between myself, the one person that could complete me, and you Lord. You know my shortcomings and my misdeeds. But you also know my faith. You know that I truly believe that there is nothing too hard for you. So Lord, if she exists, my perfect being, my other half, my true love and soulmate, please bring her to me. If you do this, I promise to forever love her with all that is within me and will forever give all of the glory to you. In your name I pray. Amen."

The Answer

Seven left his mom's house to catch the bus to work, his mind persistently drawn to the thought of finding his soulmate—his rib, his wife to be. He entered the bus, staring out the window all while pleading with God in his mind to answer his prayer.

Is it her Lord? How about her? Even if it is not your will for me to find her while I'm still in my twenties, please allow me to at least see her face, so that I know she is there and waiting for you to bring us together, he thought.

Seven looked up and down the seats on the bus and watched as people walked the street, looking desperately for a sign that his love existed. His eyes searched while his mind and body yearned. The thought of being alone became unbearable and the more he thought about it, the more he prayed that God would grant him this miracle. And one day, he felt like his prayers were answered.

A new manager started working at his part time job during the day. Being that he only worked there at night, he hadn't seen what all of the fuss was about. All the other fellas on the day shift had been speaking about this new manager for a couple of days now, but he was less concerned. As he walked into the employee locker room, he was met by some of the guys who had been eyeing the new manager of the local restaurant. She had been also shooting down their attempts to flirt with her. So, they thought to try to tempt the former ladies' man to shoot his shot as well.

"Come on fellas. Y'all need to chill. I think I'm done with all of this being with different women thing." Said Seven.

"Yeah right. And what brings you to this conclusion?" asked Ralph.

"Well I went out on Friday night, like most Friday nights. Hanging with my folks. I met this girl named Cassy and we began to chop it up and everything seemed to be good."

"Did you hit?" asked Dan

"Yeah, but that's beside the point." Answered Seven.

"Beside the point? That is the point." said Ralph.

"Absolutely the point in my book." Dan agreed.

"Wait, y'all. Hear me out. Afterwards I knew that while this was a nice young lady who had some decent qualities and a good head on her shoulders, I knew she wasn't the one for me."

"Man, what you trying to get married or something?" asked Ralph.

"Dog you trippin'. You got at least another ten to fifteen years before you should even be thinking about that," responded Dan.

"Yeah man. That soulmate crap is just that. Crap." said Ralph, a slight chuckle leaving his lips.

"Listen guys. Respect it or not, I've decided to change my ways. I'm looking for Mrs. Right, not Mrs. Right Now. I'm flattered that y'all have so much faith in me, but y'all are going to have to go it alone on this one." Answered Seven.

"Oh, you must be scared." Taunted Ralph.

"Yeah he scared y'all." Dan teased.

"The world is about to come to an end. Seven the pimp of pimps is looking for love." Kevin teased.

"Yeah soon to be sucker for love." said Ralph.

They all had a good laugh at Seven's expense, but he would not waver. He knew what he wanted in his heart. And they did not know all he had been through and the countless times he had petitioned to God. No one could ever understand his pain.

Seven shook his head and continued to put his things away in his locker. He reached out and fastened his apron, and walked onto the floor, ready to charm some tips out of his customers.

"Hey Dave." Called Seven.

"What's up Seven." Dave responded.

"Where am I tonight?"

"Up to you since you're the first from the night shift to show up."

"I'll take the back then."

"Why do you like the back so much?"

"Shorter walks man. Shorter walk to the ticket station and to the kitchen for pick up. Shorter walks mean faster service. Faster service means happy customers. And we all know what happy customers mean right?"

He looked at the managers with a smile and heard a response from an unfamiliar voice. A sweet voice, coming from directly behind him.

"Happy customers mean bigger tips?" asked Faith.

"Um, yes exactly. The only reason why I'm here." Answered Seven.

There was a pause so Dave the day manager took the time to introduce Seven to the new night manager.

"Seven, this is our new night manager. Her name is Faith." Said Dave.

"Faith, this is Seven. He is one of our best servers."

"One of the best?" asked Seven.

"As you can see, Seven is not lacking any confidence in himself."

"Hey Seven. Nice to meet you." Faith extended her hand as she greeted Seven.

"Nice to meet you as well Faith and welcome aboard. If you need anything just let me know. But for now, I'm going to get my section together to prepare for the dinner rush." Replied Seven.

Seven and Faith greeted each other with a handshake. The rest of the evening went on as it normally did. Seven's section jumped with patrons as some of his regular customers came in to have dinner. He charmed them as always. He asked them about their days at work, complimented their appearances, played with their children, all while making sure they had everything they needed for their meals. His hope was to make all customers his regulars, because he had a mission. His mission was to get as much money as possible. He always had a captive audience between, the other patrons, his colleagues, and the managers. He received praise often for how he handled his work. Unbeknownst to him, he had a new admirer.

A few hours into the dinner rush, he walked into the kitchen to check on the order for one of his tables.

"Hey Seven. Can you come here for a second?" asked Faith.

"Hey Faith. Give me a minute, okay? I need to run my table their food."

Seven grabbed the dishes of food and delivered the order to his table. He quickly returned to the register area where Faith was waiting.

"Hey Faith, what's up?"

"Hey, I wanted to ask you for a favor. Do you mind closing tonight?"

"Um, I wouldn't mind necessarily, but I rely on public transportation and the last train from this area is at ten. I don't want to get stranded here."

"Well, how far away do you live?"

"It takes about an hour and change based on the bus and train schedule, but driving should be no longer than thirty minutes."

"Oh, okay that's not bad. So, if I gave you a ride home, would you be able to stay?"

"Um, sure."

Seven paused as he looked at Faith in her eyes. He realized how beautiful she was. A slightly awkward moment of silence fell between them as they looked at one another.

"Um, is there anything else you need Seven?"

"Oh, no sorry. I'm good. Guess I should get back to my tables."

"Yes you should. Back to work…chop, chop."

Faith smiled at him as she shooed him back to work. Seven

winked at her and walked away to tend to his customers. The rest of the evening went as any other evening for Seven. He charmed his customers as he served them their appetizes, entrees, and desserts. People in people out, all served, and before he realized it, it was time to start closing up the restaurant. The rest of the wait staff were wiping down their sections, but his section was already clean and done. So, he moved on to helping the rest with the closing checklist.

"How'd you do today Seven?" asked Charles.

"I met my goal." Replied Seven.

"That's what you always say. Why don't you ever tell us how much you make?"

"Um, because that's my business and not the rest of y'alls."

"Hey Seven?" asked Greg.

"What up?" answered Seven.

"Why are you still here? Thought you were too good to close the store?"

"I'm not too good but you know I won't have a way home normally. But a few people called out so I was asked if I could stay."

"So how are you getting home then?"

"Oh, I got a ride, so I'll be straight today."

"Is it a prospect?" asked Charles.

"I bet it is." Greg teased.

"If y'all don't get out my business and get to work." Seven laughed.

He laughed and joked with the servers as they performed their duties to get the restaurant cleaned and prepped for the next day. The tables were cleaned, floors mopped, silverware rolled, ketchups married, all was now done. So, he sat and waited for his ride while all the others started leaving one by one. After a while, Faith came out with her bags.

"Hey Seven. You ready?" asked Faith.

"I am. It's been a long day for me for sure." Answered Seven.

Seven held the door for Faith to walk out, and then waited patiently as she fumbled for her keys to lock the door. Once the door was locked, Seven followed Faith to her car and got in. They pulled out and Faith headed for the highway, engaging in small talk along the way.

"Thanks again for helping me to close the store." Said Faith.

"Sure, thing. Thanks for giving me a ride home." Replied Seven.

"Not a problem. So how long have you worked here?"

"About a year. Just picking up some extra cash. I actually work during the day down the street at the cleaners."

"The dry cleaners?"

"Yep."

"What's that like?"

"It's cool. It's a job."

"What are your hours?"

"I'm there by 7 a.m., so I leave my house by 6 a.m."

"Wow. So that's why you said it's a long day."

"Yeah. Fifteen hours and counting. I can't wait to get home."

Seven settled in his seat, enjoying the comfort of being able to rest his body. He nestled into the comfort of the seat. Despite the fact that his body is weighed down with fatigue and his eyes are heavy with sleep, he was enjoying his conversation with Faith.

Faith whistled, shaking her head, her eyes fixed on the road.

"Man, that's a tough day. Why are you working so hard?"

"Um, for starters I still live with my mom. So, I'm trying to make as much money as I can to buy my own home and be independent."

"Goals. That sounds great. Any timeline you have set?"

"Yeah by the time I turn thirty. So, I only have seven years in order to get in position. My credit is good, but I want to have as much capital as possible so that I can afford my house and all that goes with it."

"That's pretty impressive. What other goals do you have? Like what's your five-year plan?"

Seven cast a glance towards her. Her question had caught him off-guard.

"Oh, so I guess you're my therapist now?"

"No, I'm sorry. We don't even know each other so I shouldn't pry."

"Yeah that's exactly what I was thinking. Like why you all up in my business like that?"

They looked at each other briefly, and Seven could tell that Faith was a little embarrassed, so he shared a smile and then burst into laughter.

"I'm playing with you. Anyway, yeah, I would like to do a lot of things. Don't quite know what I want to do as far as an actual career but I like people, I like helping people to succeed, so probably something that I could utilize my passion. In the next five years, I would love to be married, be closer to having a career, property owner, and maybe even start a business of my own. So, how about you? What's your five-year plan?" asked Seven.

"I'm really looking forward to finishing law school. I too would like to purchase my own home. Not sure if I would like to be married, but at least find the man that I would marry and start being together. Being happy, having fun, and just being in love. Overall, being successful and having fun while doing it. Those are the things that are important to me." Answered Faith.

"True. Yeah they are very important to me as well.

Especially the being in love part."

Seven sighed. At this point in life, he wished he could have someone he could bounce ideas off of, while having a good time.

"Really?" asked Faith, scrunching up her nose in contemplation.

"Yeah. Why?"

"I don't hear many dudes in their twenties saying that they looking for love."

Seven understood her response. None of his male friends showed any signs of settling down soon. They were all about having fun and sleeping around with as many women who would let them. Love was a foreign concept to most men his age—a distant idea not worthy of mention.

"Can I tell you something, without you judging me?" asked Seven.

"Sure." She replied.

"Oh, make a right at the next light. I'm at the bottom of the hill."

"Okay."

"Anyway, I'm tired of being with different women. Growing up in the climate that I did, it was all about the conquest. Another notch on the bedpost, to say I had sex with this one or that one. Bragging to my friends to feel validated as a lady's man. I'm simply tired of it all. I'd really like to find the person that is perfect for me and then live happily ever after. Truthfully, I've been struggling to find someone that I would spend the rest of my life with."

Faith looked at Seven, a puzzled expression on her face. Like she couldn't believe what he had said.

"Wow. I've never heard a man say that before. To be honest, I'm only here because my last relationship didn't work out. I moved out of town to start this fairytale and it was nothing more than a nightmare. I wasn't happy from the moment I got out there. I had dreams of being happy, starting a family, being successful, but it was all shattered when my boyfriend cheated. Truth be told, even without that happening, I wasn't happy with him. I knew that he wasn't the one for me, but I was trying to stick it out. But once he cheated that was the icing on the cake and I moved back home to my parents." Faith pulled up to the front of his house, put her car in park, and they continued to talk.

"Yeah. I had a similar experience. I didn't move away, but I proposed to a girl and I was so hoping that she was the one. In the back of my mind, I kind of knew she wasn't but it still hurt to find out that not only wasn't I number one, I wasn't even number two. She had me in a rotation with three other dudes. I was heartbroken. That's when I started praying."

"Praying?"

"Yeah. I believe God has the power to bring me to the person who is perfect for me. Who will love me no matter what my shortcomings are and forgive my failures. And I would love her the same. Our love for each other would be perfect and no one would be able to break us apart. Not even us. I have all the faith in the world that God will do this for me. Because I believe-believe."

"Wow, that's a hell of an expectation to have. I too believe God but it is up to us to walk through the doors that God opens for us. Faith without works is dead you know."

"Oh okay. I see you got some Word in you."

He was slightly surprised by her knowing a bible verse. The women he previously dealt with didn't even believe in God let alone know a bible verse. He was intrigued. Her intellect, passion, and her beauty, all made him start to wonder.

Hmm, could this be her? he wondered.

They continued to talk—really getting to know each other. It was so unintentional. Their conversation was easy. They flowed with each other. They discussed their dreams and aspirations, hopes in love, and what they envisioned their ideal situations to be. They spoke about everything. Open and free as if they were long lost friends that were catching up after years of not seeing each other. This was simple. So simple that they had not realized that it was two in the morning.

"Oh wow. Look at the time. Seven I'm so sorry. I didn't mean to keep you out this late talking your ear off."

"Yo that's crazy. I need to get up for work in three hours. I'm going to be beat tomorrow."

Seven got out the car without hesitation. He opened her back door, grabbed his things, and closed the door. He threw his backpack over his shoulder. Many thoughts passed through Faith's mind.

Dang he not going to even say goodbye? We had such a good conversation. He's unique. I haven't met anyone like him. His frame of mind, his desire for love, oh and he's sexy girl. Shut up, she thought to herself.

Seven leaned back over into the passenger window. He paused for a second looking at Faith.

"Hey thanks again for the ride. I really appreciate it." Said Seven.

"You're welcome. See you tomorrow?" asked Faith.

"Yeah, I'll be there."

"Okay great. Have a good night."

"Don't you mean good morning?"

"I suppose you're right."

"So, good morning."

"Good morning."

Faith smiled watching as Seven walked away and entered the gate to his mother's house. He unlocked the screen door, then the many locks on the front door. He turned back and saw Faith waiting to see him go in. He waved goodbye once more, she reciprocated, and he went into the house. It took him about thirty minutes to wind down and get into bed. His mind raced with thoughts as he relived the conversation he had with Faith.

"Wow. God that was weird. Are you showing me something?" he asked aloud.

He contemplated the meaning of the conversation with Faith, over, and over again. Until he ultimately fell asleep. For the few hours that he slept, he dreamt of happiness, joy, and success. The things that he had always wished for.

His peaceful slumber was interrupted by the incessant ringing of his alarm. The veil of tranquility was pierced by the shrill high-pitched tone, jolting him to open his eyes and sit up.

"Damn, already?" he said aloud, groggily.

He slowly got out of bed, stretched, yawned, scratched, and then pouted his way to the bathroom to take a shower.

Man I don't feel like doing this today, he thought.

Then, something jarred in his mind. A memory. Slowly his scowl and pouting changed—transforming to wonder and excitement.

"Lord is that you? Or am I just tripping?" he asked aloud.

He had an anticipation in his step. He quickly showered and

got ready for work. He was ready to walk out the door and catch the bus but stopped in the doorway and said a small prayer.

"Lord, thank you for another day. Thank you for your grace and your mercy over my life. I ask that you protect my heart, from things that will hurt me and provide me with strength. I also ask that you sharpen my discernment so that I may hear and see clearly the things that are for me versus those that are not. Lastly, bless my mom while she is at work and let her come home safely day to day."

He reached for the door, began to exit, and then paused once more.

"Lord? Can you also bless my dad, wherever he might be? Maybe one day we could get passed whatever is holding us back. I would love for us to really know each other. To be father and son. Even if it's only for a moment. I ask that you let *your* will be done according to that. I thank you above all. In your name I pray. Amen."

He rushed to the bus stop. His day went quickly at the cleaners. He helped the many customers that came to pick up their dry cleaning. Some of them were customers that he also served at the restaurant up the street. So, he continued being helpful and caring as it would pay off if any of them came out for dinner later in the evening. He was a master of getting tips. Before he knew it, it was time to clock out and head to the next phase of his shift. He grabbed his bag from the back and took the five-minute walk up the street to the restaurant. He walked into the locker room only to see some of his fellow servers getting ready for their shifts as well.

"What's up fellas? How's it looking in here today?

"Oh, look who it is guys." Said Greg.

"Oh it's Mr-I'm-too-good-to-close-the-restaurant-for-y'all-but-for-a-pretty-face-I'll-do-anything," Charles teased causing the group to burst out in laughter. Seven shook his head and smirked.

"Right. So, are you closing tonight too?" asked Greg.

"So tell us all sir. How did you get home last night?" asked Charles.

"Are those bags under your eyes?" asked Greg.

"Looks like he didn't get much sleep. I wonder why?" asked Charles.

"All right now fellas. Calm it down. Again I say, stay out of my business. Ain't nothing going on." Seven explained, rolling his eyes in the process. At the back of his mind, he instinctively knew that they would continue to pester him.

"Oh really? Well Faith is here. Want me to go tell her you said hi?" asked Charles.

"Whatever man. Anyway, y'all ready to get this money or not?" asked Seven.

"Oh, you already know we are forever 'bout this paper." Said Charles.

So they all laughed with each other as they walked out of the locker room and started preparing for their shift. There was a sense of comradery that Seven liked. He could put up with their incessant intrusion into his life, just to enjoy the bond that they had.

"Hey Seven. You have a sec?" asked Faith.

"Hey Faith. Sure."

"Great. Come with me to the office."

As he walked to the manager's office in the back, Seven heard the whispers and chuckles from his work friends teasing him. He turned and gave them all *the finger* and chuckled as he followed Faith to the office.

"So, I have a question for ya." said Faith.

"What's up? Asked Seven.

"How would you like to close going forward?"

"Um, actually I wouldn't."

"Why not?"

"Well transportation is my main issue. But other than that, the compensation. Closers make an hourly wage and as a server I survive off tips. So, for me to close every day, I would need to have an increase in pay. But that still doesn't resolve my transportation issues."

"Okay, well, the raise is easy. I can definitely put that in if you would commit to closing. In terms of the transportation, I think

I can help with that too."

"How? Are you going to buy me a car?" Seven joked.

"Yeah right. I can give you a ride home. If you are okay with that."

"You? Everyday? What about the days you don't work? I'll be stuck here without a ride."

"That's easy to. We both only work Monday through Friday so that should be simple enough, for now right?"

"Um, I suppose. Well, if it means more money than I'm in."

"Great."

"The first time you leave me stranded then I'm done. You pretty and all, but not that pretty," Seven joked lightly.

"Oh, you think I'm pretty do you?"

Seven didn't mean to say that out loud. He stuttered thinking of what to say next. He didn't mean to be so forward or to let his thoughts come out in the open. Before he could say anything to clean it up, Faith laughed, producing the sweetest sound he had heard in a while.

"Calm down. It's not that serious. I mean flirting with your boss is not something you should be doing, but since I am beautiful, I can understand how you couldn't help yourself." Faith joked.

"Oh really? Like I said, you pretty but you ain't *that* pretty."

"Oh yes, I am. It's okay though. You not *that* bad looking

yourself."

"Not *that* bad looking? Girl I'm the definition of GQ. Don't even play yourself."

"You cute or *whatever*. But don't let it go to your head."

"Yeah right. Let me get back to work to get this money. You don't even know how busy Friday nights are. I have an extra apron if you want it."

"An apron? For what?"

"I could use an extra busser to keep my section clean."

"Oh you got jokes. Get your behind to work before I fire you."

They laughed at each other and enjoyed the verbal sparring. It was enticing to them. She loved to challenge him and he loved being challenged, so he challenged her right back. Everyone around them could see that there was a chemistry that was developing between them. It had only been their second day working together, but they had the staff rolling.

Faith kept everyone on point in handling their responsibilities; food was out fast, and fresh, while Seven led the charge to ensure customers were getting a great experience. He even laughed and joked with customers that had been assigned other servers. He had learned that helping everyone led to better tips. They laughed and teased each other as the evening ended. Just as last time, everyone finished their work and started leaving once the restaurant was officially closed. Lost in his thoughts, Seven waited patiently for Faith to wrap up her paperwork.

Man we get along really well. I barely know her though. Talking with her is so easy. I wonder if she feels the same thing I'm feeling. But then, what is this I'm feeling? Like she is really cool like one of the homies. Stop it! Don't do this to yourself. Stop it, he thought to himself.

"You ready big head?" asked Faith.

"Big head? How you know my head is big?" Seven regretted what he just said. He didn't mean to be offensive or flirtatious on that level.

Faith looked at him up and down with a blank expression, seemingly disapproving of his statement.

"Come on let's go." She said sternly.

Seven walked to the door as Faith followed. He opened the door and held it so that she could come out.

"Hmm, well you do walk like a ball player." She joked. A sigh of relief came over Seven at her equally flirtatious response.

"Oh, you been watching how I walk huh?"

"Mhmm."

They exchanged looks and smiled as they got in her car. They continued to chat away as they drove to Seven's house.

"Hey so, since it is Friday. I was wondering if you would like to hang out for a bit?" asked Seven.

"Um, when you say hang out, what exactly do you mean Mr. Bradford?"

"Oh, so formal. Well since it's after 10 p.m. I think we are a little limited in options, but maybe we can go grab a quick drink somewhere?"

"A drink? Well, that sounds nice but, um… I don't drink like that."

"Oh, okay. I only wanted to be able to go somewhere and talk. I really like talking to you."

"You're so sweet. I like talking to you too. But I really need to get home soon. It will be pretty late by the time we go somewhere, sit down, talk, and then drive you back home."

"Yeah I suppose you're right."

Seven felt disappointed, as he had hoped to spend some more time with Faith as he really did enjoy her company and conversation. For once, he didn't even want anything other than her conversation.

"But hey, we can talk at your house. Since I have a little time to kill."

"At my house? Don't get me wrong, I really enjoyed kicking it with you, but my back is still tight after sitting in the car for five hours talking."

"It wasn't five hours stupid."

"Anyway, it was still a long time."

"Whatever. But I meant *inside* your house silly."

"Yeah I know. I just wanted to hear you say it."

Faith jokingly smacked him upside his head.

"Yeah, you know you want me." He joked.

"You wish boy!"

They pulled up to his house, parked the car and went in. It was an older house that his mom owned—worn out due to wear and tear over the years. Inside, the lighting was not great so it seemed dreary. He paused as they entered the front door and looked back at Faith.

"Watch your step. It's a little dark in here." He said.

She walked in after him and grabbed for him immediately.

"Hold my hand." She said.

"What? You scared?"

"I don't like the dark."

He could tell how apprehensive she was as her eyes fleeted around the older modeled furniture. There was a faint musty smell in the air. It was always like that due to the leak in the bathroom. But this was his home. His home for a few years now and he was proud of it. And even more proud of his mother for purchasing their very own home. Growing up, Seven and his mother were frequently on the move after she had left Sam. After his freshman year of high school, they continued to move from place to place. His mother always looked to cut expenses. There were times when Seven even went without food for multiple days at a time until his mother finally got paid. She would buy the same things; couple loaves of bread, peanut butter, jelly, occasionally some snacks because they were cheap. He carried this with him. Always thankful for the little things. He walked her to his room and turned on the light.

"Come on. Don't be shy. Welcome to *mi casa*." He said.

"Oh, you speak Spanish now? Bilingual huh?"

"You always got jokes. I like that though."

"Mhmm. I bet."

"So, here have a seat."

"On your bed?"

"Sorry, but that's the only place to sit."

"Okay, but don't you try anything."

"Anything like what?"

"Yeah ight!"

"Just sit down girl."

Faith sat on the bed and Seven took her jacket and laid it on the bed post. She rubbed her hand across his sheets as she sat there.

"Your sheets feel nice." She said.

"Yeah that's because they silk baby."

"These ain't no *silk* sheets."

"Okay, well their sateen, but don't they feel nice though?"

"Sateen? Wow. But yeah they do feel nice."

"Mhmm… I see you rubbing them."

"Whatever boy. Can I have some water?"

"Sure."

Seven went to the kitchen, rinsed out a cup and filled it with water. He left the door open and saw Faith get off of his bed and walk around his room. She took small but purposeful walks; looking at some of his pictures that were on his TV stand, running her hands on some of his things that were in his closet, glancing at the posters on his wall. While she inspected his room, he couldn't help but look at her and smile. She looked as if she was enjoying herself, absorbing her environment in every sensory way possible.

Could it be Lord? Is it even possible? Could this be her? Boy, get yourself together. You've known her for less than a week. The boys were right. I'm turning into a sucka for love. Hold it together. His mind raced as he walked back into his room with the water.

"Here you go." He said, stretching his hand to give her the cup of water.

"Thanks. Well, so what do you want to do now? You got me

in your house, in your room, and now on your bed. What next?"

"What do you *want* to do?"

Faith curled up her lips and leaned her head to the side after hearing his sly response. She couldn't help but return the same gesture.

"*Talk.*" She said slyly.

"Okay. So let's *talk* then."

He laughed heartily. He sensed that she was feeling him and after all he was really feeling her too.

"So how was your day?" he asked.

Seven reached for his remote and turned on the TV.

"My day was okay. It tends to go fast." She replied.

"Not mine. They're always long."

"Yeah I don't know how you do it."

"I'm trying to get somewhere so I have to."

"I guess."

Seven continued to flip through the channels as they talked about their respective days. Again, their conversation flowed.

"Wait! Let's watch that. Go back a channel please?"

"What this? Love and Basketball? What is this about?"

Faith slowly turned to face Seven, her eyes widened.

"You've never seen this?"

"Nah. This looks like a *love* movie. I'm more of an action guy."

"It's a cute movie, let's watch it."

Seven scooted all the way on the bed and put his back against the wall. Faith went to do the same, but Seven stopped her.

"Hey, don't get in my bed with your sneakers on. Take those off."

"Oh, I'm sorry. I'll sit on the edge of the bed then."

"You sure? This movie is over two hours long. You sure you don't want to get comfortable?"

"Yeah, I'm *sure*." She said in a stern voice.

Faith's eyes were downcast, belying her earlier confidence. Seven thought her expression was cute, wondering why she hesitated.

"Man take your sneakers off and stop playing."

Seven grabbed her foot, but she pulled back.

"What your feet stink or something?" he teased.

"No stupid."

"I bet they do. That's why you don't want me to take your sneakers off. You got athlete's feet?"

"Shut up silly. My feet don't stink."

"So, then, go ahead and take your shoes off then."

"Nope."

"Why not then?"

"Just watch the movie."

"Fine."

So, they continued to watch the movie, made commentary and offered their opinions about the characters' actions. Seven noticed that she seemed a little uncomfortable as she started to snuggle up closer to him. She leaned on his shoulder, but kept her knees bent into him so that her feet dangled off the edge of the bed.

"Just take your sneakers off girl. You making me uncomfortable by looking at you being uncomfortable."

"I'm not *that* uncomfortable." She responded.

He reached across her to untie her sneakers once more, but the angle of her body caused him to not be able to. At that moment, he realized that their faces were very close together. They looked at each other deeply. She smiled slightly and bit her bottom lip.

"Can I tell you something?" he whispered.

"Sure," she responded in a soft tone.

"You are beautiful."

Seven leaned in a little more and kissed her. She kissed him back. Very soft and sensual they continued to kiss. Before long they were wrapped in each other's arms, rolling from one side of the bed to the other. Holding each other in a tight embrace, they exchanged long passionate kisses for what seemed like forever. She wrapped her legs around his and he immediately felt her sneakers. But he didn't let that deter him. As they kissed, his mind was on how he could remove her sneakers. They rolled again, kissed more deeply, and finally he felt his toe rub up against the back of her foot. He then pushed down as hard as he could and the heel of her foot popped out of her sneaker. She sighed. He quickly kicked off her sneaker. He could feel that she had relaxed so he leaned over and pulled off her other sneaker without objection.

"Why'd you do that?" she whispered.

"I wanted to get more comfortable with you and your sneakers were in the way."

"*Mhmm.*"

The passion had ended for a moment as their attention diverted back to the movie. They continued to watch it. They laughed at the funny parts and got a little quiet during the serious parts. They exchanged eye contact, smiles, and now kisses during the love scenes.

The movie had started to wind down but something crazy happened.

"What? But he was about to get married. So, he going to throw all that away just for her?" he commented.

"But what if who he was marrying wasn't the right person? Would you marry the wrong person for the sake of being married? Only for the sake of saving the time you put in even though you know that's not the right person for you?" she asked.

"No, I wouldn't actually. When I get married, I want it to be for all time. I want my true other half. Like Adam and Eve."

"So, in this case if the right person was the one who he let get away and now is back, wouldn't it make sense to stop the wedding?"

"Yeah it does, but man that's a hell of a decision to make. And I know that other woman had to be devastated whenever he broke it to her. I would feel really bad for hurting her but would also be really happy to find my soulmate."

"Yeah. I think the same way."

"Do you ever want to get married?" he asked.

"Honestly, yeah I do. But I want to really be in love. I don't want to be the type to settle for some man that I may love but could fall out of love with. I also don't want to be the person that ends up in a relationship for 10 years and have to give an ultimatum in order to get married. I believe that when you are in love, like truly in *love-love*, which should be the easy part."

"Yeah I get it. It shouldn't have to feel forced. It should simply flow. Similar to a great conversation. Not forced like small talk with strangers. But rather the perfect chemistry."

"Yeah like that. Hmm. I think you get me Mr. Bradford."

"Yeah, I guess I do."

They gazed into each other's eyes as the credits rolled. Seven kissed her again, soft and slow.

"Mmm, your lips are so soft. Your kisses are almost perfect."

"Almost?"

They chuckled. Faith nestled into his chest as the beginning of another movie started to play. They were quiet; clearly in deep thought. At least, until Seven broke the silence.

"Hey, I thought you needed to go home before it got too late?" he asked.

"Yeah I did."

"Did?"

"Well, you know what I mean.'

"So, what are you going to do?"

"What do you mean?"

"So, are you going home? Or are you staying with me?"

She looked up, almost startled at his question. Her face went from slight shock and slowly transformed to a sly smirk. She gazed into his hazel eyes and kissed him ever so seductively.

"Um… I'm staying with you." She said in a teasing tone.

His smile widened as his heart pounded. His mind raced with all of the possibilities of what this could mean. He flirted with the possibility that this was God's plan. He desperately tried to conceal how he felt, but he knew she could feel his heart as it danced while she lay on his chest. He took a deep breath and kissed her on her forehead.

"Okay."

A Good Morning

Seven awoke to find Faith asleep on his chest. Her legs were wrapped around his. Their bodies were entangled with one another like a pretzel. He watched his hand as he rubbed her back. He pinched his own arm in disbelief as to what had occurred.

He watched her for a moment. He observed the rising and falling of her back as her lungs filled with air. It was similar to the rate in which he breathed as well. They seemed eerily in sync with one another.

Am I making this up? Nah, I'm trippin'. She's so beautiful. She feels so good and comfortable in my arms. I could hold her forever, he thought.

Her eye twitched, her arm moved, she started to stir awake.

"Good morning beautiful," he said.

"Mmm, hey you," she responded, her voice heavy with sleep.

"Did you sleep okay?"

"The *best* actually. How about you?"

"Yeah I slept pretty good myself."

He leaned over and kissed her when his mother knocked on his door.

"Seven? Morning son. I brought some snacks home. Are you up?" asked Sissy.

Faith realized she hadn't called her parents to let them know she wasn't coming in last night.

"Seven?" Sissy called out again.

"Yeah Momma. I'm up now. I'll be out in a minute."

"Okay baby. I just put everything away and I'll be upstairs."

A moment later, they got up and Seven's mom was still in the hall. "Hey Seven. Oh. I'm sorry. I didn't realize you had company. Well, come up when you're done."

"Actually Momma, I would like to introduce you guys. Momma, this is Faith. Faith this is my mom."

"Hello and good morning Faith."

"Good morning Mrs. Bradford. It's nice to meet you."

"It's nice to meet you as well. You are beautiful. Do you know that?" Sissy said, a warm smile on her lips.

"Oh, thank you. You're very pretty as well. I see where Seven gets his eyes."

Sissy giggled, nodding appreciatively.

"Hey, do you know how to cook?" asked Sissy.

"Um, yes I do."

"Great, you can come help me make breakfast."

Seven and Faith were surprised. Faith looked at Seven and then looked down and realized that she was still wearing his boxers and tee shirt. Seven shrugged and smiled.

"Okay girls. I'm gonna' leave y'all to it and go take a shower." Said Seven.

"Okay baby. And don't worry, we'll be fine in here." Sissy responded.

Seven grabbed a change of clothes and walked back out to the kitchen to head to the bathroom. As he walked by, he saw that Faith was mortified.

"So, Faith, can you hand me the skillet? It's under the cabinet on the right."

"Sure thing."

"Thanks honey. So, let me ask you. How did you and Seven meet?"

"Um, yeah we work together."

"Oh really? At the cleaners or at the restaurant?"

"The restaurant."

"Are you a server as well?"

"I'm the night manager. I only started a few weeks ago."

"So, did you know each other prior to working together?"

"No, we met recently. Oh, and here is the skillet."

"Hmm, that's odd. Thanks could you go in the refrigerator and hand me the butter while I finish cutting up these potatoes?"

She went in the refrigerator to reach for the butter. As she did, she felt embarrassed to be caught by Seven's mother so early in the morning. And while still wearing his shirt and boxers. She didn't want his mother to think badly of her but there wasn't anything she could do at this moment. So Faith simply handed her the butter from the refrigerator.

"Thanks hon. So, let me get this straight. Y'all just met recently and somehow you are in the kitchen with me cooking?" Sissy asked.

"Um, yes. My thoughts exactly." Faith responded.

"Hmm. So how do you feel about my son?"

"Feel about him?"

"Yeah feel about him. Like do you like him or are y'all *just* friends? Like what's going on between the two of you?"

"Honestly, ma'am I don't really know. Like I said, we only recently met. But it's odd. I feel really comfortable around him. The conversations that we have had are great. I enjoy his company, and despite what this may look like, I don't just go around staying the night with random men."

"Hmm, well it does look um… anyway… I only ask because

Seven doesn't do this. Sure, he has company from time to time, but he hardly ever allows someone to spend the night. He most definitely doesn't introduce them to me." Sissy responded, as she continue to chop the fixings for breakfast.

"Really? Then why am I here?" asked Faith.

"That's what I'm trying to figure out. Only thing that I could think of is that he really likes you. The fact that he left you in the kitchen alone with me, to talk, just doesn't happen."

"You think he really likes me? And why doesn't that happen?"

"It's because I tend to be really direct and honest. And yeah, he doesn't introduce anyone to me unless he really likes them. Oh, can you put the butter in the pan for me and turn on the stove?"

"Wow really? Well I guess that's good. Anyway, I like direct and honest. So, you're going to pan fry the potatoes right?" asked Faith.

"Yes, I am actually."

"I love fried potatoes for breakfast. I make them all the time."

"Okay so then how about you make the potatoes and I'll make the eggs and sausage."

"I can make it all if you want?" Faith offered.

Faith grabbed the cut potatoes, placed them in the butter, and let them simmer. After a few moments she poured some olive oil in the pan as well. She found all the ingredients she needed and started cooking.

The potatoes sizzled in the pan and the aroma of all the seasonings she added filled the kitchen and the dining room. As she moved on to start preparing the eggs, they continued to talk.

"So, do you live far from here?" asked Sissy.

"About twenty minutes." Faith responded.

"Okay. So, when did you get here?"

"It was last night after work. Seven has been closing with me, so I've been driving him home afterwards."

"Wait, did you say he has been *closing* with you? Huh. Girl… I don't know what you did to my son, but he must really like you."

"Why do you say that?"

"He hates closing the restaurant. Not just the extra work, but it's the principle of it that bothers him the most. Closing the store requires extra work. And that's extra work that he doesn't feel he is being compensated for. Especially since the restaurant was supposed to hire some folks to replace the last closers and never did. So now he says the wait staff are doing that work."

"Yeah I guess that's true."

"He said he would never close. And now he's closing.

Wow." Sissy shook her head, watching as Faith stirred the eggs into the pan.

"And you think that has something to do with me?"

"No. I *know* that has *everything* to do with you."

Faith finished making the potatoes and emptied them into a container. She added the sausage in the pan and could hear Seven opening the bathroom door.

"Okay, the potatoes are done, the sausage and the eggs should be quick. Anything else you were going to cook?" asked Faith.

"Nope just keeping it simple." Sissy replied, a pearly smile on her lips.

Though Faith had never met any of her boyfriend's mothers before, she could sense that Seven's mother liked her. *Boyfriend?* The idea ping-ponged around her head.

"So how long have you guys lived here?" Faith asked, shaking off the nagging thought from her head.

"A few years. We moved around a lot until I purchased this house."

"Since we're talking, how many girls has Seven introduced you to?

"I've met a few, but that he actually went out of his way to specifically introduce me to? Maybe two."

"Wow."

"Yes, so you should feel special."

They looked at each other and laughed. As they laughed, Seven had walked down the hall and entered into the kitchen.

"Wow, smells good in here Momma."

Faith had finished the cooking and placed everything in the serving dishes left on the counter so they could all help themselves and make their plates.

"You guys mind if I take a quick shower?" asked Faith.

"There are towels and washcloths already in there for you so help yourself," Seven said.

"Okay thanks."

Faith grabbed her clothes from Seven's room and showered. Seven and his mother set the table as they waited for her.

"So, you like this girl huh?" asked Sissy.

"Yeah, I really do Momma."

"But you barely know her."

"I know. That's the crazy part. Remember I told you how I was done running around and wanted to find someone for me?"

"Yeah I remember. But it's too soon baby. Don't you think you should slow down?" Sissy asked as she set three places at the dining table.

"Momma. I prayed, I mean I really prayed. And I think she

could be the one. I wish I could explain it better, but I'm still wrapping my head around this as well."

"A week though baby? It can't be that good."

"I'm not saying we getting married tomorrow. Besides I don't, all the way know, how she feels about me but, I think she may be the one Momma."

"Well, from what I can tell, she likes you too. Her energy is strong and positive. And she's really pretty."

"She's beautiful actually."

"Is that what this is about? You're not falling for her because of her looks are you?" Sissy turned to Seven, her hands on her waist.

"No Mom. It's way more than that. I really have a feeling that God has brought her to me. It's weird, but that's how I feel and I never felt that before."

"Well take your time baby. I don't want to see you disappointed. You've had so many heartbreaks from people in your life."

"Yeah, tell me about it. But anyways, be straight. What kind of vibe you get from her?"

"Nothing negative baby. I honestly think I could like her."

Seven lifted his head, feeling like a weight had been lifted off his shoulders.

Faith walked out of the bathroom, fully dressed, and had a

seat at the table joining Seven and his mother.

"Oh, you guys didn't need to wait for me, you could've started eating without me."

Sissy reached out and patted Faith's hand that was resting on the table. She smiled when Faith made eye contact.

"No that wouldn't have been fair hon, especially since you prepared this meal. That's not how I operate. Besides we wanted you to bless the food so that we could eat together."

They bowed their heads and held hands as Faith blessed the food that she had prepared. "Lord, we thank you this morning for another day. We also thank you for all that you continue to do for us all, even though we may not deserve it, we still say thank you."

"Yes lord." Seven whispered as Faith prayed.

"Lord I ask that you bless this food that has been prepared out of love and let it be nourishing to our bodies. Help us today to get closer to you and your will for our lives. Amen."

Seven's mom glanced at him and winked in approval. Seven smiled at his mom and then smiled at Faith. They continued to make small talk while they ate their food. Faith truly fit into their dynamic. As if she were already one of the family. When they finished eating Faith cleared the dishes and offered to clean up as well.

"No, it's okay baby. You've been very helpful and I

appreciate that. I can clean up especially since you did most of the cooking." Said Sissy.

Faith walked back into Seven's room where he was sitting on the bed.

"Your mom is really nice."

"Thank you. She thinks you are nice too."

She leaned over, hugged Seven, and nestled her head into his chest. He looked down at her, smiled, and kissed her ever so delicately.

"That's much better." He said.

"Better?" she asked.

"Yeah. I mean it's okay cause we had just woken up, but *girl.*"

Faith placed her hands over her mouth in embarrassment.

"Was my breath not nice this morning?" she asked.

"It's been better."

"What did it smell like?" she asked.

"Umm."

"Farts?" she asked again.

"Umm."

"Trash?" she asked once more.

"Well."

"Boo boo?" she asked a final time.

"No, just morning." He answered.

They both looked at each other and started laughing hysterically. She then punched Seven in the gut.

"You're mean." she yelled.

"I'm only playing."

"I know. But you got some nerve. Cause your breath was really bad this morning too."

"Really? What it smelled like?" he asked.

"Puke."

"Oh, dang and you wasn't going to tell me?"

"Well I didn't want to be offensive; besides I didn't know how you would take it."

"I wouldn't have been offended, I would've just blew my breath in your face under the covers." He joked.

"Oh yeah? And I would've licked the whole side of your face with my stinky breath."

"Then we would've both been the stinky breath bandits."

They chuckled and continued to hold each other in their arms.

"Hey, I need to go home soon. It's been a great night and morning, but I really need to check in with my parents."

"It's all good."

"I need to get gas though. Where is there a gas station in the area?" she asked.

"Oh, it's right around the corner. I can go with you." He answered ash he reached for his keys.

Seven's mom saw them leaving. "Oh, you guys are heading out?" Sissy asked.

"Yeah Momma. I'll be back in a little bit though."

"Okay baby, y'all be safe out there."

"We will. It was nice meeting you Mrs. Bradford." Said Faith.

"It was nice meeting you as well Faith. Hope to see you again sometime soon." Said Sissy.

"I think that can be arranged as long as Seven would have me." Faith replied.

They smiled and hugged each other. Seven then led Faith out of the house and they got into her car, and headed for the gas station.

"Man it is hot out here." Said Seven as he wiped a bead of sweat from his brow.

"Hey, look. A Dunkin' Donuts." Faith said enthusiastically.

"Yeah. Okay?"

"I love Dunkin' Donuts—especially their coffee. You mind if we stop?"

"Um, sure. Knock yourself out."

They parked and walked into the Dunkin' Donuts and got in

line behind an older couple. They got to the counter and ordered. Seven grabbed them each a bottle of water and handed them to Faith as she paid for their order.

Once out of the line, Seven reached to take his water from Faith, but she dumped it on his head. He stood up quickly trying to get away from the water, but Faith followed him, pouring it on his head, until the entire bottle was empty.

"Really? That's what we doing now? That's so messed up." Said Seven.

"You said you was hot. So, are you feeling better now? Or are you still hot?" joked Faith.

"No, I'm great. You should feel how great this is. Let's share the moment together!"

Seven uncapped his water. Faith saw what he was doing and tried to run away. He grabbed her quickly and threw water on her.

"I can't believe you did that. Oh, this is war!" she yelled.

"Oh, you want war? Then war it is." He yelled back.

Faith and Seven both ran to the refrigerator as they battled to grab the next bottle of water. Faith grabbed hers first and then tried to block Seven as she opened her water. Seven was able to get around her to grab another bottle himself; however, she had already opened hers and quickly flung some at him. He tried to get away and open his bottle at the same time so he reached out and grabbed Faith trying to defend the water attack. But they both slipped and fell on the floor.

They both looked up at each other and laughed in unison. They were having a great time. They had grabbed multiple bottles of water and continued their water fight. Flinging water at each other, laughing, slipping and sliding, really going for it. By the time they were done, they didn't even realize they had an audience. Both the cashier and the older couple that were in front of them had huge smiles on their faces watching them have fun. At that moment, Seven realized what they had done and apologetically went to the cashier.

"I'm so sorry, we kind of got carried away." Seven apologized.

"You think?" responded the cashier.

"Yeah I know. So, what do we owe you? I think we wasted at least four bottles of water and didn't drink any of it."

"Don't worry, I was keeping count. So, it was actually *six* bottles of water." The cashier replied, in a matter-of-factly sort of way.

Seven chuckled at the cashier and swiped his card to pay for the water. They got their order from the counter finally and both walked out to her car.

"I can't believe he let us make that mess in their store. Good thing it wasn't more customers in there or they would've probably been mad at us." Said Faith.

They got into Faith's car and pulled off. Seven was quiet for a moment, but had a huge smile on his face.

"Hey. You okay?" asked Faith.

"Yo, you are crazy girl. But can I be honest with you?" asked Seven.

"Yeah of course."

"That was honestly the most fun I've ever had. I don't expect you to understand all the way but I like how you make me feel."

"Aw. I like how you make me feel too. I can't believe we've only known each other for a little less than a week. I feel like I've known you for all of my life."

They both let their confessions simmer in the air for a while longer. It felt nice to be wanted the way they both wanted each other. It seemed like they both needed to be in that moment for a while longer, so some silence settled between them—a mutually comforting silence.

"I know what you mean. I hope that we can continue to see each other. What do you think about that?" asked Seven.

"I would like that very much." Faith responded.

"Great. So, when can I see you again?"

"How's Monday?" asked Faith jokingly.

"Outside of *work* stupid."

"I know, just playing. Um… I need to go home and change so I'll be able to come back later today. Is that okay?"

"Today? So soon?"

"Or, tomorrow, if you're going to be busy. I didn't mean to push it."

"I'm kidding. Later today would be perfect. I don't have anything going on."

"Okay great. I'll check in at home and then I'll be *all yours* after that." She said.

"*All mine*? I like the sound of that." He responded.

Faith dropped Seven off at home and then she headed home herself. Seven couldn't have been any happier when he walked into the house.

"Why are you all wet? And smiling? What were y'all doing?" asked Sissy.

"Oh, we um, had a water fight. It was dope." He chuckled.

"Um, if you say so."

He kissed his mother on the cheek, went in his room and shut the door. *No way I'm this lucky. I really think she is the one. Lord I'm so grateful. It feels right. I'm not lucky. I'm blessed. He heard me*, he thought to himself.

Seven fell to his knees and cried. He didn't know why he cried, but he was so grateful and honored to be in the position he found himself in. It was as if his life had changed in the blink of an eye.

“Thank you Lord!” he said aloud.

From that moment forward, Seven and Faith were inseparable. Everywhere they went, people would complement them on how good they looked together. For the next six months, their days were full of fun, love, and excitement. Every day, they continued to spend more time together. The more time they spent together, the more they got to know each other. And the more they got to know each other, the more they fell in love

The Invitation

Sissy and Seven sat outside, a hesitation between them. Their arms were interlocked, and their bodies frozen in place. Even without looking at Sissy, Seven could sense her apprehension. It oozed off her, attaching itself like a leech on his subconscious.

“You sure you want to do this baby?” asked Sissy.

“Absolutely Momma. God spoke to me. She is definitely the one for me. She is perfect for me, and I am perfect for her.” Seven replied.

“Okay, I’ll support you in anything that you do. I’m not trying to be negative, I’m just saying y’all only been dating for less than a year. If she is truly for you, there is no rush."

"I know Momma, but when you know that you know something is yours, why procrastinate? I'm believing God for it all. He's not a man that he should lie, so I'm standing on that."

"Okay baby. Like I said, I'll support you in everything you do."

"Thanks Momma."

"Now, are you sure you want to do this too?"

His mom looked up at the building, cocking her head to the side. Her smile dropped slightly, expressing her discomfort at being there. Seven paused for a moment, took a deep breath, and nodded.

"Yeah I have to. What do you think he wants to say?"

"Only one way to find out baby. You said you're sure you wanted to do this, so, go do it." Sissy chided, nodding towards the building.

Seven smiled at his mom, opened his car door and walked to the building where his father lived. Up the elevator, to their front door, stuck in his mind was nothing but nerves. He wondered what his father had to say that he wanted to see Seven in person. They haven't seen each other in years.

His father opened the door. Seven paused for a moment and looked at him. He'd aged since the last time he'd seen him. He even had some grey in his beard. His father stepped aside and allowed him to walk in.

"Hey Dad."

"Hey Seven."

"How you been?"

"I've been good."

"That's good. Um, where's Jumi?"

"At school. Listen, I asked you here because I need to talk to you." He motioned Seven in and they sat on the couch. "So, I was surprised when you reached out to me. Even more surprised to find out that you were going to get married. Actually, I was a little disappointed because you haven't known her very long."

"Um, disappointed? I actually thought you would be happy for me."

"Why would I be happy for you to marry someone you *barely* know?" asked Jerri.

"You *joking* right?" asked Seven.

"Not at all. You making a mistake. And I wanted to talk to you man to man. Father to son. Apparently, your mother don't care enough to tell you the truth."

"Excuse me? First off, don't bring up my mother because you don't know what she thinks or what she has said. You forfeited that right. Second, you don't even know Faith to even know if I know her or not?"

"I don't have to know her to know this is not the right choice. Son you haven't even lived a life of your own yet. You've never traveled, you barely even left New Jersey, you haven't even had your own place to live yet. What's the rush?"

"Oh, just like you don't have to know me right? You got some balls. You call me over here just to tell me this? Why would I ever think you would be happy for me about anything? You've really never cared about me."

"Now watch your mouth boy, I'm still your father."

"Watch my mouth or what? What you gonna' do? I'm not a child that you can beat on. You try to put your hands on me ever again in life and you won't like what you get back."

"I see you ain't never change. And you will never change. You the same disrespectful person that you've always been. No respect for me, your mother, not even yourself. You don't even hear what I'm saying to you," Jerri spat, his face contorting with contempt.

"Well, I guess like father like son huh? You ain't never been there for me. All I ever wanted was for you to love me. I used to dream of you riding in and rescuing me from all of my problems. As if you had the power or even the *desire* to do it. Truth is, you never got over the fact that my mother left you. That's why you always bringing her up and trying to put her down in front me. It's like the moment she left you, you decided to leave everything connected to her. Including me."

"So that's what you *think* huh?"

"No. That's *exactly* what I know."

"Son, you a wrong."

At that moment Rehi walked through the door, putting a momentary pause on the ensuing argument. Unknowingly, she plugged the crackling tension between Seven and Jerri. Over the years, she had stepped into situations that would have become uglier.

"Seven? Hey baby. How are you?"

"Hey Rehi. I'm okay. How are you?"

"I'm good. Come here and hug me." She said.

Seven walked over and hugged Rehi. He managed to force a smile on his face, but she sensed something was wrong. His pent-up anger subsided slightly.

"So, what brings you this way?" she asked.

"Actually, I was just leaving. Please tell Jumi I said hey and ask her to give me a call."

"Um, okay."

"Oh, and the invitation still stands in case you change your mind *Jerri*."

Seven turned to the door. Jerri, furious at the fact that Seven called him by his name, stormed behind him.

"Go ahead and make your life harder. You're going to make her life harder as well." Jerri screamed. Seven stopped at the door, turned around shooting a piercing look at Jerri.

"Seven, what's going on?" asked Rehi.

"Ask your *husband* Rehi. I love you guys. Take care of yourself." He responded.

Seven walked out and slammed the door behind him as hard as he could. Instead of taking the elevator, he walked to the stairwell and jogged down the first flight of steps. He slowed down to a walk as he made it to the second flight, and stopped as he got to the next.

Why don't he love me? Why does he envision me this way? He doesn't even know me, he thought to himself.

Seven covered his face with his hands and wept—trying his best to muffle the sounds. He then sat on the steps, put his head down on his knees and cried.

I don't understand it Lord. It seems like he wants me and my mom to fail only because she left him. Why is he this way, he muttered under his breath.

He picked up his head and wiped his face. Staring at the ceiling and pondering over what happened, he wiped his face again and rose to his feet. Anger, sadness, disappointment, and rejection were all the emotions that he felt.

"Screw him. I've made it this far without him. I'll make it

the rest of the way without him too." he mumbled.

Seven walked out the staircase. He wiped his face one last time as he walked to the car. Sissy could tell that things didn't go well. She rubbed his shoulder to console him but they didn't speak a word as he dropped his mother back home. He then drove to Faith's house. When she got in the car, she knew something was bothering him.

"What's wrong?" asked Faith.

"My dad. He is just so…ugh." Replied Seven as his voice crackled from the emotion he was feeling.

"What happened?"

"He's so negative when it comes to me. He doesn't believe we should get married. He said he thinks I'm going to ruin both our lives."

"Baby, it's okay. Truthfully, what we are doing is not traditional. If it hadn't been for God telling me that you were my husband, I wouldn't be marrying you. Even though he told you, I needed him to tell me."

"Yeah I get that. But it's more than he's being concerned. You had to be there to hear how he spoke to me. Like he expects me to fail. Like nothing good could ever come from me. He made me feel worthless."

Faith rubbed his face and kissed the tears that started to flow again.

"Don't worry about him baby. Trust what God has spoken to us. And even if things aren't perfect, we still are perfect for each other. Remember that okay?"

"Yeah you right."

"And my parents aren't the happiest about this either but it's not *their* decision, it's mine. So, let's put this behind us and let's go dress shopping like we planned."

Seven nodded, and wiped at his cheeks. He put the car on drive and they proceeded to the bridal shop. He hadn't expected things to turn out like this. But deep inside, his subconscious nagged at him. *What did you expect?* The thought fleeted in his mind.

As they got out of the car in the bridal shop's parking lot, Faith said, "Okay now, remember; come in, but stay in the front. You're only here because my mom and matron of honor couldn't come with me and I didn't want to reschedule. Do *not* come to the back where the dressing rooms are. You got me?" she asked waiving her finger at him.

"Yeah I got you." He replied.

Seven walked in behind Faith and had a seat. He watched people walk in and out as he waited for his bride to be to finish. Seemed like he was there for a couple of hours and then a familiar face emerged wearing a beautiful dress.

"Seven? Seven Bradford? Is that you?" asked Cassy.

"Hey Cassy. Yes, it's me. How are you?" he replied.

"I'm great."

"You look great. Oh, and Congrats! You are a great looking bride."

Seven then looked down and noticed that she was expecting. She looked like she was expecting soon too, which confused him.

"Oh, and congrats again on the addition to your family. Do you know what you are having?" he asked.

"Thanks. And no, we wanted to wait." She responded.

"That's super dope."

"Yeah it is. I'm so happy. And congrats to you too. I saw you guys come in. Your fiancé right?" she asked.

"Yeah, it's amazing." He replied with his voice full of pride.

"Yeah isn't it? It's surreal almost. Looks like we're both pursuing what we wanted."

"Yeah, that was a dope conversation we had. Dang… that was a little before I met my fiancé."

"Yeah I met my fiancé soon after too."

Seven paused again and it was obvious something was on his mind. He couldn't help but hear Jerri's words in his head. He wanted to be more than what Jerri believed of him, and certainly much more of a father than he ever had been to Seven.

"I don't mean to be rude or weird but I want to ask you something." He said.

"Sure what's up?" she asked.

Seven looked down at her belly and became nervous. He felt excitement, almost joy, in a weird way he accepted the thought before he even spoke it. "Um, it's been about eight months or so since we, um, well, you know. I don't know how to ask this so I'm just gonna' come out with it. Is this *my* baby?"

"*What*? You trippin'. I've been with my fiancé since after you and haven't been with anyone else. So *no*, it is not."

Seven lowered his eyes and a sense of sadness came over him. In a weird way, he felt like she wasn't being truthful and that this was his child.

"I just want to be sure because, I would be there. You know?" he asked.

"Seven, I know. You are a great guy. But this is not your child," she responded.

"Okay I guess. Sorry about that. It seemed like us running into each other here was happening for a reason. I just wanted to be sure."

"Um… okay. Well I'm going to go back and take this dress off because my ride is almost here. Take care Seven. And congrats again."

"Thanks. You too."

Faith came out and Seven asked her, "So you make a decision?"

"Yeah, I think so." Faith answered.

"Nice." Seven nodded, oblivious to the expression on Faith's face.

"So um… you gonna' tell me who that was or am I going to have to *ask* her myself?"

Seven laughed, the earlier fog disintegrating into amusement. He reached out and grabbed Faith by the waist, nuzzling her neck in the process.

"You so gangsta. That was an old friend. She about to get married and they having a baby so I was saying congrats. And she reciprocated as she saw us walk in."

"Mhmm. Don't make me hurt nobody."

"Oh, you don't need to hurt nobody baby. Don't nobody want no beef."

"You better believe it!"

They laughed together and walked out. Faith leaned in Seven's arms as they headed for the car. Seven couldn't help but to have another thought about the potential of that being his child.

"I can't wait to be your wife baby," Faith said.

"Good, my clothes haven't been washed in a month." Seven

joked.

"*What*??"

She punched Seven in the arm due to his joke.

"Ow. I'm playing."

"You better be punk."

"I am. Unless you gonna' do it. Anyway, I can't wait to be your husband. I love you so much."

"Yeah I can't wait to go shopping, and go on trips, and do everything that I've always wanted."

"Wait, just because we are married, doesn't mean that I've become rich overnight."

"It doesn't? Well why not? Sounds like you got work to do then."

"Yeah, I'll get on it as soon as you get my laundry done."

Faith playfully leaned over and tried to bite Seven on the arm.

"Okay, okay, stop. You play too much." he laughed.

"No, you play too much." She responded.

The Morning

The morning sunlight streamed through the blinds, casting shadows across Seven's room. It was a beautiful morning, and

Seven soaked it all in. He felt a warm rush of happiness flood within him. He had waited for this day ever since he could remember.

"Seven? Time to get up baby." Sissy's voice reverberated through his skull. He was awake, rearing to go. It seemed her voice was what he needed to push him out of bed.

"I'm up Momma. I'll be out in a minute."

"Okay. Just want to make sure you was up. You gotta' be to the church by 12 right?"

Seven got out of the bed and stretched his limbs. He rubbed the nonexistent sleep from his eyes as he walked out of his room.

"There he is. Soon to be a married man."

"Good morning Momma."

"Good morning baby. You okay? You look tired."

Sissy's tone belied the intended mood for today. Her face scrunched up, worried. Seven looked into her eyes and gave a brief smile.

"You know what Momma? I'm a little scared," he responded truthfully.

Despite his overwhelming excitement, he couldn't help but feel that something bad was lurking in the horizon. His life had never been easy, so why would things become simple now.

"Scared? Why baby? It'll be over is a couple of hours. Don't worry."

"Not of the ceremony, but for what happens after."

"After?"

"Yeah. Like I know that this is my soulmate sent specifically from God, but I'm scared that I will mess it up. You know David was selected to be king by God, but he messed that up with all the craziness that he did." Seven explained by using a story from the bible as an example.

"Yeah, but God also gave him space to repent. You will reap what you sow, but it doesn't mean that God leaves you in that state."

"I suppose you're right. But I'm so scared of messing it up Momma. I don't want to ruin what we have."

"Then don't baby. Most things are in our power to handle, the rest are decisions that build character to learn from."

Seven momentarily reflected on her words but still felt unsure. *Am I man enough for Faith? Am I worthy of her love and affection?* The thoughts penetrated his veil of excitement.

"I've seen so many bad examples of men and I'm worried that I have the ability to display some of those characteristics. I can't help but to think about my dad and how he is. Part of him is in me. I can't help but to look in the mirror and see him," Seven replied, his voice tinged with sadness. More than anything, he didn't want to end up like Jerri.

"We are both part of you baby. You have been the sweetest

child I've ever known. You've always had the biggest heart and would do anything for anyone. You even challenge me to be better."

"I don't want to fail Momma. I don't want to be married to get divorced. And I love her so much."

Sissy looked at Seven, a sad smile on her face. She sighed heavily, contemplating on the hard life they had gone through. Deep down, she understood his feelings of unworthiness. These feelings had been a product of the numerous challenges that had come their way.

"Do you want to know what I see when I look at you?"

"What? Tell me Momma. What do you see?"

"I see you. And I know you like I know myself. I've *seen* you ever since we left Sam. That moment taught me to see you for who you are. You were a great kid that turned into a young adult. A young adult addicted to the fast life—drugs, money, and sex with fast women. That is who you were. The moment when you decided to live with your dad, for a chance to better yourself, is the moment when you started to change. Even though I didn't condone how you got it, I even appreciated the gesture when you left that money out for me find it in your room. Your past is your past baby. Who you are today, is a young man, who found himself. You have found God and *He* has given you the love of your life. That means *He* knows you are ready for this. It doesn't mean that you won't make mistakes or even that she won't make mistakes. But it does mean that you will be able to recover and learn from your mistakes, as long as you *choose* to. You have the most honest and pure heart that I have ever witnessed. You take ownership of your mistakes in such a way that is rarely seen in this world. Don't ever lose that."

Sissy looked up at the ceiling and sighed. She contemplated before speaking again.

"Let me tell you something. Your dad. He is a good man. No things didn't work out between us, but we didn't break up hating each other. We were in love. And that look in your eyes you have when you look at Faith, is the same look that he had when he looked at me. Your father loves you. I know how life may have made things appear, but as parents we make decisions to the best of our abilities but honestly don't how things are going to play out. We do the best with what we have. All I can say is, the same way you trusted God for everything else in your life, you need to trust him in terms of your relationship with your dad. I promise you that if you trust *Him*, that you will have an opportunity for understanding. There is still hope for you both to get past whatever is between you guys."

"Okay…" Seven answered unconvincingly. His eyes were downcast, fidgeting with his thumbs.

"Listen, do you know why certain people always say things to demean you?" Sissy asked, placing her hands into his.

"No, I don't," Seven asked, interlocking his arms with hers.

"It's because they are jealous of you. They wish they were

you. They wish they had what you have. And every time they put you down you seem to raise up higher. Evolving in a way that people don't even recognize you anymore. God continues to guide your path. That's why it feels like you always in the fire. He has some great moments for you to experience. And today is one of those moments. I know you really want things to be better with you and your dad, but never forget, God is the father of us all. He will be with you when no one else is and he has the power to redeem the time."

"Yeah but I feel so much pressure right now. Where is that coming from?"

"That's life baby. You never run from the pressure. It's the fires of life's pressures that will reveal your true self. It will reveal your true character and love. This is what separates you from everyone else. Do you know that?"

"Sometimes. But how do you deal with that mom? When people keep you in a box based on whatever mistakes you've made. How do you overcome that?"

"Listen, as time passes you continue to mature and your love evolves. Your understanding of life and what's important will continue to evolve as you mature. It doesn't feel good when people you love and have given all of your effort to, turn around and judge you or hold a grudge against you for some mistake you made in the past. How do I overcome it you ask? I move on. If I apologized for it then whether they forgive me or not is not up to me. I did my part. So, I choose to move on."

"You make it sound so simple."

"Yeah but it's not. You have to deal with your own feelings and emotions and accept it for whatever it is. Don't ignore your instincts and what God is revealing to you about people. My whole thing now is, while I love people, is it worth sacrificing my peace for the sake of it. In some cases, yes it is. And in others, it is not. And I don't care how I'm perceived by the decisions I make for my peace. My peace of mind, peace in my heart, and peace in my home, are all way more important to me than entertaining folks who eventually will jeopardize that. Some people are who they are and will never change, but you, at your core, you have the purist love that I've ever seen. God truly broke the mold when he made you son. You gotta' know and believe that. One day, you will look back at all this and laugh. You'll be looking at Faith wondering, *how did the last twenty years fly by so fast.* Whenever your days come to an end, I'm sure your heart will be full of love and without regret because you are the type of person to pursue the things that you desire. You don't let anyone get in the way of your goals and dreams. Don't let people project their doubt, fear, and failure on you to make you think you can't do whatever it is that you have your sights set on. Okay?"

Sissy rubbed his shoulders to comfort him. Seven smiled,

letting her words sink into him. He felt a sudden weight lift off his shoulders. Her words of wisdom hit the spot, reigniting his earlier excitement.

"Okay. Thanks Momma. You always know what to say."

"It's only what I've lived baby. You live long enough and you will also have experience to draw from. Keep living baby."

"That's the plan."

"Okay, so get yourself together. I want you to walk down that aisle with your head held high. Get ready to take a bow because what you are about to do will set a trend. Pay attention to what people do after this because then you will know who is watching you."

"Watching me? What do you mean?"

"So, if everyone connected to you now starts to get married then you are their bar. Some look at you for hope and for inspiration, but others look at you out of jealousy. Like '*if he can do it then I know that I can*'. But what they won't realize is that it is God himself who has brought y'all together and not you choosing to settle down with someone. I'm telling you baby. What y'all have is special. And people won't be able to understand it because they have never experienced love on the level that y'all have for each other. People will question your relationship and loyalty to each other for years to come. Your age is only an excuse to be used to try to put out the flames of love that you guys have. Don't let it happen you hear me? Fight and fight hard for what you believe in. Don't give up, like I did."

Seven looked at his mother and was confused by what she just said. She looked away from his glance and started to walk away.

"Momma? What..."

"A story for another time baby. Now go and claim what's yours."

"I always do Momma."

"Yes you do. Now get in the shower and get ready."

"Okay. Wait, how are you getting to the church?"

"Oh, I rented a limo so I'll meet you guys there."

"Oh, okay fancy."

"Well you know, my only son doesn't get married every day. This is a once in a lifetime event. Time to put on for this."

"Mom you so crazy."

"Oh, and when you gonna' get the rest of your stuff?"

"Huh? Oh you putting me out now?"

"No, but hey, you about to be a married man. Besides, you got your own place now. So, you know, I don't want to interfere with your independence. I can pack it up in the limo if you want?"

"I can't with you lady. I'll get my stuff out of your house Momma." Seven laughed.

"That's my baby. Never scared to be independent." Sissy

chuckled in return.

Seven and his mom laughed and hugged each other one last time before he headed to take a shower.

"Hey, you're your own man now and I'm proud of the man that you are becoming."

"Thanks Momma!"

I Do

Seven stood with tears in his eyes as he watched his bride walk toward him. All turned and watched her walk slowly passed them. Some taking pictures, others in awe of the moment, but all on their feet as the vocalist sang. His smooth voice filled the church as he sang Ray Charles' version of "You Are So Beautiful". Each note perfect, and the song itself embodied what Seven had been feeling in his heart as he watched her walk down the aisle.

He nervously panned the room and smiled, recognizing all the family and friends that came to support their union. For a brief moment, he felt a sadness creep up in his heart, due to an obvious absence. His head dropped slightly and Jerri's words would play again in his mind.

You are going to ruin her life.

He picked up his eyes and continued to look around the

room. He saw his friends, uncles, cousins and aunts, as they watched in anticipation. He then panned around the room some more and his eyes landed on his mom. She mouthed to him, "Head up high", as if she knew what plagued his mind at that very moment. He nodded and smiled. By the time his bride made it to him, he had already wiped away the tears that had escaped his ducts. He clenched in his hand the vows he had written the night before, as a surprise, but he could feel that his sweaty hands had moistened it.

Lord, please don't let me mess this up, he prayed within his mind.

It was time for the vows to be said, and as the minister motioned for them to repeat after him, Seven asked for the mic to say his own words. He grabbed the mic as Faith stood in anticipation trying her best to not mess up her makeup from crying.

"Faith, you are my world, my life, my everything. We started this journey without a clue as to what we would become, but we would be friends before we would ever become anything else. It was so seamless how we clicked. Unbeknownst to you at the time, I had been praying for God to send me my wife. And he sent me you. If God is the oxygen I need to survive, you are definitely the lungs by which I need to breathe *Him* through. Some will say that I'm a lucky man, and I understand what they mean, but the truth is, luck had nothing to do with it. You are the Eve to my Adam and God himself made you specifically for me and no one else. My friend, my cheerleader, my love. I love you more than all the words in all the books, and I look forward to spending the rest of our lives together."

The crowd erupted into hushed whispers, stifled sniffles and brief claps. Faith's lower lip quivered as she looked into his eyes. Seven sighed and smiled, thankful for the blessings he had received thus far. Soon after, the minister finalized the ceremony with the announcement that had everyone on their feet.

"And for the first time, I'd like to present to you all, Mr. and Mrs. Seven Bradford!"

Chapter 10: Ezekiel 18:19

"Yet you say, 'Why should not the son suffer for the iniquity of the father?' When the son has done what is just and right, and has been careful to observe all my statutes, he shall surely live."

"Seven? You okay baby? Seven? You're scaring me baby. You okay?" asked Faith.

It was only hours after they reached the hotel. Their honeymoon hadn't really started yet. Seven locked himself in the bathroom. Faith could hear him weeping so loud and hard from outside of the door that she felt the hairs on her arms and neck stand up. "Come on baby. Please. Let me in."

Finally, the door opened and Faith quickly rushed in to see what had happened. Seven stood in the doorway, face full of tears, and his eyes were bloodshot and puffy.

"Aw baby, what's wrong?" she asked again.

She put her hand on his shoulder and he fell into her arms. He cried and cried. She walked him to the bed and he laid down while she rocked him as if he were a baby.

"Whatever it is, I'm here. It will be okay. God got you and so do I."

He wept and moaned as he clutched and cleaved tightly to her. Her shirt had become drenched with his tears. He cried as if he had lost someone. The more she spoke to him and assured him that she was there for him, the more he cried. Not knowing what else to do, she prayed.

"Lord, whatever this is Lord, please let it pass. You said in your word that weeping may endure for a night but joy comes in the morning. Help us get to our morning time. Greater is *He* that is in us than he that is in the world. Lord you said if we acknowledge you in all of our ways you would deliver us from all of our fears. Well, Lord we meet you here and need your help. Right now, Lord. You said, by your stripes we are healed so Lord please heal whatever is aching. Fix whatever is broken. Have your way at this moment for we know that no weapon formed against us shall prosper as we already have the victory. I count it as done and receive it even in my mind. In your name I pray. Amen."

At the end of her prayer Seven's weeping had reduced to sobs. The intensity of his tears had slowed.

"Can you bring me a towel baby?" he asked.

She brought one to him and he blew his nose. "You okay baby?" she asked.

Seven nodded. Tears still slowly fell down his face as he wiped them away with the towel and looked at his now wife.

"He didn't even bother to show up." Seven said. Faith looked at him and now understood what this was about. It was about Jerri. She sat next to him and rubbed his back. "After all the things he had already missed in my life. All the things he already didn't do. I wanted my father to be there for me at this moment. The moment that changes me in every way. That I could be changed as a person, as a man. My wedding day. And he didn't even come."

"It's okay baby. So many people who love you were there."

"Yes, but they are not my *father*."

"True, but they love you nonetheless. Your mom is so happy for us. Even happier than my parents. You are loved baby. Regardless of where the love is coming from. It doesn't matter if it's not from who you'd had hoped to receive it from. When the dust settles I think you will find that your dad does love you. There has to be a reason why things are the way that they are."

Seven contemplated Faith's words for a minute. She was right in all respects. For a brief moment, the hurt and pain of not having his father there absolved.

"That's true. My mom is so proud. I've never seen her this happy. I'm glad I was able to put a smile on her face. After all that I put her through as a teen."

"She is so proud. I mean, she showed up in her own limo like it was a red-carpet event."

Seven smiled. "You know what though babes? He never really been there for me. The truth is, he may never be. And I may never truly know why. And I think I'm going to need to be okay with that. I'm not saying that it won't bother me as time goes on, but

I do recognize that it's very likely a relationship won't ever materialize."

"Well, you never know baby. But I understand what you are saying."

Seven sighed, wiped the final tears from his eyes, and stood.

"I'm sorry baby. I needed to get that out of my system or I would've been sad the entire time."

"It's okay. You don't have to apologize."

"You're the best thing to ever happen to me. And I look forward to our forever," he said.

"You always know what to say to me to make me blush," she responded.

"Do I now?"

"Mhmm."

"So, are we going to go check out the island, or are we going to break in this room a little?" he asked jokingly.

"We got all week to see this island." She replied in a sly voice.

"Well come over here then."

******

"So, you see? He was completely heartbroken. But God

stepped in and filled the void." said Faith.

"Well, if y'all had all of this love and was so meant to be, then how come you never had a child?" Jumi antagonized.

"Jumi!" yelled Jerri.

"What Dad?"

Faith lowered her head. Though what Jumi said hurt, it was the truth. That was the one thing they missed in their relationship. The ability to start a family.

"I… I don't know. I just could never get pregnant. But hey, we are planning to see a specialist and I'm sure we'll be pregnant soon. We both wanted to start a family. It's the right time."

"Yeah I bet." Said Jumi.

"You want to know the one thing that scared him the most about starting a family?" asked Faith.

"Nope, but I'm sure you're gonna' tell us anyway," answered Jumi.

"Being a father like Jerri."

"I'm not going to sit here and let you keep coming for my father."

"Trust me, if Seven were here he would have a lot more to say than I do, since we on the topic of *your* father. He's only ever fathered you."

"That's not how I remember it at all. What about the time I

helped him get a job, or the time I gave him money when he needed it, or the time I even helped him get out of jail? I guess no honorable mentions for that stuff huh? I may not have been there physically every day but I have been there for my son. I think that there is a lot lost in translation." Explained Jerri.

"Sorry to interrupt you Dad, but I don't like you," Jumi said to Faith.

"And I never understood why. I've never done anything to you," replied Faith.

"For Seven's sake, can you two please relax?" Jerri interjected.

Faith sat in the chair and Jumi walked over to the window. "You know what? No. Since we having this *family discussion,* Jumi, what is your problem with me?" asked Faith.

"You wanna' know? You really wanna' know?" asked Jumi.

Faith nodded and folded her arms.

"Because I think you took advantage of my brother. He was broken, gullible, and looking to be loved. And I think you came in and carried him away. Away from everyone. After y'all got married, we barely even heard from him anymore. He didn't call, he didn't come over, it's like he disappeared."

Jumi lowered her head and a tear rolled down her face. "Through all that he had went through in his life, I really wanted to see him happy, but I never thought that I wouldn't actually *see* him."

Faith looked at Jumi in her eyes, and the anger melted away. She understood the real problem. Jumi missed Seven.

"Jumi. I am not the reason why Seven reacted the way that he did. Honestly, he always has tunnel vision when he's focused on something. At times he didn't speak to his mother for a week or two. After we got married, the first few years we were focused on us and being happy. Soon after that, he was focused on his career. He put in a lot of hard work to become as successful as he has. More importantly, he was focused on the things that made him happy and less focused on the things that gave him pain." Faith explained.

"So, you saying he left me out because I caused him pain?" asked Jumi.

"No, not directly. Seven loves you Jumi. So much. The challenge for him is that he always wanted to have a relationship with Jerri. And you are forever connected to Jerri and it's a hard reminder that he was not. I really think you guys all need to talk when we find him. He can better explain it than I can," said Faith.

"If I'm being honest. I know he was envious of our relationship. And I never understood why Seven and Dad could never get along. But after he moved back to his mother's place, we started to have our own independent relationship. So, through the years we really became closer. And I liked that."

"Yeah I know. He told me about that as well. He actually

loved it. Because what he realized was that you both were lonely as only children in your respective households. Maybe he more than you because you have a big family but he loved the bond that y'all created. He also felt the sting of not having his father while you did. Every time y'all would talk on the phone, it was inevitable that he would hear Jerri's voice in the background. For years, he felt like it was being rubbed in his face. Not by you, but more by life, because it was a painful reminder of what he didn't have," Faith explained.

"I can understand that. But then when you guys got married, he dropped off the face of the earth. And I was angry because I felt like you stole my big brother away from me," Jumi replied.

"Listen Jumi, it wasn't like—"

Before Faith could respond, Jumi cut her off.

"You wanted the truth. That's the truth."

"Well, okay… thanks for sharing that. I'm sorry if I presented in any way that reinforced that feeling. I always kind of knew it wasn't anything personal towards me, but still wasn't sure what the problem was. But listen, Seven's heart and feelings are very complex. It hasn't been easy to maneuver through his pain and triggers. Even for me. I've been telling him for a few years now that he needed to have a conversation with the both of you."

"Um, I did speak to him when I was first diagnosed with Cancer," said Jerri. "I called him about two months ago when I first found out. I felt bad because I have wanted to call him so many times before, but just couldn't."

"Why couldn't you call him before then?" asked Faith.

"I don't know. I think I was upset with him. The last time we spoke he was pretty disrespectful and I wasn't happy about it. Being diagnosed with cancer really shook me up. If worse came to worse I didn't want to leave this earth without talking to my son. So, when I was diagnosed Jumi gave me y'alls number, I called right away just to hear his voice," explained Jerri, a side-smile creeping on his lips. Faith and Jumi glanced at each other briefly.

"Yeah, I remember that day. He was so happy to hear from you and then he was super sad because you basically told him that you was going to die. Or, at least that's how he felt. He has been so stressed about that since that day," said Faith.

"Dad, other than that what did y'all talk about?" asked Jumi.

"He had told me that he forgave me. He said he was in therapy with one of the pastors at his church and it helped him to forgive all the people in his life that hurt him. Myself included."

"And what did you say in return Dad?"

"I said thank you and I apologized for not being there in his life. I also explained the reason why I missed most of his childhood. The truth is, I had always intended to be there for him. His mother and I had made plans for me to go into the military so I could take care of them financially. What ended up happening was that his mom sent me divorce papers while I was in the military. The reasons for it were a bit murky but I complied with signing the papers. By the time I was out of the military, and readjusted to start trying to be in Seven's life, he had to be around nine or ten. With so much time passed, I honestly didn't know how to move forward. I remember going to see them while his mom was with the Sam character. I was devastated that he didn't really know who I was. So I reacted poorly. And I apologized for that as well. It was a hard conversation to have and we both had some moments in which our emotions got the best of us. But all in all I think we are on the right path to trying to repair our relationship because he was able to understand that I didn't just skip out on his childhood. It was much more complicated than that." Jerri explained.

"I also didn't want to bring up too much of the past because I didn't want to get all into it in one phone call. I realize that we are similar people and I didn't want to argue and rather stay as much as possible on a positive note. I really think we are in a better place from that one conversation. Besides we have time to get through it all. I'll be sure to open up more and talk to him as soon as I'm out of here," Jerri explained further.

"I'll tell you one thing. He has really forgiven you Jerri. The moment he heard your voice, he became that same little boy that always wanted his father. He loves you. He has always loved you. Even when he would call you out on things, it was out of love. He always had such a high expectation of you as a kid because he felt you had to be able to provide something better than the situation he was in." explained Faith, moving closer to Jerri's bed. She could feel a sense of mutual understanding growing between them all. This was a moment that she wished Seven was here to experience and be part of as well.

"That's my son. And I love him too," replied Jerri.

"So, you know. He fasted for an entire week when you told him about your diagnosis. He fasted and pleaded with God to heal you. He wouldn't eat, he barely slept, he couldn't focus on work, and he was totally focused on you. Because he was so fearful that he was going to lose you before y'all could totally re-establish your relationship," said Faith.

"Really? Wow. He did that for me?" asked Jerri, his lower lip quivering.

"Yes he did." Said Faith.

"Wow. I didn't know that either. Faith, thank you for sharing all of this with us. I'm sorry that I've been holding this against you for so long. And you're right. We all need to sit down and talk about all of this. More importantly, him and Dad, so that they especially can understand and process this. It's great that the initial conversation went well with you guys. I think it will help us all understand each other and be able to move past the pain of it all," said Jumi.

Jumi walked over to Faith and hugged her. They shared a

moment of compassion that had long since been needed. All they had needed to do was talk to each other.

"I forgive you. That's the one thing I can say that I have learned from my husband, is how to forgive. Now, is there anyone you may know that can get a hold of him?"

They shook their heads as they had exhausted all avenues trying to locate him. Jerri started to worry again. His dream was so vivid. He shook his head the more he thought about its meaning. Tears formed in his eyes.

"Lord, I love my son. I've hurt him in so many ways. I feel like I was there for him as best as I could be at some times, but also feel like I've abandoned him at some points. I know he felt disappointed in me on so many levels, but Lord if you give me another chance, I promise I would make things right. Please Lord, find my son and bring him to me. Forgive me Lord, please give us the chance to walk in our roles of being father and son. Lord, I beg you. Hear my cry. Please Lord." Jerri prayed aloud.

Chapter 11: Hope-Less

Who is this man? Am I trippin'? He seems so familiar, thought Hope.

In that same moment, Seven quietly awakened to see Hope standing over him. Their eyes locked on one another's. He didn't budge. Neither did Hope. They continued to stare into the windows of each other's souls. His eyes began to light up, the frown and confusion was erased from his face as his cheeks began to rise and his forehead softened. His smile was so radiant and infectious that she couldn't help but to smile as well. He looked at her with such contentment in his eyes. Such approval and pride, she couldn't help the multiple thoughts that flooded her brain once more.

Why does he feel so familiar? Why does he seem so pleased to see me? Does he know me? She continued to think to herself.

He sat up, lifted his arm, and reached out to touch her face. With his hand, he rubbed her cheek. A tear rolled down his face. Barely able to speak he started to whisper something. Hope leaned in more to understand what he had tried to say.

"I'm sorry," whispered Seven.

"Sorry? For what?" asked Hope.

"I should've fought harder."

"Fought harder? For what? I don't understand."

She was unsure of what he meant but nevertheless she grabbed his hand and held it. As he sat up, she could see his facial expression had changed. His infectious smile faded, his forehead hardened, his eyes closed. Suddenly, he fell back down on the gurney and he let out a huge sigh. Another tear ran down his left cheek as the heart monitor went off.

"Doctor! We lost him!" Hope yelled.

The doctor rushed to his side. "Hand me the Defib and stand back!"

He placed them on his chest. "Clear!" He rubbed the paddles together once more to make a new attempt to revive him. Then he started CPR.

Hope looked on in shock. She was unable to move. Hands at her side looking on as the doctor tried to revive him. It's as if she was witnessing his soul leave his body; his life coming to an end. All her training flew out the window.

"God please save him," she mumbled.

He lay there. Unresponsive. Before long the doctor gave up. "Time of death 2:33 p.m."

Seven was no more. His time on Earth had expired. Hope walked to the gurney and grabbed him by the hand. "No," she whimpered.

The doctor then walked over and touched Hope on the back

of the shoulder as she leaned over Seven's body.

"Hope, did you know him?" the doctor asked.

As she looked up at the doctor to answer, she just cried. Tears streamed down her eyes, unabated. She was so confused. Her heart was crushed, as if she'd known this person. She wondered what was wrong with herself. She never got that emotional over losing a patient.

"What is his full name? Do we have any next of kin on record that we can notify?" asked the doctor.

"Seven. Seven Bradford was his name." said one of the other nurses.

"Bradford? That sounds familiar." He said.

"Doctor. That's Jerri Bradford's son. The one who awoke in recovery screaming his son's name," said Hope.

The doctor frowned and shook his head. The coincidence was too daunting. He rubbed Hope's shoulders in an attempt at comforting her, remaining strong for the both of them.

"You are right. I'll go and speak with them," replied the doctor.

Hope shook her head profusely. She needed to get herself together and do her job.

"I can handle it doctor. I've been speaking to his family most of the morning and they all have been looking for him."

"Are you sure? You have been emotional."

"Yes, I'm sure. I can speak with them."

"Okay, let them know that I will be down in a moment."

"Will do."

Hope found her way to Jerri's room. As she entered, Jumi and Faith were hugging each other.

"Excuse me, you guys. I needed to have a word with you all." Hope said as she entered.

"Hey Nurse Hope, how are you?" asked Jumi, her eyes lit up.

"Hey Jumi, I'm doing okay," she responded, refraining from displaying any emotions through her voice. Hope needed to make sure that she broke the news in a professional manner. From her training, she knew she needed to be the solace of their strength as they absorbed the news.

"My dad seems to almost be his old self again."

"That's great. He certainly looks much better."

Hope walked over to the side of his bed and checked his pulse and heart rate. She looked through his charts to double-check his vitals.

"How's your pain level?" she asked.

"It's about a three," answered Jerri.

"That's good. You should be able to go home soon. In the

next day or two, but the doctor will come to speak to you in more detail about that."

"Oh, okay that's great," he replied.

Faith approached Hope. "Hi I'm Faith. I know this sounds a little weird, but do we know each other from somewhere?" she asked.

"Um…I don't think so," replied Hope, confusion settling on her expression.

Jumi spoke up. "Now I normally don't agree with my sister in law often, but there is definitely a familiar vibe about you. I told you before but I thought I was buggin' but now I'm not so sure since she also sees it."

Hope took a deep breath and spoke. "Listen guys, I'm so very sorry. But Seven, was involved in a very bad car accident."

"What? Well, where is he, can we go see him? Where is my husband?" Faith asked, as panic started setting in.

"Please, let me explain. His car was run off the bridge, and it fell into the river. When the ambulance brought him into the ER, he had a very weak pulse and we did all that we could to save him. But I'm sorry, there was nothing else that we could do," she said sadly.

"Wait, *what*? What does that mean? I want to see my husband! Where is he?" Faith cried.

"The doctor will come to see you all in a minute. I just

wanted to be the one to let you all know being that you have been trying to reach him for most of the morning."

Hope felt a chill as she spoke. She cast her eyes downward rubbing her shoulders in the process. Just then, Faith noticed her birthmark. Faith grabbed her arm. Hope jumped back, startled by Faith grabbing her arm and inspecting it.

"I'm sorry. I noticed the mark on your shoulder. It looks familiar and I wanted to get a closer look at it. I shouldn't have grabbed you like that." Faith said as she apologized.

"That's okay. Listen, is there anything I can do for you guys?" asked Hope.

Jumi looked at Faith and hugged her again. They both cried as the realization of Hope's words sank in. They hugged each other and cried even more. Hope shed a tear as well. For some odd reason, she felt connected to them. They all were so immersed in their own feelings that no one immediately noticed that Jerri was grimacing in pain as he held his chest. He had turned on his side, as he held his chest, and gasped for air.

"I can't breathe," he said. But he wasn't able to project his voice loud enough for anyone to really hear him. "I can't breathe. I can't breathe." Gasped Jerri.

Hope wiped the tears from her eyes and looked up. She initially focused on Jumi and Faith. They were sobbing together. She then looked across the room and observed Jerri lying on his side. She walked slowly toward him as she tried to see his face.

"Jerri are you okay?" asked Hope.

"I can't breathe. Help me. I can't breathe," said Jerri.

"Okay I want you to try and calm down. Try to relax. I want you to take a slow and deep breath for me. Can you try to do that?"

He took a slow and deep breath as Hope coached him. And another. After a few more, he seemed relaxed and the pressure in his chest started to subside. At that moment, another nurse and the doctor came into the room.

"Hey Jerri. How are you feeling?" the doctor asked solemnly.

"A little better, Doc."

"That's good. I'm going to check you out okay?"

"Sure." Jerri responded with a whimper. He allowed the doctor to check him. He then cried out.

"Seven. I'm sorry baby boy. I'm sorry." He cried profusely while the doctor examined him. "I wanted to apologize and I didn't. I'm sorry!"

"Seems he had a slight panic attack after hearing the news," Hope whispered to the doctor.

"Okay. I want to have an EKG done to be sure but that's very common when people experience loss," he whispered back, the mood in the room an all too common occurrence.

Jerri sat up in his bed and screamed so loud that other nurses came into the room to see what was happening.

"I'm so sorry. I should've fixed it while I had the chance. I'm sorry that I let you down and wasn't there for you. Please forgive me. Forgive me please God!"

His head sank in his chest and he cried. He was inconsolable. The guilt he felt was apparent as he pleaded and pleaded for forgiveness. The emotions were high as Faith and Jumi both cried out in denial.

"When can we go and see him doctor? I want to see my husband!" yelled Faith.

"We are moving him now to a room so that you all can see him. We will be back when he's ready. I'm so sorry for your loss," replied the doctor.

The doctor turned and left. And so did Hope. She felt drained and couldn't wait to go home. *This was such a crazy day. I need to go home and go to sleep*, she thought. Hope left the hospital and returned to the bus stop once more lost in her thoughts. She sat on the bench and instinctively pulled out her pen and took a pull. She exhaled and her body relaxed. Before long, the bus arrived, and Hope walked up the steps, entered the bus, and spoke to the bus driver.

"Hey Sam."

"Hey Hope. You look a little frazzled friend, how was your

shift today?" he asked.

"Never a dull moment. That's all I can say. Someone passed away today and it really affected me," Hope sat down and placed her things in the seat next to her.

"Really? Wow. I'm sorry to hear that."

"Yeah me too."

"Did you hear about the car accident this morning on the bridge?"

"Yeah. That's who actually died. We tried to revive him but ultimately we lost him."

"Aw that's sad. I'm sure his family is torn up."

"Yeah it's pretty bad. Their father Jerri came in for emergency surgery so I had been his nurse the whole time. When Seven came into the ER, I had no idea that they were even related. It was such a crazy day."

"What did you say his name was?"

"Seven. Seven Bradford."

Sam was speechless—in shock at what he just heard.

"You sure that's his name?" he asked.

"Yeah. Why? You know him or something?"

"Not for a long time. But yeah."

Sam was clearly shaken by this news. He had not seen Seven or Sissy in years. He often thought of his time with them and felt bad about the way he treated Seven as a kid.

"You okay Sam?" asked Hope.

"Um… yeah. That's just a shock is all. Hey you think you could find out the details around the services and let me know? I would like to go and pay my respects."

"Um… I'm not sure. It's not like I know them like that. You know what? They will probably post it in the obituaries. So maybe you should look there?"

"Yeah you probably right. I'll look out for it."

Hope laid back in her seat. She closed her eyes. The bus rocked back and forth with the occasional jolt from hitting the many potholes in the road. Before she realized it, Hope was sound asleep.

"Broadway and Carrol!" yelled Sam.

Hope opened her eyes at the sound of Sam's voice booming through the bus. This was her stop. She quickly stood, grabbed her things, and shuffled down the steps.

"Thanks for waking me Sam. See you tomorrow," she said.

"No worries. I'm sure you'll finish cutting that grass when you get home," he mused.

She laughed as she exited the bus and walked home. As she walked into her apartment, she dropped her bags by the door, pulled out her pen, and as soon as she put it to her lips her phone rang. She looked down and saw that it was her mom calling her. It was their daily routine so even though she was reluctant to do so, she answered.

"Hey mom."

"Hey baby. How was your day?" she asked.

"It was a rough one. I had someone scare the crap out me. One of our patients awoke in the recovery room screaming, like violently screaming for his son. It was so crazy." Hope explained.

"Shut up. Seriously?"

"Yeah it was really unsettling. Even the doctor was taken a back."

"Dang that is unsettling. Did he say why he was screaming for his son?"

"No, he didn't go into detail, but he begged and pleaded for us to reach out to him. But it gets deeper. I went to speak to his daughter, Jumi, and I told her what happened and that they needed to call his son. But she said she couldn't get ahold of her brother for some reason."

"Hmm. That's interesting."

"Yeah, so the patient's name is Jerri. And his son's name was Seven. She said she even went to his house and still couldn't find him."

"Did you say the son's name is Seven?"

"Yeah, why?"

"Oh no reason. It's a unique name I guess. Like who names their child after a number? Anyways go ahead and finish the story."

A brief silence ensued, causing Hope to stop pacing back and forth and sit on her plushy couch.

"Mhmm, well yeah I thought so too initially. But listening to you now, I have weird feeling that you know something more than what you are saying. So, spill the beans. What do you know?"

"Um, I don't know what you mean."

"Don't play with me Mom. In my twenty-five years of life I come to know when you are not telling me all of the truth."

"Um."

"Cassandra Cassy Smith. What do you know? Tell me now." Hope yelled.

"Girl, who you think you talkin' to? I am your mother and don't you forget that." Cassy yelled back.

"How can I ever forget? I grew up most of my life wishing I had someone else for a mother. You're the one who needs to remember that you are a mom. It's bad enough you won't tell me about my father, but then for you to be how you are makes it even worse. I've been on my own since being a teen. Yeah, we lived together, but you sure as hell ain't raise me."

"That's it! I've had enough. You are not going to keep talking to me like this!"

"Go ahead, hang up, Mom. Matter of fact leave me alone. You are dead to me. Just like Seven is."

"Wait, what did you say?"

"I said Seven is dead. That's right. The man you claim to not even know. The one that for some reason connected to my soul the moment our eyes met. He died in front of me. He has, or shall I say he had, such an infectious smile. Just like mine. His eyes, same color as mine. His cheeks, his lips, even his nose, are like mine. And now, he's dead."

"Dang, I'm sorry to hear that, but listen to me, I don't know him."

Cassy remained adamant, her tone of voice fueling Hope's rebuttal.

"Mom. When are you going to start being able to open up? You never want to tell me the truth about anything. Whenever I want to talk about a sensitive topic you never want to and you shut down on me. You continue to hide. That's why I'm so confused. Why I don't even know who I am. Because you won't tell me. To be honest, at times I hate you for it. All my life, I only wanted to know more about where I came from, why I'm the way I am but because of your unwillingness to share that with me, I feel like I'm forever going to be confused and conflicted."

Hope's mother felt really guilty. The more she thought about what Hope was saying the more she felt bad.

"Mom, was Seven my father? I think that he was. You know why I think that mom? We don't only share similar features, but we also share the same birthmark. With his last breath, do you know what he said to me?" she asked.

"No," Cassy answered, her voice shaking. "What did he say?"

"He apologized. Apologized for not fighting harder for me. He was my dad wasn't he? Tell me the truth!" she cried.

Her mother became quiet. She didn't know what to say. Her mind became cluttered with thoughts.

"Fine don't tell me. But know that I will forever hate you for not telling me the truth about my father!" Hope sobbed.

How is this possible? God please forgive me. I thought I was doing the right thing, Cassy thought to herself. Her heart continued to race as she contemplated telling her daughter the whole truth. The secret that she had been hiding from Hope for all of these years just blew up in her face. She took a deep breath and let out a sigh. "Okay. I'll tell you."

"I'm *listening,*" Hope responded sarcastically.

"Seven and I were cool. We weren't really dating just had a night of fun. When I first met him, I found him funny, charming, and definitely good looking. We met hanging out with a group of mutual friends drinking and smoking. It was about ten of us. So over time, I ended up talking to different people within the group and before long we found ourselves sparking up a conversation with each other. So, we were smoking and chattin' it up about life, faith, our futures, and many other things. When at some point, he looked down at his phone and became quiet. I asked him what was wrong since I noticed that his demeanor had changed. '*Oh nothing, it's just my life*,' he responded in a solemn tone. He then got up from where we were sitting and walked out to the back porch. I followed him out there and he asked, '*Do you ever wonder where you come from? Like, who your people are? And what's your purpose*?'"

"I replied saying '*Sure at times.*' Even though I didn't," Cassy continued, "because I knew where I came from. Even though your grandfather passed away while I was still a young girl, I have very vivid memories of us and was pretty close to both my parents' family. I sorely wish that he were still alive though. I loved my dad and he loved me so much. Like I could actually feel his love. He made me feel so safe and protected and cared for."

Cassy sighed as she continued explaining the details to Faith.

"So, we sat, and smoked, and drank, and more importantly we talked. Talked for a very long time, before we even realized how much time has passed. Even though our circumstances were different we both very much wished our fathers were actively in our lives. So, we created somewhat of a connection over that—at least for the moment. It's hard to explain, but I felt like I knew him, like really knew him and that he knew me as well. It was such a deep conversation. By the time we walked back into the house, everyone else had already left. So, while we were there alone, and having seemingly created a connection through our pain, disappointment, and hopes and dreams, we ended up being intimate that night."

"Great, so you were sleeping around with random people now?" Hope snapped in a snarky tone.

"Girl you ain't much different today than I was back then so watch your mouth. But anyway, yes we ultimately had sex at the party," Cassy replied.

"Well, what happened after that?"

"So, me and, um, this other gentleman started seeing each other a little after that and ended up dating exclusively for a few months and decided to take it to the next level. We fell in love quickly. We did everything together. But as the months passed my belly began to grow. I initially didn't think anything about it, but my belly grew so quickly that I realized something was wrong. So, I took a pregnancy test and it was positive…" Cassy's voice trailed off.

"Were you nervous?" Hope asked

"Extremely. I didn't know where this would lead or if he would even want to still be with me. We always practiced safe sex. But I had to tell him because as God is my witness, I have never loved anyone as much as I loved him. And he loved me back. I started shaking and crying while apologizing and he simply hugged me and said that he would be honored to raise a family with me. He didn't even ask if you were really his or not. He was the perfect gentleman. But truth be told, I believed he knew all the while. He really didn't care about that."

"So, what happened? Did I ever meet him? I don't remember him at all. All I ever remember growing up, is me and you, no one else."

"Well, we had moved in together and planned to get married. Everything was great. I remember that he dropped me off at the bridal store for me to start looking at dresses. I made him drop me off because I didn't want him to see the dress until our actual wedding day. But the craziest of things happened. While I was in the store, I saw *him* again."

"Who? Seven?" asked Hope.

"Yes. And this would be the last time I would ever see him. It was definitely a freaky weird moment because he was with someone, but we both recognized each other at the same time. He was walking into the store with a woman. He stopped and sat in the chair at the front, and she kept walking to the back of the store."

"What did you say?"

"I said nothing. We made eye contact, and then I focused back on my dress. He eventually walked over to me. He complimented me on how I looked in the dress. He congratulated me and asked when I was getting married. I told him soon, but I noticed the whole time he was looking at my belly. I was hoping that he never asked me about my pregnancy since I hadn't seen him since we had sex that night. But he eventually asked the very question that I was dreading. He asked if the baby was his. I looked him straight in his eye and told said no."

"Why did you do that? Why wouldn't you tell him about me? You robbed me of my father mom," Hope cried.

"Baby, in my mind, you were going to have the father of all fathers. Because my soon to be husband loved me so much. It was real love and not only infatuation. He made me feel loved, safe, even adored. I hadn't felt that way since before your grandfather passed away when I was a girl. And just like that, I was a little girl all over again. He was definitely my soulmate."

Cassy cried as she relived the memories. Hope was quiet while her mother collected herself. She slowly gathered her composure and wiped her face with a tissue that she had in her hands.

"Hope, this man was all the father that you could've ever wanted."

"But he wasn't. I never met him. So, what happened?" Hope chided.

"We were all set to be married. All of the arrangements were made. We were literally just waiting for the date to come and for me to re-size my dress once I had given birth to you. This truly was the happiest moment in my life. Then about a week after you were born, I was home with you, and he called and asked if I needed anything from the store. I didn't really need anything, but remembered that I had wanted him to play the lottery. So, I told him to pick up some lottery tickets on his way home. And that would be the last time I'd ever hear his voice, let alone, see him alive. Apparently, someone robbed the store after he walked in. Long story short, he was shot and died in the hospital."

A heaviness weighed on Hope's chest. She hadn't thought about why her mom was so closed emotionally. She immediately regretted all the years she had been quick to insult her mom. More tears threatened to cascade down her cheeks.

"Wow, I'm sorry mom. I'm so sorry this happened to you. I can't even imagine how that must've felt. I'm sorry I was rude earlier. All of this makes me sad and upset. I really wanted to know who my father was. Did you ever tell anyone else about my father?"

"Baby my life was shattered. I was in pieces. I had a thought to try to reach out to Seven after you were born. But I had no idea where he was or how to even go about finding him. We had mutual friends so I did think about putting the word out that I wanted to speak with him, but before I could even do it, your aunt had told me that she seen him at a mutual friend's house."

"Really? Auntie had seen him? Wait, she knows about all of this and she never told me?"

"Wait, before you get all angry with her too, let me finish. Your aunt actually questioned me about you after you were born. She was the first to say that you looked exactly like Seven. But I lied to her and said you were not his. It wasn't too long after that, that she ran into him. Of course, he asked how I was doing and how was the baby. Your aunt, as only she could, took it upon herself to say to him that he was your father. She later told me that he was furious. He yelled at her saying that he asked me and I said you was not his, so how dare she come and lay that on him after he just got married."

Hope sighed as she continued to listen to her mom explain the events that impacted her.

"Baby, it was the guilt of all of this that pushed me over the edge. I lost my soon to be husband—the love of my life. And that feeling alone was hard for me to process. And I didn't want to be seen as the girl who didn't know who her baby daddy was. It made me feel like I was on an episode of Maury. I was embarrassed to then go to Seven and say you were his child—especially after I had already told him that you weren't. I was young and broken at the time. I know it sounds wrong, and looking back, maybe it was the wrong choice, but I felt like it was the right thing for everyone at the time. Including you. Besides, I didn't really know Seven like that even though I admired his passion and how he thought about things. Who I knew, was the man I was about to marry. How was I supposed to know that he would be killed?"

Hope took a moment to let what her mom was telling her sink in. Thoughts and emotions tumbled around in her, making it hard to focus on one thing. She still had more questions, so she pushed on.

"I hear what you are saying Mom, but it's hard for me to know that you still had a chance to allow my father to be in my life all those years ago, and you chose not to."

"Yeah, I know, I'm sorry. I truly am. Ultimately, I only had a short period to think about it. Shortly after the funeral, I was heartbroken. Most of that time after that, I was in a fog and didn't know whether I was coming or going. I did all that I could to not think about any of it. To not have to deal with the reality that the two men that had ever truly loved me were both gone. And not just gone, but gone forever. My world was upside down. That's why I've been so sick over the years. I should've talked through it long ago. I just didn't know how. I apologize baby for what you had to endure while I was going through all of that. I am so sorry for not being stronger for you. But this was my reality and the harshness of it…"

Cassy cried through the phone, tugging at Hope's heartstrings.

"I'm sorry that you went through all of this Mom. I truly am. I understand a little about why you did the things that you did, but I can't help but to realize that you allowed me to experience the same pain. I grew up always wondering who my dad was. Being envious of the few kids who actually had relationships with their dads. Father daughter dances at school, him being able to see me on my prom day, my graduations from high school and college—missing whatever relationship advice he could've given me from a Dad's perspective. I always envisioned him grilling my, would-be, boyfriends in an effort to protect me. I longed for him to tuck me in at night as a little girl making sure I went to sleep. In my head, he wouldn't have been a jock kind of dad that pushed his girls to be more like boys for the sake of athletics. But rather I fantasized that we would be loving and caring and supportive in anything that I would've wanted to do or become. He would've been a girl-dad. By the time I was twelve, I used to daydream about this all the time. Especially after you started being sick all the time and me having to take care of you."

"I'm so sorry baby."

Hope sobbed even more as her mother apologized. "I wanted a childhood mom. You not only robbed me of a dad, but you robbed me of being a little girl and doing things that little girls do. Do you even know why I became a nurse?" asked Hope.

"I'm sorry baby, but no…" answered Cassy

"I became a nurse because I've seen you so sick so many times that I felt like I needed to know how I could save you in case you were about to die. My entire being has been over-shadowed by the need to take care of you. I haven't had the chance to even think about what I really would like to do with my life. It's because of you that I have no identity. I've had enough of all of this," Hope said, a tone of finality in her voice.

"Hope baby, I don't know what else to say… but… I'm sorry."

"And now that he's gone, it hurts even more because, I don't even have any memories created with him in order to cope with his death. Instead of memories, all I have is what I've always had. Questions. You know what? I'm sorry Mom. I gotta' go. Bye."

Hope picked up her pen and took a puff, held it for a moment, and then let out a huge cloud of smoke. She took off her clothes and climbed in her bed. Tears fell from her eyes as the day's events replayed in her mind.

All this time I suspected that my father was out there. I can't believe my mom hid this from me, she thought.

Hope cried until she fell asleep. Her dreams were influenced by the moments of the day. Seven was on her mind the entire time she slept. She was so devastated that she even cried while she slept. She would fall asleep, see his face, and then wake up again. She tossed and turned like that for what seemed like hours. Finally, she couldn't take it any longer and got out the bed. Then a thought crossed her mind. *Jerri.*

******

The doctor returned to Jerri's room to speak with them all.

"Mrs. Bradford?"

"Yes doctor?" Faith answered.

"We are ready to take you to see your husband's body."

"Are we all able to go?" she asked.

"Yes you may, however we would need to get a wheel chair for your father-in-law."

"Faith, you should go ahead first. We can go after," said Jumi.

"You sure Jumi?" she asked.

"He's your husband. You deserve to be with him uninterrupted. Besides we should wait here until Sissy arrives. This way you can have your time with him because once she gets here, she'll need some time as well."

"Thanks Jumi."

"You're welcome. Take your time."

Faith hugged Jumi and then followed the doctor to the room where Seven's body lay. With every step, her heart broke into more pieces. Her best friend, her heart, the love of her life was no more. She walked closer and placed her hand on his face. *He's so cold*, she thought.

She looked over him and closely inspected his features. In

disbelief, she fell on his chest and cried. She stared at his face unable to wrap her mind around what had occurred. She rubbed his face and kissed his cheek. Tears rolled down her face again. She felt even worse when the realization that they were trying to start a family and never was able to, sunk in. At that moment, she felt so much guilt.

"I will always love you baby. I will never forget you. I'm so sorry that we never had children. I know how much you wanted to be a father. To be able to love someone that came from you. You had so much love in your heart. You were far from perfect, but you were perfect for me. You would've been the perfect father too," she whispered. She kissed his cheek again and something caught her attention. The crescent shaped birthmark on his shoulder.

Faith slowly walked out the room to speak to the doctor. "Hey Doctor I have a question for you." Faith and the doctor walked down the hall. "Is Hope around? I wanted to thank her for her help today."

"No, actually she went home. She… um… took all this a little personally so we excused her for the rest of her shift. I will be sure to pass your thanks along to her when she comes back in. Is that okay?" asked the doctor.

"Yes, that's fine. Thanks. Do we know when my father-in-law will be released?"

"We were planning for the end of the day tomorrow, but I

want to see how he is doing in light of everything that happened today."

"Okay. Well maybe I'll see Hope tomorrow?"

"Um… it's possible but I'm not sure if she'll be in or not."

"Okay. I think you can bring everyone else in now."

Hours had passed and Sissy had arrived to the hospital. Faith, Sissy, Jerri, and Jumi all mourned the loss of their brother, their son, their husband and friend. Rehi also came to the hospital after Jumi had told her all that had happened.

"It seems as if time is standing still. I've never expected to be in this position. Where I would be mourning the loss of someone so full of love and compassion. I feel so numb, like it's a dream. Like, Jumi, is this really happening?" asked Faith.

"Yeah. It is. I'm devastated, but the funny thing is, I can't even process my own feelings. All I can think about, is you and Sissy," Jumi replied.

"Me?"

"Yeah, you. I know how much Seven loved you. And if you love him as much as that boy loved you, then I know you are hurting bad now. I was really just being a jealous little sister all of these years. He's my big brother. The only brother that I have… well, had."

"I forgive you. I really do. Besides the only reason why I

didn't kick your butt already was because I knew how much Seven loved you. He spoke of you constantly. It was his mom, Jerri, and then you on his pillow talk top three."

Jumi laughed inadvertently and hugged Faith again. She wiped the tears away from her face.

"Thanks Faith," said Jumi.

"No, thank you." Faith responded.

She nodded and Jumi winked back. They both felt a sense of relief.

"Seven would've loved to see that. To see you both love on each other." Sissy said as she wiped tears away from her face.

"Seven I'm sorry. Son, I'm sorry. I'm so sorry!" Jerri sobbed.

Hope walked up to the door and knocked lightly. Faith was exhausted, numb, and confused in her thoughts. Faith walked to the door and opened it. She stood in the doorway and stared at the face that stared back at her. She examined every inch of the face in front of her. The round cheeks, the wide nose, even the way that she stood at the door. While those were all similarities, the one that stood out the most were the eyes. The exact light brown almost hazel color. She shook her head in disbelief and walked back to where she was sitting clearly lost in her own thoughts.

"Umm…hey guys. I know this isn't a great time for you all,

but I needed to come see you guys," explained Hope.

"Thanks Hope. I know I for one appreciate that. Seems like you have been with us all day today. First with my dad and now with my brother," said Jumi.

Hope simply nodded and walked over to speak to Jerri.

"Hey Jerri, how are holding up?" asked Hope, placing her hand on his shoulder.

"I'm just sad. I feel like I wasted the time we had together. He was my son and I barely even knew him," he replied.

Sissy watched as Hope spoke to Jerri. She didn't say a word but watched her closely and inspected her every move.

"It's okay. I'm sure he loved you." Said Hope.

"How can you say that? You don't know us. Why am I even talking to you? Why are you here?" asked Jerri.

"Jerri, relax," said Sissy.

"No. Why is she making comments about something she clearly knows nothing about?"

"I'm sorry. I didn't mean to upset you, but I'm speaking from a place that I do know about. I have never met my father, but I love him with all my being. I've never spent one day with him, never spoke to him, and never saw his face. But that doesn't change how I feel about him. Besides, Seven was rushing to be here for you right?" Hope asked.

Jerri nodded his head to acknowledge her question.

"Okay see. He loved you," Hope felt that she was about to become emotional. "Well, okay I need to go now. I'm sorry for your loss."

"Wait," Sissy said. "I have a question for you. Why do you look like my son?"

"Sissy?" Faith shouted.

"Faith, you can't tell me you don't see the resemblance."

"I mean, yeah, but really? Like right now?" asked Faith.

"Sissy, I'm distraught over the loss of my son too, but to imply that this is my granddaughter is ridiculous!" Jerri said.

"Ridiculous? No, I don't think so." Faith interjected.

"Sissy? Faith? We are all hurting over this. Maybe you both should take some time to think this through. Not right now," said Jumi.

Hope sat quietly as they talked about the coincidence. She felt out of place but she had to wait. Suddenly, they all turned to her for answers.

"I know how this sounds. But did either of you even see her shoulder?" asked Faith.

Faith looked at Hope and gestured to her to lift her sleeve. Hope slowly complied and raised her sleeve revealing her birthmark. Faith grabbed her by the arm and brought her over to her husband's body. She looked at her shoulder and compared it to the one on her husband's shoulder.

"Look. It's the same mark. Even in the same location." Faith explained.

Hope couldn't believe they were all coming to the same conclusion at the same time.

"For what it's worth, I had never met Seven prior to today. Nor had I even heard of your family. I have been without a father for all of my life. I always wondered who he was and who my other family members were. Never had one conversation with him at any point, nor did my mother mention of him."

"See, told you. She ain't kin to us," said Jerri.

"Please let her finish." Replied Sissy.

"That is until today. When you all came into surgery, I had no idea who any of you were. When he came into the ER shortly after, I had no idea who he was. Of course I couldn't help but to notice the similarities in our features, but I see so many people in and out of the hospital they all start looking alike. He was barely hanging on for life and we had to remove his shirt to work on him. It was then, that I noticed the birthmark on his shoulder. That caused me to pause and think. Because this was odd. The same mark in the same area is really coincidental. For most of this, he was not conscious, but when we revived him, he was stable for a very short period of time. I was cleaning him up and something dropped. I bent down to pick it up and then that's when it happened?" Hope explained.

"What happened?" asked Faith.

"He was coherent and looking at me. I saw his eyes and he smiled. It was like looking into a mirror. Then this feeling came over me. I can't even describe it really but I felt like I knew him. He reached out and rubbed my face."

"See all she had is a feeling." Said Jerri.

They all looked at Jerri sternly and he stopped talking again.

"Did he say anything?" asked Faith.

"How long was he alive? Was he in pain?" asked Sissy.

They both asked simultaneously. Hope glanced between the two, her nerves on edge.

"It all happened so fast. But I'll never forget what he said to me," explained Hope.

"What did he say?" asked Faith.

"He cried and he told me that he was sorry. Sorry for not fighting harder for me. What I didn't realize at the time, was that there was a moment when he saw my mother somewhere while she was pregnant with me," Hope continued.

"The bridal store," Faith blurted out.

"Yes. The bridal store. She told him that he wasn't my dad..." Hope's voice trailed off.

"Every so often I would think about that day. Because he never really told me what they spoke about. He only said that it was someone he knew a little before we met," said Faith.

"My mother explained it to me for the very first time today. This is why I really came back here today. I had to see you all for myself."

Hope glanced around her, letting the news sink in.

The Repass

The funeral was hard on everyone. All of Seven's family showed up. Even Sam was there. Seven was well-liked by many, not so much by others, but everyone paid their respects nonetheless. It was especially hard for Faith, Sissy, and Jerri. But for different reasons.

Faith lost her husband, but he was much more than just her spouse. He was truly her friend, her best friend, her partner in all that life had to offer. The good, the bad, and the ugly—he was there with her, a steady force in the relentless challenges of life. From the very first day that they hung out, till now, they were inseparable. They failed together, they prospered together, and through it all, they prayed and believed together. Her loss was great.

Sissy was sad, but was in better spirits than the others. As close as Faith was to Seven, she, was that much closer. Even though Seven was no longer alive, she had no doubt that he died with love in his heart. She couldn't explain it, but she knew that he was the happiest that he had ever been in his lifetime. So, she found solace in that thought. She also found peace in knowing that he created a life. Sissy looked forward to getting to know her as Hope was all that was left of her son.

For Jerri, what he lost was an opportunity. An opportunity to make an experience with his son. The realization that Seven died on the way to the hospital to see him, especially grieved him. Even though their relationship wasn't ever fully developed, Seven still loved him. And Hope helped Jerri to understand that. Her words stuck in his mind as he continued to battle the guilt he felt. So the opportunity he lost to have a full relationship with his son, was reborn, in the form of his granddaughter. And that gave him much joy and optimism.

Hope grieved but her feelings were a little more complex. While she was sad that she hadn't gotten to know her father, she appreciated now being able to get to know *of him*. She sat in a corner, all on her own, watching everyone. Some laughed, others cried—emotions all occurring due to the memories created with Seven. And hearing those memories gave Hope life. She absorbed it all. They were all talking about her dad. And her father's name, was Seven.

As she sat and took it all in, Faith, Sissy, and Jerri walked up to speak with her.

"Hey there. You okay?" asked Faith.

"Oh hey. Yes, I'm okay. How about you? You okay?" asked Hope.

"I'm functional."

"Yeah. I can't even imagine how you feel. You guys have been together for so many years and now he's gone."

"Yeah. We made a lifetime of memories. I feel like he's still with me though. So many things that I had actually forgot about are all now coming back to me. We had so much fun. I've laughed out loud to myself at least five times today just remembering something he did or said."

"Wow. That's priceless. I wish that I had that. But can I tell you something?" asked Hope.

"Sure." Faith replied.

"I know everyone is sad and will miss him, but without this happening, I would've never even known who he was. I would've had no knowledge of who my father was. So, I feel relieved in a way to hear so much about him. I'm slowly getting a sense of who he was."

"Hmm… I never thought about it like that, but yes, you're right. Your dad had a way of seeing the good out of bad situations as well. I guess you are more like your father than either of us may realize."

"Really? You think so?" Hope asked, her voice laden with expectation.

"Absolutely. No one knows him better than I do. Well, maybe Sissy here, but that's still different." Faith chuckled.

Sissy rolled her eyes playfully at Faith's comment.

"Well I knew him first. That's right. He hung around with me way before he was even conceived." Jerri joked while they looked at him and shook their heads.

"That makes me feel good—special even." Hope replied.

"Good. Besides, you are all that we have left of him. We have nothing but time. So, I want you to think about it okay?" said Sissy.

"Think about what?" asked Hope.

"Sticking around. Staying connected with us." Faith replied.

"Oh yeah I'm definitely here for that."

Faith, Sissy, Jerri, and Hope embraced each other, a bond slowly forming between them. The air around them crackled, as they felt as if Seven was there standing with them. They smiled at each other, placing their hands together.

"Great. Now, there's something that I think your father would want you to do." Said Faith.

"Really? What?" asked Hope.

"Think about your life. All of it. The good, the bad and the ugly. The sooner you come to make peace with your past the sooner you can start effectively planning for your future. And if you are like him, you have a bright one ahead of you. So, what was your life like?" asked Faith.

"My life? Hmm… that's a long story," Hope sighed, wondering where to start.

"The word of the Lord concerning us."

To everything there is a season, and a time to every purpose under heaven:

A time to be born, and a time to die; a time to plant, and a time to pluck up that which is planted;

A time to kill, and a time to heal; a time to break down, and a time to build up;

A time to weep, and a time to laugh; a time to mourn, and a time to dance.

A time to cast away stones, and a time to gather stones together; a time to embrace, and a time to refrain from embracing;

A time to get, and a time to lose; a time to keep, and a time to cast away;

A time to rend, and a time to sew; a time to keep silence, and a time to speak;

A time to love, and a time to hate; a time of war, and a time of peace.

Ecclesiastics 3:1-8

Made in the USA
Middletown, DE
06 August 2020